Horace Stebbing Roscoe John

Audubon

The Naturalist of the New World

Horace Stebbing Roscoe John

Audubon
The Naturalist of the New World

ISBN/EAN: 9783337341428

Printed in Europe, USA, Canada, Australia, Japan

Cover: Foto ©Raphael Reischuk / pixelio.de

More available books at **www.hansebooks.com**

AUDUBON

The Naturalist.

Boston:

Crosby, Nichols, Lee and Co.

AUDUBON,

THE

Naturalist of the New World

HIS

ADVENTURES AND DISCOVERIES.

.

BY

MRS. HORACE ST. JOHN.

REVISED AND CORRECTED, WITH ADDITIONS,
AND
ILLUSTRATED WITH ENGRAVINGS BY J. W. ORR,
FROM ORIGINAL DESIGNS.

BOSTON:
CROSBY, NICHOLS, LEE AND COMPANY.
1861.

PREFACE.

THE materials of this narrative have been derived from Audubon's works, from the recollections of his friends, and from fragments published in the United States. The writer's object has been, exclusively, to follow the adventurous American through those episodes of romance and discovery which constituted his career as a naturalist.

Those unacquainted with the enthusiasm which carried him onward in the project of his life, may be at times startled at the extreme vigour of his descriptions; but when it is recollected that his original language was French, and that in rendering his thoughts and feelings in English, he found it wanting in the sweetness and vividness requisite for the expression of his poetic imagination, and to illustrate the beauties of nature as he felt them, then his style will be fully appreciated, and the reader will follow him through his career, wondering that nature had so many beauties before unknown to him.

It has been found necessary to correct the English edition in many particulars of fact, and in the order of events, which are better known on this side the water. Some additions have been made by the American publishers.

CONTENTS.

CHAPTER I.

CHAPTER II.

CHAPTER III.

X CONTENTS.

CHAPTER IV.

CHAPTER VII.

CHAPTER VIII

CHAPTER IX.

CHAPTER X.

CHAPTER XI.

CHAPTER XII.

CHAPTER XIII.

CHAPTER XIV.

CHAPTER XV.

CHAPTER XVI.

CHAPTER XVII.

THE BUFFALO.

CHAPTER XVIII.

THE OPOSSUM.

CHAPTER XIX.

THE BEAVER.

THE JAGUAR.

CHAPTER XX.

THE ROCKY MOUNTAIN GOAT.

CHAPTER XXI.

THE GRIZZLY BEAR.

CONTENTS.

AUDUBON

THE NATURALIST IN THE NEW WORLD.

CHAPTER I.

A RARE combination of beauty with grandeur characterizes the aspects of Creation
in the New World. Varied as they are, yet
ever peculiarly rich and often sublime, it would
seem indeed as though nature had designed to
cast this her favoured land in a fresh mould of
marvellous beauty.

Widely differing in its features, the American
territory, from the charm of its contrasted scenes
offers equal attractions to the most antagonistic
lovers of the beautiful. There are vast forests,
roofed with dense foliage, the lofty stems in their
delicious retreats, interlaced with numberless
vines, or gaily crowned with perfumed flower
garlands. Brilliant blossoms of every hue and

odour mingle their loveliness with the stuartia's snowy purity, the majestic form of the magnolia, or richly scented clustering orange, irradiating with golden light the dark verdure of gardens and groves.

Birds of splendid plumage and graceful flight congregate in multitudes, telling their aerial passage by the wondrous melody of their song.

Tempting fruits and berries, ripened by genial warmth and brushed by gentlest breeze—all these are elements of many a sunny scene, which breaks like a gladdening land of promise on the gaze of a loiterer, midst the western woods.

Alternating with the pathless intricacies of the wilderness are vast untrodden prairies. Over these some hermit wanderer might roam, following only the track of the Indian, undisturbed for miles by human sight or sound, greeted now and then but by the buzzing wings of the beetle —a prey for the night hawk, whose skimming undulations are seen around, or by the more unwelcome howling of distant wolves.

To those delighting in the freedom of the waters, how inviting the waves of the imperial Mississippi and Ohio! Pursuing the gracefully winding course of these rivers, from which verdurous islands rise, glistening in the light, like emeralds gemming a breast of snow, some Crusoe-minded mariner too, might contentedly once have wandered. In sight of lofty hills, bordered by forests, he would have heard only the bells of the cattle, pasturing in the valleys beyond, the horn of the boatman, or the hooting of the owl.

Or, to adventurous spirits, yet more tempting perhaps might seem those sterile wilds—the homes of the Esquimaux. Upon their rugged shores vast tracts of snow dappled country are seen clad with stunted vegetation of firs or tangled creeping pines. Innumerable beds of richly tinted mosses relieve the desolation of huge mountain ridges, and the barren aspect of these wastes.

Far above the boisterous waves of the St. Lawrence, towers a line of crag and cliff, like a granite bulwark of the waters. From its summit open all around, in gorgeous array, fertile valleys, thickets clothed with green, and glassy lakes, over which hover birds of varied wing, and banks of snow backed by mountains, mingling their gray tints with those of the cold northern sky. On the numerous low islands dotting the western coast of these regions, are multitudes of cormorants and other aquatic wanderers, their sable wings sailing with astonishing rapidity over the waters, or spread to seek their nests among cliffs washed by the surge.

But whether on northern or southern soil,

there is attraction for the lover, no less than the student of nature in the New World. Sources of poetic inspiration and of scientific interest abound, from the genial land of Louisiana, to the inclement regions of Labrador. A very intellectual El Dorado for the Naturalist,—no more propitious element could be imagined, for the nativity of Audubon, the Genius of the woods.

For him nature breathed an irresistibly persuasive language, and allured, as with a magic charm the loving soul of her disciple—favoured inhabitant, he thought, of retreats where surely she must have lingered to scatter her costliest treasures, and display her most winning grace. Gratitude for such a birthright added fresh zeal to the warmth of his love. Recognizing, moreover, divinity in the impress of beauty on the earth, this love was elevated into worship of the great Spirit of Truth and Light, which brooded over the troubled waters, and still ordains the invariable harmony of the Universe.

To this worship was doubtless owing that entire dedication to his calling, which crowned him with such distinguished honours in his vocation, as Naturalist.

The traits even of his childhood appropriately characterized him for this, his chosen career. Woods, brooks, and wilds were his favourite haunts.

Welcoming the coming seasons, or watching with .special wonder and delight the return of the bright-liveried birds to their retreats, were employments which had for him an unequalled charm. Such ecstacy even did he experience when gazing on the shining pearly eggs, imbedded in softest down, among dried leaves, or exposed on the burning weather-beaten shores of the Atlantic, that an intimacy with such objects, not of friendship merely, "but of ardent passion bordering on frenzy," he felt assured must accompany his steps through life. This conviction increased with advancing years, fostered by the paternal companion who shared and sympathized in all his congenial pursuits. He longed to understand nature, and the hidden agency by which the spells of her enchantment were wrought. In order for this he must ally himself with her—he must devote himself to her; be the constant companion of her changing moods. Only through this allegiance could he make her his. He resolved; and wedded to this object of his dearest desire, during life he cherished it faithfully and well. Vicissitudes and trials had only power to stimulate him in his course. Yet disappointment awaited him for many years. He was inspired with an ardent wish to possess the productions of nature. This haunted him, and incited that creative impulse through which

1*

the artist strives to embody the idealism of his loving thought,—thus reproducing the beautiful objects of the material world mirrored by his imagination.

To appease this desire the father of Audubon presented him with a book of ornithological illustrations. Received with avidity, it only increased the desire to produce a work of the same character; but the sorest mortification attended this effort. His production, Audubon, tells us, had no more resemblance to nature than mangled remains on the battle-field to the forms of living men. But with the unwearied assiduity of true genius, he persevered in these attempts. "To have been torn from the study," he says, " would have been as death to him." Hundreds of such sketches were by his request the materials for bonfires on the anniversaries of his birth—seemingly the sacrificial offerings of his young fancy at the altar of that artistic truth he would so zealously and devoutly serve. Patiently he continued in his endeavours; various plans of study were successively adopted and as surely abandoned. Early in life he was taken to France for the purpose of education. There he had David for his master, who gave him as models gigantic human features and colossal animal representations, the curious mythological devices of some ancient sculpture. But no classical bias

induced him to appreciate these strange productions of antique taste. Such exercises were immediately laid aside. By living, breathing
nature only was he arrested. To him she was
manifested in all her wisdom, and he was thus
furnished with a thousand infallible sources of
enlightenment. Creation he could unweariedly
study, and from perpetual contemplation acquired a skill in his delineations which at length
brought him success beyond his most sanguine
expectations.

With fresh energy and delight he returned
from France to the glorious woods of the New
World. Inspired by their atmosphere, he commenced again the studies of his early youth,
even with more enthusiasm than before his sojourn in France; which enabled him to complete
that marvellous collection of drawings perpetu-
ated in the "Birds of America." This work is
one of unequalled magnificence, and in the tints
of its gorgeous illustrations, as in illuminated
characters, the fame of its author remains in-
scribed. From this period his exertions were
unremittingly continued. Difficulty, toil, privation, and even danger, often attended his researches, pursued as they were throughout the
entire extent of the American territory. Rude
swamps, dreary solitudes, wild barren regions—
these were of necessity the resorts of the natu-

ralist, no less than the gladsome scenes of his native soil. To roam, furnished only with his wallet and fowling piece, from day dawn till compelled by darkness to seek the shelter of some copse or shade in the unknown waste; there, beside the fire kindled by his own hands, to partake of his frugal meal; friendless and alone, to be surprised perhaps by the resistless fury of the elements—lightning, storm, and thunder—causing the wreck of nature round his unsheltered resting-place—menaced by the ferocity of wild animals or the inhospitality of his own species;—such were his customs, and the conditions essential to his vocation.

Successive intervals present us with various phases of this great man's career; yet always we see the rare truthfulness of his nature, and his high-souled faith transparent in that dauntless nobility which made him display equal freedom of action, as well as equal affability and ease, in the camp of the Indian or the settler's hut as in the assemblies of refined society. He visited successively all the most distinguished capitals of Europe, and we gladly find him welcomed, encouraged, courted, and honoured by the great and good of the earth. But with yet more gladness we follow him, unchanged, through the vicissitudes of his destiny, retaining the simplicity of taste, the freshness of sentiment, the cor-

dial feeling and geniality of heart, which as a
richer endowment even than his intellectual superiority, distinguished so specially and so hon-
ourably the renowned Poet Naturalist of the
New World.

Through an amiable modesty, Audubon himself permits many details of his life to be veiled
in obscurity. This, which may reasonably be
supposed to increase the difficulty of the bio-
grapher in following minutely and accurately
his career, is not, however, an insurmountable
impediment. From strict attention to the various
sources from which information may be gathered,
it is comparatively easy to follow, step by step,
the fascinating story, edifying from the example
it affords, and replete not only from its scientific,
but from its moral value, with interest and importance.

CHAPTER II.

AS Audubon advanced towards manhood, his father desired to present him with some enduring evidence of the affectionate regard he had ever manifested. An estate, or, according to American phraseology, a plantation, in the beautiful State of Pennsylvania,* surrounded by woodlands, meadows, and verdurous hills, was the appropriate token selected. This spot offered many an enticing subject for the artist's pencil.

Rambling at dawn, to return wet with the fresh dews of morning—rejoiced if the bearer of a feathered prize—Audubon here passed delicious days in the pursuit of his favourite studies.

His plantation reposed on the sloping declivity of the Perkioming Creek. Along the rocky banks, it was his habit fondly to loiter. There he could watch the sweet flowers cordially unfolding their beauty to the sun, see the contemplative kingfisher perched with dignity on some

---

* At that time Pennsylvania was a slave state, and the farms were called plantations.

stone or spray, reflected in the clear water beneath; the fish hawk and white-headed eagle,
their elegant aerial motions raising the thoughts
to that heaven towards which they soared.

A small cave, scooped by nature in the rock,
was his studio. Some paper, pencils, with a
volume of Edgworth's tales, or La Fontaine's
charming fables, were its contents. Here, when
swelling buds and blossoming trees—spite of
snow-flakes on the earth and chill winds—told
the approach of spring, the birds returned to
their nests in the rock, over the arched entrance
of his retreat. Already the glowing rays of the
sun coloured richly every object, when entering
one morning his accustomed sanctum, a rustling
sound told the arrival of the pewee fly catchers,
his appearance had disturbed. Courteously he
withdrew to leave his retreat occupied by the
little pilgrims. Daily he returned to behold
them fluttering in and about the cave, darting
through the air and enjoying, apparently, by
their fluttering motions and erected crest, the
most agreeable converse. Before a week the
pewees and their guardian were on terms of
such intimacy, that Audubon, determined to enjoy the company of so affectionate and amiable
a pair, spent the greater part of the day again
in his cave with them. Delighted, he observed
them repair the nest, and warm it by an addi-

tional lining of some large soft feathers of the goose, picked up by them along the water's edge. Meanwhile, the emotion of their twittering notes and gentle expressions of tenderness in their caresses, seemed to anticipate their future joys. As long as the plantation remained to Audubon, a pewee's nest continued in his favourite retreat. This species of bird is abundant .in the Floridas, as also during winter in Louisiana and the Carolinas. It almost invariariably forms its nest in caves or the rocky banks of creeks.

And now the enthusiastic passion, hitherto awakened only by birds and flowers, was kindled in the presence of a nobler breathing nature realizing more than all of material beauty beheld before, as well as the highest idealism could conceive. He loved; and we may conclude, that "his affection" was *not* "light as the feathers he delineated," since soon he was a husband, and through existence continued tenderly mindful of the relationship he owned. Of this, we have ample testimony, notwithstanding the long intervals of absence his occupations necessitated. We have treasured reminiscences and brightening glimpses of returning dearly-cherished joys glittering like sparingly-scattered gems over the restless and often troubled current of his way.

At this time, his feelings were wounded by

the irritating remarks of some well-meaning friends, who, ignorant of his genius, and deaf to its charmed voice, opposed the prosecution of his pursuits. Doubtless, he was not only admonished, but censured as heedless of interest and of duty. Happily he found solace in the sympathy of the chosen companion of his life, who, during the solitude of separation, also found *her* consolation in the sustaining conviction of the nobility and worth of an affection like that of Audubon's, ever unaltered by trial.

To Louisville, one of his favourite abiding places, Audubon repaired immediately after his marriage. It was situated on the banks of La Belle Rivière. Graced by the famed rapids of the Ohio leaping over their rocky beds—by the mountains of the Silver Hills, bounding on the opposite side a Swiss-like view, miles in extent.

On the north, one of the many beautiful streams which adorn the State is the Beargrass Creek, loitering through a shady wood of majestic beeches, interspersed with walnuts, oaks, elms, and ashes, which extend on either side its course. It was the resort of many a lounger in the balmy, sunny days of that climate, and it was also a favoured spot in the country, for the celebration of the great day of the American people, the Anniversary of the Declaration of Independence.

Then in the warmth of summer, when har-

2

vests are ripened into gold, and orchards bow their laden branches, gentle breezes waft the scent of richest flowers, and the woods are melodious with song, the free-hearted Kentuckians assemble to enjoy the pleasures of a Barbecue. No invitation is given, because every one is welcome. For a week or more, all have been busy clearing an area for the assembly. The undergrowth cut down and the low branches lopped off, the grass alone is left—a beautifully enameled pavilion. Wagons loaded with contributions from every inhabitant of the State; oxen, hams, turkeys, venison and fowls, wend their way to the spot. Flagons of every beverage, and fruits of every kind arrive too for the feast. Columns of smoke from the kindled fires rise above the trees, fifty or more cooks bustle to and fro, while waiters disperse dishes, glasses and punch-bowls, and vases crimsoned with rich wines. Everything announces a banquet, as joyous groups emerge from out the dark recesses of the woods. White-robed maidens on their palfreys, and youthful horsemen on prancing steeds advance like the brilliant *cortége* of a tournament.

Soon the whole arena resounds with merriment. A huge cannon gives forth a salute, and a thousand cheers mingle with its echoes. It is succeeded by orations, sometimes eloquent, and always patriotic. The visitors then proceed to the tables groaning under the choice stores of Kentucky's prolific land. To toasts and speeches succeed the dance—groups in fairy-like attire, fluttering in the woodland recesses, looking like the meeting of divinities of classic story, or the genii of mytholigic lore.

In the hilarity of the fête, all unhesitatingly mingle—no ball-room etiquette, artifice or pomp to alloy their pleasures. Some, ignoring the dance, show their dexterity at the rifle, or display the swiftness of their fine Virginian coursers; hunters relate their exploits, and travellers tell their tales.

At length comes the preparation for departure, when, loth to separate, the lover hastens to escort his fair one, friend seizes the arm of friend, families gather into loving groups for their homeward journey, and so ends a Kentucky Barbecue.

A rare fertility characterizes the State of Kentucky as it verges southwards toward the lands of Tennessee. Here a sweep of the so-called "Barrens" may be seen enamelled with flowers, numberless, and richly dyed, over which the south wind blows, wafting their fragrance, or clothed with magnificent crops of Indian corn, from ten to fifteen feet in height, of tobacco, or of wheat waving and golden.

This luxuriance contrasts picturesquely with the northern portions of the country. These, dreary and wild, present only hills of sand, or lines of rugged cliff, amidst which here and there a torrent dashes with menacing roar, and far winding gorges, dark and deep, are suddenly disclosed by the juttings of the crag, to the dismay of the travellers. Savage wildernesses, too, terrible as Dante's solitude, are there, which, abounding in legendary interest, are renowned in Kentuckian story, and form not the least attribute of these strange romantic regions. There it was that the Indians, driven from their original territories, or hunting grounds, took up a position to wage a relentless war with their aggressors, whose strength was tested in many a fierce encounter with the swarthy Shawnees. Still to these memorable tracts does many a "sporting party" resort, where the remains of rough built tents tell of the invincible hunter-warriors, who once held them as their own. Dauntless heroes of a different race existed, however, ready to dispute the possession of every inch of Kentucky land with the tawny settlers. Harrod and Boone were distinguished among them, but even they were surpassed in bravery, by one whose matchless skill in contest, whose ruthless ferocity and indomitable daring were so remarkable, as to be regarded by the savages

as the result of some fearful supernatural agency.
The superstition acted naturally to their detriment, and increased the power of Will Smith,
the Forest Chieftain, who, victor in repeated contests, they looked upon as the evil genius of their
race—an instrument of vengeance sent by the
Great Spirit. Their timidity in facing so terrible an enemy was the cause of an irresolution in
their attacks which usually brought defeat, and
facilitated, of course, the means of escape for the
conqueror. Sometimes unexpectedly on the
rear of his enemy, at others ahead of them, or
incomprehensibly in the very midst of the fray,
it seemed indeed as though the warrior had a
" charmed life." True it was that a spell hung
on the existence of this extraordinary man, who
lived under the shadow of a great and inextin-
guishable sorrow. The bitter remembrance of
this it was, which, inciting a ceaseless desire of
revenge, was the secret of his restless and sanguinary career. The blight of misery, as a
plague-taint, separated him from his fellow
men.

Sternly and isolated he lived, for ever haunting
the war path or the hunting trail of the Indians,
from which their bravest leaders disappeared.
Few among the border people approached or
ventured to address the dreaded chieftain. A
mystery surrounded him, which was the source

2*   B

of perpetual conjecture, increased by the very
circumstance which appeared to render it improbable it should ever be solved; for this singular
being maintained a silence as unbroken as though
he were dumb, through which he was commonly
known as the " Silent Hunter."

This appearance of sullen reserve distanced all,
and those who otherwise would have compas-
sionated his sorrows, or perhaps even willingly
have shared his singular fortunes, now denounced
him as a ruthless and reckless adventurer; very
different would have been their judgment, could
they have penetrated the enigma of his solitary
life, and known how cruelly scarred had been a
heart once quickened by the kindest and liveliest emotions. Misfortune, which at one dread
stroke had deprived him of the realization of
happiness on earth, seemed to have deadened
every human hope and sympathy, and crushed
every social instinct within his heart.

The son of obscure emigrants from the Old
World, his first unhappiness was to be left an
orphan at an early age. The next, to be ap-
prenticed to a farmer in North Carolina, a miserable miser, who not only subjected the poor
boy to deprivations and the most arduous toils,
but proved a traitor to the conditions of the indentures by which he was bound. These in-
cluded the privilege of receiving a general school

education, instead of which young Smith was not taught its merest rudiments. Will, owing in great part to his capacity and inclination for study, combined, doubtless, with the combative impulse often accompanying it, resolved, nevertheless to become a scholar. Happily, to aid his good intention, he found an instructress, whose amiability and skill rendered the task of learning rather a pleasure than a toil. This was Mattie Saunders, the farmer's daughter. Often Will's eyes would unconsciously wander from the page to her earnest blue eyes, and then would come such sweet gentle tones of remonstrance, that he really could scarcely be sorry for the offence. Still he made rapid progress, and before long the pupil became the teacher.

In this studious companionship, as time went on, more than letters were learnt, though little did either Mattie or Will imagine how important an influence would be exercised on their destinies, by the hours which glided so swiftly and carelessly by. They loved unconsciously, and the sweet secret of their breast was first made known to them by the father of Mattie, who perceived the condition of affairs, and revealed to them their mutual misery.

From the time of its discovery, the direst tyranny, not to say atrocity was practised by Saunders towards the poor boy. Deprived of the very necessities of existence, he was driven in the midst of winter to sleep with but a single threadbare covering, on some hay in a barn! Such was the endurance to which he bravely submitted for his dear companion's sake. His sole consolation was the sympathy expressed by Mattie, during his stolen interviews with her. She, no longer permitted to see poor Will, had her gentle heart lacerated, by the knowledge of the persecution he suffered, without the ability of alleviating the misery, of which she knew herself to be the innocent cause. Meek-spirited and tender, she was but little fitted to oppose the unremitting severity of her father, who, having amassed for her a considerable fortune, imagined he did sufficient for her happiness by zealously guarding it. His daughter, even on the approach to womanhood was rigorously watched, for the idea of a moneyless suitor was distracting to him. His malignity, awakened by the affection subsisting between Mattie and Will, was mercilessly visited on the forlorn orphan boy. The patient heroism of love alone could have induced Will, naturally of a bold and defiant temper, to yield to the degrading servitude he owned. But to break from it was to part from Mattie—that thought was more grievous than all. So he endured and hoped for long, till the increasing severity of the bondage became unbearable. Incited by a burning indignation he resolved to escape, and stealing to Mattie's room one night, told his intention. The child lovers had little time to indulge their grief—one burst of tears—one clasped embrace, and they parted. Mattie's only consolation, the last words of her lover, that "when he was a great man, he would come back and make her his little wife."

With a few crusts and some scraps of clothing, Will set forth on his journey to the American capital. Curious vicissitudes awaited him. His scanty store was soon exhausted, and he was compelled to beg his bread, and seek some wretched shed for shelter at night.

On one of these occasions it was that he was discovered by the excellent Judge Campbell, who, an early riser for the charitable purpose of looking to the welfare of his cattle, as well as of his household, on visiting his stables, was amazed to find there a pale, miserable looking boy, emaciated with deprivation and hunger. The good old man could not refrain his tears, as he exclaimed, " Never while I have a crust must this be." Removed to the Judge's dwelling, for days the poor orphan vacillated between life and death, unable to explain his unhapy situation, or express his gratitude to his deliverers. From the time that Will Smith was received into the

Judge's family, he was treated as one of its members.

Through a strange coincidence, the very first case met with by the Judge, on setting out for the Circuit was that of the "Commonwealth *versus* Samuel Saunders, for unlawfully making away with the indentured child, known as Will Smith." Campbell, delighted with the idea of retribution on the persecutors of his *protegé*, whom he loved as a son, gave it his immediate attention, and compelled minute investigation of every particular of the affair.

The trial was a singular and terrible scene. Campbell, severe and implacable, sat like another Brutus, resolved for the sentence.

Mattie, too, the timid Mattie was present, pale, heartsick, and agonized by conflicting feelings. The novelty of her situation, and its publicity, were sufficient alone to overwhelm her gentle nature, in addition to which she had the misery to witness her parent's disgrace, and was distracted by the conviction, that Willie, her sole hope and only friend, was lost to her for ever. Saunders, trembling and conscious, awaited the verdict, which came as a death knell on his ears, as in a solemn tone of denunciation "guilty" sounded through the unbroken hush of the court. At that instant the sound of carriage wheels told an arrival, and sent a murmuring agitation through the crowd. The excitement was told by the eager curiosity of the people's gaze, to learn the cause. Even Mattie was roused from the stupor of despair into which she had sunk. A strange vague hope awoke in her breast, and scarcely could she conceive the marvellous reality, as she beheld enter one whom she could not mistake, but so pale, attenuated, as to seem indeed rather a spectre than a living being. But it was the lost one, her well-remembered companion, whose sudden appearance created a sensation impossible to describe. His persecutor, horrified at the sight of what he conceived to be an apparition, swooned, and was taken from court.

The result was, that the conditions of the boy's indentures were declared by the jury to be forfeited, and the sorest sting of all to the miser— he was compelled to aid in the support and education of the boy, until he attained his majority.

A new light thus broke on the horizon, hitherto so dark and troubled for Will Smith. Diligent in improving the advantages afforded him, before long he enjoyed the honourable position of a successful young barrister, and the old Judge on his retirement, had the satisfaction of seeing his own career renewed in that of his adopted son, as he listened often in an ecstasy of admiration to his brilliant vigourous oratory.

But the most delighting triumph of all to Will was, that he could now claim his blue-eyed love, Mattie, as his own. In defiance of opposition, he took her for his bride. Years of unalloyed happiness were the reward of his trials and his toils. Care, sorrow, endurance were forgotten, even ambition slumbered, while he basked in the contest of his new-found joy.

But changes awaited him. The noble contest for freedom and independence arose, and then all that was elevated and unselfish in his nature awoke. Wealth, ease, were relinquished with the ready consent of Mattie, joyful if her beloved remained at her side. Will's services in his country's cause were unremitting and effectual. His sincerity was proved by the sacrifice of his entire fortune; for the conclusion of hostilities saw him a beggar, the result of his hardly earned possessions flown! Energy and enterprise he knew must open a fresh path of progress for him. The glorious lands beyond the Alleghanies offered the best resource; and thither he resolved, if Mattie would accompany him, to repair. He met with no remonstrance from his sweet wife. Her whitening cheek alone told the one pang of consent.

The journey was long and arduous, but the travellers found compensation in the stimulus of novelty, as well as in the charms of the lovely scenes presented by the new-found lands, already bearing a semblance of civilization from the numerous forts and settlements which appeared. Will, having arrived on the borders of the Sinking River, deposited there his family with a powerful guard in camp as their defence, while he, careful to secure further supplies, pressed on to meet his friend Boone at a given spot. Six days only he was absent, six eventful, memorable days. Doubly long seemed the separation to Will's loving heart. He hurriedly sought the spot where all that was precious on earth to him remained—consecrated as home by one blest presence.

He perceived with astonishment the camp broken up, and the few remaining emigrants retreating. Hastening after them, he sternly demanded his wife and children of those whom he had constituted their guardians.

"You will find them where you left them; ask the Shawnees, they can tell you the rest," was the reply. "Traitors," exclaimed Smith, "you have neglected your trust, they are murdered!" Then with a sudden spring at the throat of the hunter who had spoken, he hurled him to the ground, and without turning to see the result, the wretched man returned to the camp.

He was found there stretched on the floor be-

3

side the lifeless remains of his Mattie and his children, whom he alternately embraced. He then rose, and silently and with an awful solemnity proceeded to work for hours, until a grave was formed, large and deep, in which he placed side by side his treasures. Their youngest-born lay on the fair mother's breast, the eldest with the death frown of a hero on his brow, still grasped the rifle with which he had vainly sought to combat the deadly foe! The miserable father, having completed his task, erected a small pile of stones where reposed the remains of his all of earthly bliss. Then snatching up his rifle in one hand, with the other he waved a farewell to his companions, and disappeared following the track of the Shawnees.

He never left that track. For years he haunted the hunting grounds of the Shawnees, slaying them as they slept, or as they sat at their feasts, or as they groped in the paths of the forest. Gradually, such numbers had fallen under his terrible rifle, that he was dreaded as the phantom of murder, and the Shawnees deserted their old resorts on the banks of the Green River. As the last of their canoes dropped down the stream, a bullet struck one of its crew, who fell into the water, dead. The others looked up, and saw their fearful enemy retiring into the forest. A simple stone sarcophagus, such as are common in Kentucky, marks the resting-place of the "Silent Hunter," whose singular and melancholy history has more than once lent its romantic interest to fiction.

CHAPTER III.

AUDUBON continued to make valuable additions to his collection, until his portfolio was enriched by nearly two hundred drawings. He received the most friendly assistance from Galt, the botanist, Ferguson and others. Thus welcomed and encouraged, perhaps no epoch of his life was happier; nor can we imagine pleasanter pictures than those afforded by the hours of hospitable entertainment, friendly intercourse, and communings of love at Louisville. One circumstance which occurred during his residence there, in 1810, seems to have been especially remembered by him. He was surprised by a visit from the celebrated Alexander Wilson, author of the American Ornithology, of whose existence even he had been in ignorance until then. The peculiarity of Wilson's countenance and appearance was vividly retained in Audubon's memory, impressed probably more particularly from the strangeness of the connected circumstances.

His long hooked nose, keen eyes and prominent cheek bones, were unfavourably united to a stature not above the middle height. His dress, consisting of a short coat, trousers and waistcoat of gray cloth, was one unfrequent in that part of the country. His object in calling was to secure Audubon's patronage and a fresh subscription for his work. Audubon, on the eve of assenting to his request, was arrested by an interrogation from a friend, with an acpanying suggestion—that his own drawings were far superior. Whether from vanity, which too willingly corroborated the assertion, or a conscientious conviction of its truth, Audubon then declined to subscribe.

The astonishment of Wilson, on examining the collection of Audubon was as great as had been his on recognizing a fellow labourer. Pursuing the same objects and proposing the same ends, they had remained in entire ignorance of each other's inquiries and achievements; and like too many students toiling in solitude to laborious discoveries, were surprised and disappointed to find them forestalled.

Audubon strove to efface the annoyance, evidently caused through his dissent, by every friendly demonstration to Wilson, even offering to allow him to publish the results of his own researches, which he had not the intention of doing himself at that time, with the condition

3*

only, that their origin should be mentioned. The proposal was, however, declined. Wilson departed, leaving Audubon disagreeably perplexed as to what reminiscence of this singular occurrence would be retained by him. To his regret he was enlightened, afterwards, on reading the following paragraph in "Wilson's Ornithology."

"March 23d, 1810.—I bade adieu to Louisville, to which place I had four letters of recommendation, and was taught to expect much of everything there; but neither received one act of civility from those to whom I was recommended, one subscriber, nor one new bird; though I delivered my letters, ransacked the woods repeatedly, and visited all the characters likely to subscribe. Science or literature has not one friend in this place."

This bitter record of disappointment,—certainly, in some measure justified by Audubon, —then, apparently, under the happiest auspices, for his own success, was felt by him as a lasting alloy in his pleasurable associations with Louisville. After a residence there of two years, Audubon's next dwelling was at Henderson, on the Ohio, whither he repaired in 1811. Remarkable fertility of soil characterizes the Kentuckian State. The beauty of its borders, extending along the margin of the most magnificent of rivers, its forests, streams, springs and caves, its verdurous heights and charming valleys must have rendered this abiding place nothing inferior in attraction, to Louisville. Here he remained for several years, and unfaltering in enterprise, added fresh stores to his ornithological lore. Among the most interesting of his observations were those relative to the character and habits of that bird of romantic tradition—the passenger pigeon. The flight of this bird is performed with singular rapidity. With shrewd caution, it breaks the force of its descent by repeated flappings as it nears the earth, from dread of injury on alighting too suddenly. Its migrations, which are for the purpose of securing food, and not on account of temperature, do not, therefore take place at any fixed season. It remains for several years in Kentucky. This is owing, probably, to the exuberant fertility of the soil, the passenger pigeon requiring, apparently, a plentiful supply of food, equivalent to its powers of digestion, which are as extraordinary as its capacity of flight.

These aerial passengers, travelling at the rate of four hundred miles in six hours, are enabled, if so inclined, to visit the whole European continent in two or three days. They are facilitated in the object for which they fly—the discovery of food—by the keenness of their vision, so that when skimming a barren track, they soar high, with extended front, in order to survey hundreds of acres at once.   Finding the earth abundantly supplied, they fly low; and, when enticed to alight by a particularly plentiful spot, they hover round in circles to review it.   The dense mass they then form, presents, during its evolutions, the most beautiful appearances; now a glistening sheet of azure,—when their backs are in view; and, again, by sudden simultaneous change, a canopy of rich deep purple.   Lost for a moment, midst the foliage, they again emerge, and, flapping their wings, with a rushing noise, as of distant thunder, sweep through the forests to see if danger is near.   Their aerial motions are so extraordinary as to resemble the action of military discipline.   In the process of throwing up the withered leaves, in search of food, the rear ranks pass continuously over the main body, alighting in front, in such rapid succession, that the whole force seems still on wing. If menaced by a hawk, they rise suddenly with the might of a torrent, and pressing into a solid mass, dart forward in undulating lines, descend and sweep close over the earth with wonderful velocity, mount perpendicularly in a vast column, and, when high aloft, wheel and twist within their lines, which then resemble the coils

of a gigantic serpent. Multitudes are seen, sometimes, in groups, at the estimate of a hundred
and sixty-three flocks in twenty-one minutes.
The noonday light is then darkened as by an
eclipse, and the air filled with the dreamy buzzing of their wings.

Not unfrequently a terrible massacre of these
birds takes place, when an armed company of
men and boys assemble on the banks of the
Ohio for their destruction. Great pomp attends
the cruel victory—a camp is formed, fires are
lighted, and overpowering is the din and confusion of the contest. Enormous quantities are
destroyed, and the remains left unappropriated
on the ground. Spite of these devastations, the
number of the birds is always doubled, and often
quadrupled yearly.

But more terrible to the winged tribes, than
forest crusades, sweeping with desolation through
the woods like tornadoes, are the earthquakes,
which menace a traveller over those vast and
dreary plains—the famed Barrens of Kentucky.
Wandering over them one November afternoon,
Audubon was surprised by a sudden and strange
darkness, spreading from the western horizon.
Regarding it as the forerunner only of one of
the hurricanes, a storm to which he was well
used, without further apprehension, he merely
spurred his horse to reach the sheltering roof of

a friend not far distant. But the animal with the intuition of fear, instead of hastening, proceeded slowly, and with a caution, as if treading a sheet of ice.

Imagining that he faltered, Audubon was on the point of dismounting to lead him, when the animal, spreading out his fore legs, hanging his head and groaning piteously, appeared as if arrested by the stroke of death. Audubon, already dismayed at his desolate situation, the melancholy of his solitude, and the misfortune of his failing horse,—his only companion and assistance—now beheld with awe the extraordinary appearance of the elements, the whole creation seeming under the influence of some strange and calamitous phenomenon. Shrubs and trees were agitated from their very roots; the ground rose and fell in undulations, like the waves of a stormy sea, ready to engulph all within its grasp. At that perilous moment what must have been the sensations of Audubon; transfixed with terror, rocked to and fro upon his shuddering horse, the subterranean roar of the convulsion, mingling with the vision of a menacing abyss, which he anticipated every moment would open for his destruction. Separated by miles from his family, apprehensions for their safety added fresh tortures to his situation. Should he ever return to seek them? Would they still exist to greet him? Imaginations, hopes, fears, rose rapidly and flitted alternately —a phantom-like company—before his mind, which, tumultuous and bewildered, shared the agonizing struggle of creation around. Speedily as it rose, the vision of despair passed by. In a few minutes the heavens, serenely sunlit and glad, seemed to express to the eye of Faith the immutability of the eternal promise.

Audubon's horse, relieved from its fears, no longer needed the spur, but galloped as if as eager as his master to escape another such adventure. These visitations are generally followed by slighter shocks, which occur almost every day or night for several weeks. Gradually they subside into little more than mere vibrations. One of these happening during Audubon's visit to his friend, was, strangely enough, not only unattended with calamitous consequences, but through the unfounded apprehensions to which it gave rise, an additional incentive to the rare merriment which renders a wedding in the western country a truly festive occasion. The ceremony having been performed, supper over, and instruments tuned, dancing became the order of the moment. It was kept up till a late hour, the guests encouraged by the hilarity of their host. Being a physician, his urbanity was opportunely increased by the preservation

of some drugs in jars and phials, lancets, ampu
tating knives, and other sanguinary apparatus,
which, filling a corner of his large and solidly
built log house, had a few days before narrowly
escaped destruction through the shock. At
length all retired to rest—some to be haunted
by bright faces, sighs and smiles; others to sink
into pleasing dreams or oblivion as delightful.
But oh! "that on night so blest such awful
morn should rise!" Instead of tender accents
and soft sighs, gentle ears were greeted at dawn
by the rumbling noise of the agitated earth.
Unhesitating demonstrations of true terror were
exchanged for the silently endured apprehensions, or timid avowal of less overwhelming emotions. Young and old anticipating instant destruction, rushed wildly into the grass enclosure
fronting the building, terrified at the creaking of
the log-house, to mingle again in a general assembly—this time, however, as disorderly and
incongruous as that of the spirits meeting in
Macbeth.

Meanwhile the full moon slowly descended
from her throne, attended by a stately retinue of
dark clouds intervening, as if to conceal from
her placid saintly gaze the confusion of the scene
below. Thus the ladies in their frail and partial
attire were happily veiled in appropriate obscurity, and recognitions to the discomfiture of the

following morning avoided. The earth continued
to heave before the wind, the birds to fly hither
and thither, while the doctor was mindful of the
gallipots in his store-room.

In the bewilderment of his distress, forgetful
of closing the door, spreading out his arms, jumping before his glass cases, and pushing back the
falling jars, he assisted the catastrophe with so
much success, that, before the shock was over,
all his possessions were lost. The ladies, conscious at length of their dishabille, and intimidated now from a different motive, fled in dismay
to their several apartments.

In the mountains, or more sterile portions of
the Union, as in the open Barrens of Kentucky,
it is that the curious note of the whip-poor-will
is heard. It is seldom seen during the day, when
it seeks some shady spot for its slumbers, having for a couch, generally, the low branches of
trees and shrubs. Commencing its labours with
the disappearance of the sun, it then passes over
the bushes, sweeps repeatedly in different directions over the fields, and skims the skirts of
forests, alighting occasionally on the ground, to
secure insects as its prey. Its flight is low, light,
and swift. So noiseless is the motion of its wings,
as to be inaudible by a person, even within a few
feet of it,—it is recognized in the darkness only
by the low murmuring sound it utters, and the

4

gentle undulation caused in the air by its passage.

By Audubon, wandering midst solitudes where the grandeur of nature acquires sublimity from the eternal repose of all around, its loud, clear notes were gratefully welcomed, when, exhausted and hungry, after a day of uninterrupted toil, the darkness of night compelled him to set his camp in the wilderness. Under such circumstances, more melodious than song of nightingale, was the cheering voice of the whip-poor-will—his sole companion. For the whip-poor-will continues to sing several hours after sunset. It then continues silent till early dawn, when, along the declivities of the mountains, and through every valley, its shrill note re-echoes till the clouds which darkened the fair face of nature are dispersed, and break into gladness at the sun's majestic coming. Hundreds of these birds then assemble in the woods, and emulate each other in a chorus. They receive their name from the fancied resemblance of their note to the words whip-poor-will. Their migrations southward, as well as their toils, are performed by night. Audubon unhesitatingly pronounced this species distinct from the night hawk.

About the middle of March, in the forests of Louisiana, the song of the chuck-will's-widow, its interesting relative, may be heard. It is seldom seen beyond the limits of the Carolinas, but abounds in the lower portions of Alabama and Georgia. Repairing thither from Mexico, and still warmer regions, it may be regarded as the sign of Spring. The resorts of these birds are deep ravines, shady swamps and pine ridges. If surprised in their roosting places—for the most part the hollows of trees, where they lodge, in company with bats—instead of trying to make their escape, they heroically assume the defensive, retire to the farthest corners of their retreat, ruffle all their feathers in great rage, and open their mouths to the widest while they utter, menacingly, a snakelike hissing. These birds show a remarkable attachment to certain localities for their rest or enjoyment. Like the whip-poor-will, so accustomed are they to take their ease in a dim retreat till twilight, that, if seized and brought to the light of day, they open and shut their eyes, as though unable to bear it. As swift as its relative when on wing, the flight of the chuck-will's-widow is even more graceful and elevated. It is performed by easy flappings, combined with sailing and curving motions, so elegant, that when seen soaring in the air over cotton fields or sugar plantations, mounting and descending with the dexterity and grace of a Taglioni, accompanying its evolutions with a low murmuring sound, it seems a very flying fairy of the night. During these nocturnal journeys, in pursuit of food, suddenly its course is checked—a moth or beetle secured—when, continuing its flight, it passes and repasses hundreds of times over the same ground. Alighting on the tallest plant, it utters its note with unusual vivacity. Again on wing, it gives chase to insects in the air, at intervals skilfully poising itself upon the trunks of trees, in this manner ingeniously seizing the insects on the bark, while enabled, at the same time, to inspect the whole tree in search of prey. The curious sound of its clear and powerful note—chuck-will's-widow—repeated six or seven times in as many seconds, forerunning, as it does, a calm and peaceful night, comes, borne along the winds with a soothing pensive pleasure to the listener. Its song is seldom heard in cloudy weather, and never during rain. It is singular, that though this bird exhibits the domestic affections in a remarkable degree, it forms no nest for the preservation of its young. A little hollow, carelessly scratched among dried leaves, is the only deposit for its eggs. · This seems, indeed, rather the result of extraordinary instinct than of neglect, since, owing to no appearance of an aerial habitation existing to attract attention, the eggs are seldom found, without great difficulty. Should they be meddled with, it is instantly perceived by the parents, who, ruffling their feathers, with every sign of distress, and uttering a low plaintive cry, fly close along the ground, bearing the eggs in their mouths to some other verdurous and hidden retreat.

The wooing of these amiable birds is attended with demonstrations as elaborate as those attending the courtesies of the most refined society. A permissible degree of pomposity is showed by the male, who, alighting before his love, with drooping wings, sings his appeal, with the most persuasive eloquence, whilst the lady, at first, silent and coy, is soon won ; when, leaving the branch, they gambol through the air together.

4*

CHAPTER IV.

DURING the residence of Audubon at Henderson, his attention, notwithstanding his numerous ornithological researches, was not unfrequently directed to other kinds of scientific pursuits or exercises, more properly termed, perhaps, by the inhabitants of the State, Kentucky sports. The origin of that peculiar inclination and aptitude shown by the Kentuckians for the warlike diversions of nail driving, squirrel barking, and candle snuffing, is not improbably the long and sanguinary contest between the Virginian settlers and the Indians, which took place before the superiority of the former could be established in the State. The settlers, incited by the indomitable courage of their renowned leader, and attracted by the wild luxuriance of the uncultivated soil, pressed with the unequalled enterprise of Americans, regardless of endurance, danger, or defeat, towards the shores of the Ohio. With an axe, a couple of horses, a heavy rifle, and store of ammunition, but with very light provision, trusting

to the exuberance of the land to supply his wants,
a man sets forth with his family. Guided only by
the sun through dark and tangled forests, they
pushed on, till compelled by weariness, they
sought repose on the bare earth at night. Numberless streams were crossed on rafts, women and
children imitating the courage of the adven-
turers. Luggage and possessions were landed
with greater difficulty, for the cattle, tempted by
the rich pasturage, roved away, causing a delay of days. Meanwhile the wanderers were
tortured with dread of the prowling ruthless Indians harassing their march or menacing their
slumbers. Some, travelling under pleasanter
auspices were attended by wagons and negroes.
An advance guard cut a way for them through
the woods, and when overtaken by night, the
bold hunter attachés of the party, loaded with
the dainties of the forest, hastened to their place
of encampment.

Then it was that the sounds of merriment told
all was well. Soon the flesh of buffaloes or
deer was laid in deliciously-cooked slices before
the embers, while cakes, flavoured by the rich
viands, were quickly baked. Wagon-loads of
comfortable bedding were unloaded, and horses
too had their pleasant recreation midst the luxuriant undergrowth of the woods, caparisoned
only with a light bell to guide their owners in

the capture of them the next morning. With such intervals of joyous sociality months passed before the journey westward was accomplished, occasional skirmishes occurring between the intruders and the wily Indians who sometimes crept unperceived into the settlers' camps. Still cheerfully they pressed on, till at length the land was cleared for a permanent residence. On reaching the banks of the Ohio, some, in primeval fashion, constructed arks for a home on its inviting current. These arks or flat boats, thirty or forty feet long and ten or twelve in breadth, were considered so stupendous as to hold men, women, children, cattle, poultry, vegetables, and a host of miscellaneous wares. The roof or deck constituting a farm yard, was covered with hay, ploughs, carts, and agricultural implements—the spinning wheel of the matron morever conspicuous among them.

In these floating habitations, containing their owners' all, the emigrants, fearful of discovery by the Red Skins, denied themselves even fire or light by night, so fearful were they of a surprise from the ferocious and ever watchful foe. Many an encounter, to the discomfiture of the Indian hordes, ensued ; for, to the exercise of the settler's courage on these occasions is probably owing that extraordinary skill in the use of the rifle exhibited by the Kentuckians in their sports.

A common feat among these is driving the nail. An assembly then mount a target, in the centre of which a nail is hammered for about two-thirds of its length. Forty paces is considered a proper distance for the marksmen. The bending of the nail is indicative of some skill; but nothing short of hitting it on the head is satisfactory: this is called " driving the nail."

In the flat land, thickly covered with black walnut, oaks and hickories, beyond the rocky margin of the Kentucky river, it is that the squirrels are seen gamboling on every tree. To hit with a rifle shot the bark of the tree immediately beneath the squirrel, and through the concussion to kill the animal, constitutes the cruel diversion of " barking a squirrel."

There are frequently sporting expeditions for practice in the woods, when fires may be seen blazing through the thick foliage of the trees, to enable a marksman to shoot at the reflected light from the eyes of a deer or wolf at night.

In snuffing the candle, such dexterity is attained as to enable a rifleman, six times out of seven, actually to snuff a light without extinguishing it. When it is considered that a Kentuckian, with the same ease with which he snuffs his candle dispatches his enemy, and that every man in the state is used to handle the deadly weapon from the time he can shoulder it, it will be evident that the Kentuckians are no contemptible antagonists.

But yet more formidable than to contest with such a foe is to encounter that terrible phenomenon known in the State where it is so frequent as a hurricane. Audubon, surprised by one on his journey from Henderson, appears to have retained as vivid an idea of its awful grandeur as of that of the earthquake. It is preceded also by a thick haze in the atmosphere, from which he would have inferred a recurrence of the same catastrophe, but that his horse exhibited this time no inclination to stop and prepare for it. Having arrived at the verge of a valley, Audubon dismounted to quench his thirst from a brook close at hand, and while leaning on his knees, close to the earth, he heard a strange murmuring sound, far in the distance. Raising his head, he observed towards the south-west, an extraordinary phenomenon, of a yellow-tinged oval spot on the horizon. Before he had time to reflect upon it, a sharp breeze agitated the trees, increasing rapidly, till the smaller branches were soon falling to the ground.

In two minutes more the whole forest was in fearful commotion. The creaking noise of the huge trunks pressing against each other from the violent gusts of wind, seemed the announcement of some terrible convulsion. Torn by the blast, the noblest trees of the forest bowed their lofty heads, the cracking of their branches and the heaving of their massive stems preceding the crash of their entire destruction. Others of enormous size, rent up at once entirely by the roots, fell in one vast heap of ruin to the earth. Some, with colossal branches, like giant arms, outspread for the conflict, offered a momentary resistance, to be suddenly snapped across the centre; while the victorious tempest, carrying in its current a mass of twigs and lighter foliage, whirled around a cloud of dust which obscured the air.

The groaning of the desolated forests mingled with the storm, as hurrying, with shrieking war-cry or sullen howl, along its desolating track, its tumult could have been equalled only by the roar of the Niagara cataract. Speedily, as it arose, the fury of the hurricane subsided, though for hours the air was thickened by the abundance of lighter foliage, still swept around by the gale. An odour, as of sulphur, then filled the atmosphere, and the greenish lurid sky looked down upon the huge heap of vegetation, which, in shapeless masses, marked the course of the hurricane. So rapidly had it advanced, that before Audubon could take measures for his safety, its violence menaced the very spot on which he stood. With consternation he was compelled to watch its awful progress, and grateful to the Divine Disposer, he beheld at length nature assume her wonted aspect, and found himself uninjured. Having business of an urgent nature, instead of returning to the adjacent town, he boldly followed the pathway of the storm, so tangled as to cause him innumerable difficulties; nevertheless he pursued his way, now aiding his horse to leap the mangled remains of trees, now scrambling himself through the shattered branches by which he was hemmed in. For hundreds of miles the traces of the hurricane were visible; its ravages perceptible even on the mountain summits adjoining the great Pennsylvanian Pine Forest.

Audubon's wanderings, thus prolific of extraordinary events, were not less so of amusing incidents, necessarily connected with the many remarkable characters who met his observation. One of the striking among them was that of the renowned and dauntless leader of the emigrant bands into Kentucky, Daniel, or as he was courteously termed in the state, Colonel Boone. It was Audubon's fortune to remain under the same roof with this extraordinary man, whose appearance and gigantic stature well befitted a hunter of the woods. His chest was broad, and prominent muscular power displayed itself in every limb, while the expression of his countenance, which was bold and ingenuous, indicated courage, enterprise, and strength. Audubon, who occupied the same sleeping apartment with him, was indefatigable in his questionings, in order to elicit some account of his companion's exploits. The Colonel, after merely laying aside his hunting shirt, and arranging a few folds of a blanket on the floor, remarked that " he would rather lie there than on the softest bed." He then assented to Audubon's request, by relating an occurrence which befell him while on an expedition to the Green river in Kentucky, where none but sons of the soil were looked upon as lawful proprietors of that State.

He had extinguished one night the fire of his camp, and lain down to rest in security, as he imagined, when seized by an indistinguishable number of hands, he was immediately pinioned, as if about to be led to execution. To have resisted, when in the power of the crafty Redskins would have been dangerous as useless. By suffering himself to be quietly removed, the Indians were convinced of his fearlessness. Meanwhile, his mental ingenuity was incessantly exercised for some stratagem of escape. On his arrival at the camp, great rejoicings were shown, and he was warned by unequivocal gestures, that before another dawn, one mortal enemy of the Redskins should have ceased to live.   The squaws, who amused themselves with ransacking his hunting shirt for booty, now succeeded so well in their search as to find a large flask of Monongahela (strong whisky), while a barbarous grin on their ferocious faces told their delight at the discovery.   A silently disguised satisfaction filled the Colonel's heart at the prospect of their intoxication.   Wishing the bottle ten times as large, or filled with aquafortis, etc., he beheld it pass from mouth to mouth, midst songs and outcries of wild revelry.   He observed also, however, with a depression which made his hopes sink, that the women, his least formidable antagonists, drank far more freely than the warriors.   At the report of a gun in the distance the men suddenly jumped to their feet, and singing and dancing were for a while discontinued, for a consultation between the warriors and their wives, of which the Colonel plainly perceived he was the cause.   In a few minutes the men departed, leaving the squaws alone, as he hoped, to guard him.   In five minutes more the flask was drained, and very soon he beheld, with inexpressible delight, unmistakeable signs of intoxication manifested by the tumbling snoring company.   The Colonel following the example of the assembly, from a very different motive, rolled over and over towards the fire, and thus succeeded in burning the cords by which he was fettered. Springing to his feet and snatching up his rifle, he thus effected his escape; for once, sparing the life of an Indian and mindful of his own. A cut of the Colonel's tomahawk in the stem of an ash, was made to commemorate his adventure there, and if the innovations of time, and the inroads of an equally ruthless civilization permit, the curious or interested may prove the authenticity of this anecdote.

As Audubon rambled one day beside his favourite river, he observed a man landing from a boat, with what appeared a bundle of dried clover on his back. No sooner had the exclamation "What an odd-looking fellow! an original, surely!" crossed his mind, than he perceived the stranger approach him in haste, and with astonishment, heard him inquire for the house of Mr. Audubon. With the cordial hospitality which characterized him, Audubon instantly replied, "Why, I am the man, and will gladly lead you to my dwelling."

The traveller thus happily relieved from all perplexity as to his entrée, actually clapped his hands with delight. He then took from his pocket a letter of introduction, which he presented. Its contents were—

" My dear Audubon,
" I send you an odd fish, which may prove to
be undescribed. If so, I hope you will let me
have an account in your next letter.

> Believe me always your friend, B.

With an amusing simplicity worthy this Cin-
cinnatus of science, Audubon unhesitatingly
asked the bearer " where the odd fish was?"

Perplexity was now his, when, with perfect
good humour and self-possession, Monsieur de
Thouville, in whose presence he was, replied,
" I am that odd fish, I presume, Mr. Audubon."
To their mutual relief, the house of his host was
soon reached. Audubon, desirous to put his
friend at ease, was on the point of ordering a
servant to the boat for Monsieur de Thouville's
luggage, who prevented him, however, with the
remark, that he had none but what he brought
on his back; at the same time loosening the pack
of weeds which had first attracted Audubon's
attention.

The stranger naturalist then, while engaged
in pulling his stockings, not up but down, to
cover the holes about his heels, indulged his
loquacity in the gayest manner imaginable.
After relating the distance he had walked, and
his passage on board the ark, he expressed also
his regret that his apparel should have suffered;

but at the same time, he eagerly denied the offer
of any clean clothes; and it was with evident
reluctance he accepted an invitation for ablution.
It is not difficult to conceive the interest and astonishment excited among the inmates of Audubon's habitation, by the singular appearance
of this scientific professor. A long loose coat of
yellow nankeen—on which the inroads of time
were plainly visible, stained as it was with the
juice of many a plant—hung about him like a
sack. A waistcoat of the same, with enormous
pockets and buttoned up to the chin, reached
below, over a pair of tight pantaloons, the lower
parts of which were buttoned down to the ancles.
The dignity he acquired from the broad and
prominent brow which ornamented his countenance, was somewhat diminished by the forlorn
appearance of his long beard, and the mass of
lank black hair which fell from his shoulders.
His striking resemblance to that equally eccentric savant, Dick Roberts, must certainly have
crossed the mind of Audubon, if, as is not improbable, that extraordinary man had ever met
his observation, whilst enjoying the hospitality
of Allerton. The surprise of the ladies was involuntarily manifested in the exchange of sundry critical glances which, to a tenacious egotist,
would have spoken volumes. Soon, however,
their astonishment was converted into admiration

5*

at the agreeable ease and rare enlightenment of the stranger's conversation.

Having visited Audubon expressly for the purpose of seeing his representations of birds, which he had heard were accompanied by those of shrubs and plants, his impatience to inspect the portfolios at once was very evident. He was struck with the drawing of a plant which appeared new to him. With a characteristic scepticism, however, which led him to believe only in his own discoveries, or such as, owning the prestige of age, had, according to Malebranche's expression, acquired a "venerable beard," he denied the existence of such a plant. As it was very common in the neighbourhood, Audubon promised to show it to him on the morrow.

"Why to-morrow?" exclaimed he; "let us go now." On reaching the bank of the river, he was convinced of the truth of the representation. Plucking the plants mercilessly one after the other, he danced, hugged them in his arms, and crying out that he had not merely a new species, but a new genus, he seemed on the verge of delirium from delight. Yet was his incredulity in no degree diminished with regard to other matters. Again within doors, the windows were opened to admit the summer air. The light of the candles attracted the insects, and among them a large species of Scarabœus. Audubon having one, showed it to his guest, assuring him that it was so strong, that it would crawl on the table with a candlestick on his back.

"I should like to see the experiment made, Mr. Audubon," De Thouville replied.

It was accordingly done, the insect dragging its burthen till, on reaching the edge of the table, it dropped to the ground, and then took to flight.*

All had retired to rest, when Audubon was surprised by an uproar in the naturalist's apartment. On reaching it, to inquire the cause, what was his surprise at the now still more singular appearance of his guest, no longer attired in costume eccentric, or otherwise. Running about, he was engaged in a sanguinary contest with the bats, which had entered by the open window— his only weapon the handle of Audubon's favourite violin, which had been demolished in the fray. Uninterrupted by the entrance of his amazed visitor, he continued his extraordinary gyrations. Round and round he went, with the monotony of a dervish, till so exhausted as to be scarcely able to request Audubon to procure one of the animals for him, as he felt convinced that they belonged to a " new species."

---

* See Dalton's "British Guiana," in which a similar experiment is described.

A small rap on each of the bats from Audubon, brought him specimens enough. The contest thus arrived at a successful issue, Audubon departed, not without a wondering glance at the scene of warfare the room presented. The remains of the stricken birds were strewn over it, and a confused heap of plants which, a little while since, carefully selected into groups, were now in irrevocable disorder.

De Thouville remained some days under the hospitable roof of his new friend, during which these fellow-labourers diligently pursued their respective occupations. He naturally desired, before departing, some memorial of the time and place, which might also assist his researches in vegetation, and enrich his possessions. The Cane Brakes, which formerly spread over the Kentucky State, interspersed with plants of every description, tempted the imagination of the naturalist. Little was he aware of the difficulties of effecting a passage through those formidable mazes, where the hunters cut a pathway with their knives, and underwood, heavy perhaps with sleet or rain, which comes down to the discomfort of the poor traveller, as he bends the foliage, and presses his way through. At De Thouville's urgent request, however, the companions set forth, Audubon not without a sly and somewhat malicious resolve to gratify his

KENTUCKY CANE BRAKES.   Page 57.

wish, even at some cost to himself. That he might not be intimidated at the outset, Audubon cleared the way by cutting down the canes. Difficulties increased as they proceeded. Having passed the rubicon, the poor naturalist continued to wade his troubled way with many a regret and groan. Through knotted vines and intricacies of cane, they proceeded, till, coming on the misshapen mass of a fallen tree, they were about to precipitate themselves through it, when suddenly from its centre a bear rushed forth, angrily snuffing the air as though intent on the first prey that should present itself. Poor De Thouville, his ebbing energies exhausted as well as his moral powers, by fright, attempted to run, but fell terror-stricken among the canes, to remain jammed between their stalks, as if pinioned. Audubon, repressing his merriment, in order to give the active assistance for which De Thouville loudly shrieked, actually succeeded in persuading him, spite the misadventure, to continue the expedition. But fresh terrors awaited them. The way became every moment more tangled. Heavy clouds, portentous of a storm of thunder, were observed by Audubon with malicious delight, but with dread by his companion; who, panting, perspiring, and sighing, seemed about to surrender in despair. Still the thunder roared, and dashes of heavy rain, while they drenched the travellers, rendered their pathway a very morass. The withered leaves and bark of the canes stuck to their clothes as they plunged through, while briers and nettles penetrated still further. To De Thouville's repeated inquiry, whether they should ever emerge alive out of so horrible a situation, Audubon returned exhortations and admonitions to patience and courage. Tumbling and crawling, the memorable march was continued by the poor naturalist, who, once well out of the maze, emptying his pockets of fungi, lichens, and moss, never again expressed a desire to enter it.

One evening, he was missed from the circle at Henderson. Grasses and possessions were no longer in his room. Whether he had been drowned in a swamp or devoured by a bear, was matter of conjecture, till a letter, some time after, assured Audubon that this eccentric naturalist still existed.

CHAPTER V.

FOR many years subsequent to his marriage, Audubon engaged in various branches of commerce, doubtless from a conscientious sense of the obligation his new position imposed.

That they should have proved unprofitable, is scarcely matter of surprise, with one whose whole mind was enamoured of entirely opposite pursuits. Nevertheless his enterprise was not unproductive of advantage; for it was while ascending the upper Mississippi on a trading voyage, during the month of February, 1814, that Audubon first caught sight of the beautiful Bird of Washington. His delight as he did so was extreme. Not even Herschel, he says, when he discovered the planet which bears his name, could have experienced more rapturous feelings. Convinced that the bird was extremely rare, if not altogether unknown, Audubon felt particu-larly anxious to learn its species. He next ob-served it whilst engaged in collecting cray fish on one of the flats of the Green river, at its junction with the Ohio, where it is bounded by a range of high cliffs. Audubon felt assured, by certain indications, that the bird frequented that spot. Seated about a hundred yards from the foot of the rock, he eagerly awaited its appearance as it came to visit the nest with food for its young. He was warned of its approach by the loud hissing of the eaglets, which crawled to the extremity of the cavity to seize the prey—a fine fish. Presently the female, always the larger among rapacious birds, arrived, bearing also a fish. With more shrewd suspicion than her mate, glaring with her keen eye around, she at once perceived the nest had been discovered. Immediately dropping her prey, with a loud shriek she communicated the alarm, when both birds soaring aloft, kept up a growling to intimidate the intruders from their suspected design.

Not until two years later was Audubon gratified by the capture of this magnificent bird. Considered by him the noblest of its kind, he dignified it with the great name to which his country owed her salvation, and which must be imperishable therefore among her people. "Like the eagle," he thought, "Washington was brave; like it, he was the terror of his foes, and his fame extending from pole to pole, resembled the majestic soarings of the mightiest of the feathered tribe. America, proud of her Washington, has also reason to be so of her Great Eagle." The flight of this bird is distinct from that of the white-headed eagle; it encircles a greater space, whilst sailing keeps nearer to the land, and when about to dive for fish, descends in a spiral line, as if with the intention of checking every attempt at retreat by its prey.

Audubon's commercial expedition, rich in attractions for his scientific observation, were attended also with the varied pleasures which delight a passenger on the waters of the glorious Mississippi. Interesting in its magnificence, even beneath a cold winter sky, with keen blasts whistling around, infinitely more so is it in the freshness of the spring season, the radiance of summer, or above all the brilliance of autumn. The vegetation adorning its shores is then enchanting. There the tall cotton tree mingles its branches with those of the arrow-shaped ash, the pecean or walnut. Huge oaks overspread the densely tangled canes, from amongst which vines of various kinds spring up, intertwining the trunks and stems with their tendrils, till stretching from branch to branch the whole expanse is covered, as with a canopy of vegetation, illumined with rich hues of crimson, brown, and gold. Adorning the distant prospect of hills arise noble pines, magnolias or hollies, waving their lofty heads in the breeze.

Fresh scenes of interest are continually disclosed by the frequent windings of the river, as you speed along its rapid current. Now the wail of the forest seems to mourn the impetuous, relentless waters, which, by their constant inroads, have swept the beautiful verdure from her borders, which once sheltered, with its overspreading masses, the grief of the cypress, like a veil the sorrowing nun. Again, the desolate camp of the Indian is in sight, or about the numerous fairy islands which decorate the stream boats are visible, sometimes gliding silently, at others swiftly, stemming the waters like attendant genii of the scene. Thousands of birds enlivening the adjacent woods gratify the ear with their sweet mellow notes, or dazzle the sight, as in their gorgeous attire they flash by.

Among the pendant branches of the tall tulip the brilliant oriole gracefully moves, seeking its food among the opening leaves and blossoms. Arriving from the south, this beautiful bird enters Louisiana with the spring. He then seeks some suitable place in which to nestle, generally the gentle slope of a declivity. Having found the desired spot, he commences chirrupping, as though congratulating himself upon the discovery. Anxious to furnish himself with a comfortable residence also, he proceeds to form his nest, in the construction of which astonishing sagacity is displayed. First securing the longest dried filaments of moss, with the aid of bill and claws, he fastens the one end to a twig, with as much art as a sailor, and then secures the other a few inches off, leaving the thread floating in the air like a swing, the curve of which is, perhaps, seven or eight inches from the branches to which it is suspended. The Baltimore oriole is thus frequently called the " hanging bird," from the peculiarity of its nest. " Much difference is distinguishable in these structures; some, from their solidity and elegance, showing superior skill in the craftsmen, while others, more slovenly, have their habitations ill contrived. The women in the country are under the necessity of narrowly watching their thread, and the farmer of securing his young grafts, as the bird frequently carries off both."*

The oriole's helpmate then comes to his assistance, and, after inspecting the work her companion has done, commences her labours by placing some fresh threads of a fibrous substance in a contrary direction, thus forming a graceful fabric of network, woven so firmly that no tempest ever can carry away the nest, without breaking the branch also. As if aware of the heat which must in those regions shortly ensue,

* Wilson's American Ornithology.

these birds form their nest only of the Spanish moss, instead of the warmer materials often used, and build it so as to be freely ventilated by the air. They are careful, moreover, to place it on the north-east side of the tree. On the other hand, should they proceed as far as Pennsylvania or New York, their nests would be composed of the softest, warmest substances; the intense cold, which sometimes succeeds the frequent changes of the atmosphere in those places, rendering such caution necessary for the preservation of the brood. Two singular instances of the capacity of birds for architecture were met with by Mr. Gould, in the bower bird and the spotted bower bird of Australia, which build "bower-like structures for the purpose of a playing ground or hall of assembly." The bower of the latter birds is considerably longer than that of the first, more resembling an avenue. Having an external coating of twigs, it is lined with tall leaves so contrived as to met at the top. Paved with shells and stones, these enticing little habitations are adorned also with brightly coloured feathers.

Equally interesting is the habitation of the tailor bird, so minutely described in that repository of rare and curious information, the Journal of the Asiatic Society of Bengal. A nest was found woven stoutly of cotton, thickly lined with horse-hair, and supported between two leaves on a twig. These leaves placed longitudinally on each other were stitched in that position, from the points to rather more than half way up the sides with a strong thread; this was spun from the raw cotton by the bird, leaving the entrance to the nest only at the upper end, between the stalks of the leaves, where they joined the branch of the tree.

When migrating, the flight of the Baltimore oriole is performed high in the air, above the tops of the trees, and sometimes, when the sun declines, they alight singly among the branches to feed or rest.

Their song consists not unfrequently of eight or ten loud full clear notes, is extremely melodious and pleasing. Their movements differ materially from those of other birds. They may be seen clinging by the feet around a stem in such a way, as to require the full extension of their legs and bodies, in order to reach some insect. Again they move curiously sideways for a few steps; or, gliding with elegant and stately motions, are seen with their blended glossy plumage and vermillion-tinted breasts, glittering among the leaves. They resort in the summer season to ripe fruits, such as strawberries, cher-ries, mulberries, and figs for food.

Deserving of enumeration, from the pecu

liarity of its attributes, with the most singular among specimens of American ornithology, is the umbrella bird mentioned by Wallace.* "In size equal to the raven, it is also of a glossy black. The male in particular has a singular crest on its head, formed of feathers two inches long, thickly set with hairy plumes, curving over at the end. These can be erected and spread out on every side, forming a hemispherical dome, completely covering the head, and beyond the point of the beak."

But linked with the Mississippi are associations of very different interest. Contrasted with the poetic charm of beauty or melody in birds and flowers is many a tradition dark with crime. One of these it is which has handed down the name of Mason as the terror of peaceful navigators on the Mississippi and Ohio. On Wolf Island, not far from the confluence of these rivers, this pirate had his settlement, and leagued with a band of associates who spread from Virginia to New Orleans. Issuing from his ambush on every propitious opportunity, passing boats were waylaid, to be rifled of their cargoes, or perhaps deprived of their crews, who mysteriously disappeared. Horses and negroes, the principal traffic of the gang, were, besides

* Travels on the Amazon and Rio Negro.

provisions, the favourite booty. The unscrupulous depravity of these emigrants, the refuse population of other lands, made them willingly retreat to regions on the extreme verge of civilization, where they imagined they could indulge, unmolested, their evil propensities.

Fortunately, a formidable power existed for the punishment of their lawlessness. It was that body of energetic and honourable citizens who—vested with powers suited to the necessities of the occasion—courageously undertook to preserve order on the frontiers, under the name of Regulators. On the commission of an offence by some delinquent, an assembly of them immediately takes place for the purpose of investigation and judgment. Should the offender prove regardless of the first sentence, which is generally simple banishment, his cabin is burnt down, and he receives a severe castigation. On a repetition of great crimes, the delinquent is shot, that the recognition of a comrade's head fixed on a pole may deter others from following his example. Against the notorious Mason, these Regulators engaged. Though, through their watchfulness, many of his haunts were discovered, he yet contrived, by the aid of his numerous spies, to escape. One day, however, having mounted a beautiful Virginian horse— his booty—he was recognized by a guard, who passed him as if in utter ignorance as to who he was. Mason thus pursued his way at ease till, reaching at dusk his accustomed resort, the lowest part of a ravine, after hobbling his horse, he esconced himself in a hollow log for the night.

He was observed all the while by the Regulator, who, marking the place and hut with his practised eye, galloped off for assistance, and soon the criminal was surprised in his retreat. In desperation, he defended himself with such valour, that the armed band, finding it impossible to secure their victim otherwise, at length struck him down with a rifle ball. His head, stuck on the broken branch of a tree, remained a monument of the affray. The followers of Mason, thus admonished by the fate of their leader, were not only intimidated from the commission of equal crimes, but soon altogether dispersed.

CHAPTER VI.

ON his return from the Mississippi, Audubon found himself obliged to traverse one of those vast prairies which form a striking characteristic of his country. His dog, his knapsack and his gun were his sole provision and company. Guided by the track of the Indian throughout the day, he wandered, gazing only on the monotony of the vast expanse, unvaried by one glimpse of human shape or habitation, till at length the sun disappeared beneath the horizon.

Then the roar of wild animals in the distance, the flapping of the night birds in their flight, and the buzzing of insects, were the only sounds which greeted his ears. As darkness gradually enshrouded the whole extent of the prairie, his desire increased to reach some hut or woodland, in which to shelter for the night. Suddenly a fire-light in the distance caught his sight, sufficiently near for him to perceive, from its glare, that it proceeded from the hearth of a small log cabin. Before it a tall figure constantly flitted, as if busied in some domestic occupation. Audubon hastened to the spot, and presenting himself at the door of the dwelling, asked hospitality for the night of the woman whom he had first seen. The answer in the affirmative was calculated rather to scare away an intruder, than invite a guest, from its hoarse, impulsive tone, which caused Audubon involuntarily a chill of repugnance. Her appearance, moreover, might have dismayed any but the stoutest heart. About her tall, gaunt figure, her miserable attire was heedlessly gathered. The roughness of her manner and the audacity of expression were also well suited to the large proportions and muscular limbs of this Meg Merrilies of the woods.

Audubon, taking advantage of her response, however, walked in and seated himself before the fire. The next object which met his view, presented a very different aspect. A young Indian, of the most symmetrical form, leant in an attitude so motionless as scarcely to seem even to breathe. His head rested between his hands, and his elbows were on his knees, as though in suffering or deep thought. A long bow was near him, and some arrows and skins of racoons lay at his feet. Audubon, anxious to learn the cause of his remarkable quietude, and whether or not it proceeded from the apathy of his race,

addressed him.   He answered by raising his head
and pointing with his finger to one of his eyes,
while with the other he gave a significant glance,
explanatory of the action.   His face thus revealed,
though covered with blood, might be seen, never
theless, to be unmistakeably handsome, dis
figured as it was by the accident which, an hour
before, had impared for ever its singular beauty.
While discharging an arrow at a racoon in the
top of a tree, the shaft had split upon the cord,
and sprung back with such violence in his eye,
as utterly to destroy it.

Audubon's attention was directed next to the
peculiarly comfortless and barren aspect of his
strange abode, without a single bed on which to
recruit his weary limbs; some untanned bear
and buffalo skins were the only invitation to repose.   As he received no voluntary courtesy
from his hostess, he was anxious to let her know
of the hunger of which he was so painfully sen-
sible himself, and, to propitiate her, drew forth a
rich watch from his vest.   This told, apparently,
with electric force upon her feelings; for he
was instantly informed of the existence of cakes,
venison, and other dainties, from which to make
an excellent repast.   But, first, he was compelled again to gratify her curiosity by another
sight of the watch which she beheld in wonder.
She received with ecstasy the gold chain, which

Audubon presented to her; and hanging it with barbaric pride around her brawny neck, she expressed, at the same time, how happy the possession of the watch also would make her. Meanwhile, Audubon, more intent on satisfying his appetite than securing his ornaments, paid little attention to her antics.

In this deceptive case he would have remained, but for the extraordinary—and what to him appeared unaccountable—movements of the young Indian. Though seemingly in the greatest suffering, he rose from his seat, and, failing to attract Audubon's especial attention by passing and repassing before him, at length pinched him violently. Audubon looked up, about to exclaim in anger at the pain, but was checked by a glance which sent a chill through his blood. The Indian then seating himself drew a knife from its scabbard, examined its edge, and again taking its tomahawk and filling the pipe of it with tobacco, from time to time, exchanged expressive looks with Audubon, when the back of his hostess was turned. He now understood the warning, and was well aware, that though enemies encircled him, the Indian was none among them. Under an impromptu pretence, he soon walked out of the cabin.

After priming his gun, he returned to the hut, where, making a pallet of bear skins, and calling his dog to his side, in a few minutes he feigned a deep slumber, while awaiting the issue of the adventure. In a short time two youths entered, bearing a stag on a pole. Having laid down their burden, they asked for whisky, of which they drank freely, all the while increasing the ferocity of their gestures.

The mother then spoke in a low tone concerning the watch, and a conversation ensued which it was easy to interpret. Audubon then gently tapped his dog, and beheld with indescribable relief the splendid eyes of the faithful animal sagaciously raised, as though aware of the impending danger, alternating towards his master and the trio in conversation. The looks of the young Indian, too, reassured him.

Yet it needed all his fortitude quietly to observe the menacing proceedings, for with surprise and horror he beheld the wretch, whose cupidity had been excited by his possessions, take up a large carving knife, and proceed to the grindstone to whet its edge. A sickness of soul crept over him as he observed her sharpening still more and more the deadly instrument with which she was about to take advantage of his defenceless condition.

Approaching him cautiously, she appeared contemplating the readiest method of dispatch.

The moment which might, spite his endea-

7

vours at self-defence, be his last, was at hand, when suddenly the door opened, and two stout travellers, armed with rifles entered. Offering them a hearty welcome, Audubon instantly made his situation understood. The Indian danced for joy, and the culprits were now the captives. The return of a bright and rosy dawn brought their merited punishment, that which Regulators usually employ for such delinquents. Their cabin was then fired, and its contents became the possessions of the young Indian.

But if Audubon, during his wanderings, had sometimes cause to be suspicious of receptions afforded him by the foresters, he had often reason to appreciate with gratitude their friendly hospitality. With these simple inhabitants of the woods, no sense of expediency or compulsory courtesy alloys the kindly welcome, which springs solely from the generous impulse of their hearts. The shelter and refreshment of their humble dwellings and homely fare is unostentatiously offered. Their hospitality, mingled thus with no pompous condescension or officious attention, is received and remembered with peculiarly pleasurable impressions.

Such an impression was retained by Audubon of an incident which he met with during his travels, when accompanied by his youthful son. They had walked several hundred miles, when, approaching a clear steam, they gladly observed a habitation on the opposite side. It proved to be a tavern, which they reached by crossing in a canoe. There they resolved to spend the night, and as they were much fatigued, arranged with their host to be conveyed in a Jersey wagon some hundred miles further. The rising of the moon was to be the moment for departure. "That orbed maiden with white fire laden," soon spread her silvery light over the woods. Their conductor, then armed a long twig of hickory, took a foremost seat in the wagon. Off went the travellers at a round trot, to be hurried fearlessly over tree trunks, stumps, and ruts which lined the road, till they danced in the vehicle like pease in a sieve! A bright dawn seemed the herald of fair weather; but soon the cheerful tenor of their way was interrupted by a change. Rain fell in torrents, thunder roared, and lightning flamed, till night set in black and dismal. Cold and wet, with little disposition now to loquacity or mirth, the wan-derers were compelled to pursue their course, with no better prospect than braving the still threatening elements throughout the night, as they had done, in the open cart. To stop was plainly to seal such a doom. Onward they went, till, on a sudden, a curve in the course of their march brought the glimmer of a light, appar-

ently not far off.   At the same moment the barking of dogs fell gratefully on their ears in the solitude.   They exchanged a salute, and no sooner
had they done so than a pine torch glared across
the gloom.   Without any ceremony of questioning, the negro boy by whom it was borne enjoined
the travellers to follow him.   The door of a
dwelling was soon reached, when a tall fine-
looking young fellow desired them to enter.
Spite the humble dimensions of the cabin, no
more inviting refuge could be imagined.   It had
evidently only been recently constructed by the
inmates, a young couple, who with the amiable
simplicity of wood-doves, had sought this humble shelter in which to tell all the happy tale of
love.   It was built of logs of the tulip tree,
neatly carved, and slabs of wood, white as snow,
formed the floor.   A large spinning-wheel, with
rolls of cotton, occupied one corner, and sundry
garments, its produce, testified the ingenious industry of the young matron.   A small cupboard
contained a stock of bright new crockery, in
dishes, plates, and pans.   The table and other few
pieces of furniture shone bright as polished walnut could be.   The only bed it contained was of
domestic manufacture.   A fine rifle ornamented
the mantel-shelf.   The ready activity and cheerful unremitting attention shown by the young
wife towards the strangers proved the sincerity

of her pleasure in sharing her husband's expressions of hospitality.

The wanderers, seated by the fire, had fresh
clothes, warm and dry, presented to them in return for their drenched garments. The blaze of
the wood logs illumined the cottage, and the
sight of poultry told of good cheer, when the
host expressed his regret "that the travellers
had not arrived three weeks earlier; for," said
he, "it was our wedding-day. My father gave
us a good house-warming, and you might have
fared better; but if you can eat bacon, with eggs
and a broiled chicken, you shall have that. I
have no whisky; but my father has some excellent cider. I'll go for a keg of it—it's only
three miles, so I'll be back before Eliza has
cooked your supper." In a minute, through the
pouring of the rain, which fell in torrents, the
galloping of his horse was heard. Meantime the
negroes ground some coffee, and bread was
baked by the fair young wife. The cloth was
set, and all arranged, when the clattering of
hoofs told the husband's return. He entered,
bearing a two-gallon keg of cider. His eyes
beamed with benevolent pleasure at the adventure, while, seated by the fire, he filled a bowl
with the sparkling juice. Supper over, part
of the bedding was arranged for the guests.
Sweetly they slept till the return of morning,

7*

when, after a hearty breakfast, they pursued their way, now with a brighter atmosphere and more buoyant hopes. The young woodsman headed the party on horseback, till beyond the difficulties of the road, when, after a friendly farewell, he returned to his dear Eliza and his pleasant home.

CHAPTER VII.

DURING April, 1824, Audubon visited Philadelphia, with the view of continuing his researches eastward along the coast.

Up to this time, though so diligent a student, he appears to have entertained no definite idea of any beneficial or advantageous result of his efforts. Never, indeed, did he dare to indulge the hope of becoming in any degree useful to his kind, much less did he dream of the rare success which should one day signalize his name. Yet to this end did the irresistible impulse of his genius unconsciously incite him. Led on by the pure attraction of his love, as the disciple of science, heroically and patiently he followed on, until at length her best rewards were gratefully bestowed.

On visiting Philadelphia, his only friends in the city, were Dr. Mease, whom he had known in his youthful days, and Dr. Richard Harlan, long his friend, and whose friendship continued through the lifetime of Audubon. By them, Audubon was introduced to the illustrious nataralist, Charles Lucien Bonaparte; and, through that medium, to the Natural History Society of Philadelphia. Lucien Bonaparte he seems ever to have affectionately regarded as his earliest patron. Through him he first conceived the idea of his great work, and was incited to arrange his drawings, already classified into three distinct departments, in a form suitable for publication. The suggestion was long a mingled source of delight and torment to Audubon. Sometimes happily absorbed in the most pleasing dreams, he fancied his work already multiplying under the hands of the engraver. Sometimes he speculated as to the possibility of his visiting Europe again, to ensure that end. At another, glancing over the catalogue of his collection, all the difficulty of the magnificent scheme presented itself. Only the more impossible it seemed from the grandeur of the design, and from the intensity of his desire to accomplish it. Then gloomy and depressed, he asked himself how could he, unknown and unassisted, hope to accomplish it? This was the critical moment of his career. As yet, his partial achievements, though full of promise, met with but little of the patronage so abundantly awarded to more matured success, which, itself a sufficient stimulus, needs not the encouragement. The temptation was, should he abandon his pursuits, so long cherished, so dearly prized? That he felt to be impossible. To follow them at any rate were preferable, and thus renewed, in spirit, with fresh resolve, alternations of feeling no longer tormented him. Dividing his collection into separate parcels of five plates, he improved the whole carefully as much as was in his power. He then determined to retire further from the haunts of men, while nothing that his labour, time, or means could command, should be left undone, to ensure the realization of his plan. Wisely he toiled, in solitude, and self sustained. He continued to explore the forests, lakes, and prairies, in order to enrich his collections, even penetrating to the Great Pine swamp. In reaching it, he was rattled by his conductor down a steep declivity, edged on the one hand by perpendicular rocks; on the other, by a noisy stream, which seemed to threaten the approach of strangers. The thick growth of pines and laurels rendered the swamp one mass of darkness. But, with his gun and note-book, Audubon struggled through its mazes, now lingering to enrich his portfolio, while wild turkeys, pheasants, and grouse hovered about his feet, now beguiling his toil by listening to the poetry of Burns, read aloud by his companion while he polished some sketch in hand.

On one occasion, during his wanderings, when

Audubon's ingenuity was put to the test, his talents as an artist stood him in good stead. While on the shores of Upper Canada, his money was stolen from him by an adventurer, with all the adroitness of a London pickpocket. To continue his journey without an increase to his few remaining dollars would have been impossible; so putting his portfolio under his arm, and a few good credentials in his pocket, on reaching Meadville, he perambulated the principal streets, in the hope that a little pardonable vanity in his species, would favor his design, and induce many a one to sit for his portrait. Looking to the right and the left, he seemed examining the different physiognomics with the critical gaze of a painter, till at length, meeting with what appeared a likely subject, attitudinizing in a doorway, he begged to be allowed to sit down, as he was much fatigued. Receiving an assent, he very cunningly remained perfectly quiet, with his portfolio in a prominent position, till at length, the dandy asked "what was in that portfolio?" On exhibiting its contents, he was complimented by the young Hollander, his companion, on the execution of his drawings of birds and flowers, when Audubon, showing him a very agreeable sketch of a friend, asked if he would like such a one of himself?

The Hollander not only assented, but promised

to procure him other sitters, if his own portrait were satisfactory. As it proved perfectly so, the artist's room was soon filled with the aristocracy of the place. After a few days sojourn, the itinerant portrait painter, attired in his gray coat, his long hair flowing loosely over his shoulders, was enabled, with a light heart and a well replenished purse, to pursue his journey. After a lapse of eighteen months, spent in varied adventure, Audubon returned to Louisiana, where his family then were. Again he diligently applied himself to his vocation, and investigated now every nook of the vast extent of woodland around that fertile and beautiful State. In this, his favourite resting-place, Audubon loved to loiter. Here, magnificent abundance in verdure, fruits and flowers, tells the richness of the soil. Huge cypresses interlace their broad tops, till no sunbeam can penetrate their shade ; in the swamps of matted grass and lichens, turtle-doves coo in hundreds on branches of trees—alligators plunge into the pools, and the scream of the heron, and hoarse cry of the anhinga, contrast with the soft melodious love notes of a thousand forest warblers.

Amidst the enchantments of such scenes, Audubon added many a treasure to his discoveries. He pronounces the rich notes, powerful, mellow, and varied of the Louisiana water thrush, a resident of the low lands, nothing inferior even to our boasted nightingale : its voice is heard afar from out the depths of the brakes. The peculiarity of its song resembles the sounds of a piano ; for, beginning in an upper key, it passes through the scale down to the lowest bass note, with the skill of an opera artiste. In its habits as in its appearance, it differs from the common water thrush. The latter is proverbially shy—the former so unsuspecting as to allow of a person's near approach. While the bird found in the eastern or northern regions wades through the water, that of the south merely skims over it. In flight, it glides smoothly through the air, and does not ever soar high. The hermit thrush, so called, probably from its peculiar love of secluded spots, is another resident in Louisiana, where it abounds even during the winter months. It prefers the darkest, lowest solitudes, till the floods, which inundate the swamps, compel it to retire to higher lands. Its movements resemble those of our red-breasted robin—after hopping a few steps, it raises its head and looks sagaciously round. The nests of this bird are always found on the low branches of trees. A soft plaintive note is the only utterance of this aerial hermit.

A favourite with Audubon, not only above its fellows, but beyond all the feathered tribes of the forest, was the wood thrush. As the harbinger of returning serenity in the elements, its wild notes were welcomed by him with peculiar pleasure. Often it was his fate to pass the night in some wretched hut, so ill constructed as to leave him entirely unprotected against the storm. The wavering sparks of his log fire, extinguished by the dense torrents of rain, which enveloped the whole Heavens and earth in one murky mass, defied his best efforts to rekindle them ; the sole light that met his eyes, were the red streaks of the thunderbolt, which, scathing in its course the stateliest trees close around him, was followed instantaneously by the crashing, deafening sounds of their destruction, and the rolling echoes of the tumult far and near. On such a night, desolate, indeed, was Audubon's situation ; far from the sweetest shelter of home, and the objects dearest to his heart. Weary, hungry and sad, he had the misery, above all, of anticipating the destruction of those treasured possessions, for which so much was relinquished and endured, as the water, collecting into a stream, menaced them by rushing through his camp, forcing its miserable inhabitant, shivering as in an ague, to stand erect and wait while, tormented with mosquitoes, with a martyr's patience, the return of day ! How did his memory return to the peaceful, happy days of his early youth, the delights of his home and

8

the embraces of his family, questioning if ever again he should behold them. Then as the first beams of morning spread over the dusky mass of foliage, the musical notes of the wood thrush —that joyful herald of the day, broke gratefully upon his ear, as if to re-assure his doubting spirit. Fervently as he listened did he bless that Being who created this companion to console his solitude, cheer his depression, and sustain his faith under all situations. His fears vanished at the inspiring strain of the songster, and were replaced by buoyant hopes. The heavens gradually cleared. The gladdening rays of the sun rising from the distant horizon dissipated the gray mist spread over the face of nature, and increased in intensity, till the majestic orb shone in complete effulgence on the sight, as the clear fresh notes of the thrush were heard, echoed by all the choristers of the wood. From its habits, this thrush might be denominated also a hermit of the forest ; for solitudes overshadowed by lofty trees, or the borders of murmuring streamlets, are its favourite resorts. There, delighted with the charms of seclusion, it pours forth its mellow song in "full throated ease," and its music may be heard to perfection. It is scarcely possible to listen without that tranquility stealing over the soul, which the serenity of the scene, as well as the melody of the song, inspires. Though possessing but few notes, these are extraordinarily distinct, powerful, harmonious, and clear. Gradually they rise in strength —then fall in gentle cadences, so as to be scarcely audible, expressing alternately all the emotions of the lover, who at one moment exults in the realization of his hopes, the next pauses in doubt as to his fate. It is a peculiar habit among this species of bird to challenge each other from different parts of the forest, as if in rivalry, when their music is more than ordinarily effective, exhibiting a remarkable skill in modulation. These concerts which occur during the "leafy month of June," take place generally towards evening, so that the notes of other " curious chaunters," who have retired to rest, may not interfere. The wood thrush glides swiftly when on wing, and performs its migrations in a manner characteristic of its love of seclusion, singly and without ever appearing in the open country. It is frequently seen in other parts of the States but is a constant resident in Louisiana, where the whole of its species congregate from different parts for the winter. The sight of a racoon causes these birds much distress, and through the mournful "cluck" with which they follow these animals at a respectful distance, they are unfortunately recognized by the hunters, for their flesh is extremely delicate and juicy.

But unrivalled, perhaps, for powers of melody and grace of motion is the mocking bird, which remains in Louisiana throughout the year. Arrayed in his soft plumage, delicately blended, with movements airy as a butterfly, his tail expanded, and his lovely wings outspread, he may be seen mounting in the air. Describing a circle around his beloved, he alights and approaches her with beaming delighted eyes. After gently inclining himself, as if courteously bowing, he again soars upward, and pours forth an exulting song of conquest, as if his full breast were about to be rent with delight, his notes flowing more softly and richly than before, in varied modulations of wonderfully brilliant execution. Alighting as at first, he then mounts higher in the air, and glances around with a watchful eye, lest any intruder should mar his bliss. Then gaily dancing through the air, as though to assure his companion of the plenitude of his love, his song flows afresh in imitation of every other warbler of the grove, and may be often heard to mimic, even quadrupeds, with ease. There appears to be no foundation, however, for the assertion of his ability to imitate the human voice.

At a certain note from his beloved, the mocking bird, in order to know her wishes, ceases his song. They then mutually inspect the sweetbrier bushes or orange tree of some garden for a place in which to prepare a nest. Frequently the mocking bird may be seen bearing food in his mouth for his companion, when he flies to the nest to secure her caresses and thanks. Dewberries, garden fruits, and sometimes insects, form their food. These birds are especially careful of their young, and should they perceive that some intruder has visited their nest, they may be heard with low mournful notes condoling together. Different kinds of snakes ascend to their retreats, and frequently destroy the brood, when not only the pair to which the nest belongs, but many other birds of the tribe league together for revenge, fly to the spot, attack the reptile, and either force him to retreat, or else deprive him of life. So much veneration is felt for the mocking bird throughout Louisiana, that one is seldom permitted to be shot.

Returning with the promise of Spring, and the very first genial rays of the sun, as early as the ninth or tenth of March, the ruby-throated humming bird appears in the Louisiana woods; visiting in turn prairies, fields, orchards, and secluded shades of the forest, may be seen this bright aerial wanderer in its gorgeous chameleon hues, sparkling in the air like a fragment of the rainbow. Naturalists unite in describing rapturously this most exquisitely apparelled winged

8*

creature. "Now it flutters from flower to flower, to sip the silver dew—it is now a ruby—now a topaz—now an emerald—now all burnished gold!" *

Fluttering with airy graceful motion from flower to flower, it speeds on humming winglets so lightly as to seem upheld by magic. The dazzling beauty of its delicate form, clothed in plumage of resplendent changing green, is increased by the brilliancy of its throat, now glowing with fiery hue, now transformed into a deep velvet-like black, as throwing itself onwards with inconceivable vivacity and swiftness, it darts like a gleam of light upon the eye. Skimming on fairy wing, it carefully approaches the opening blossoms. Poised in the air, its sparkling eye peeps cautiously into their inmost recesses, like a skilful florist, careful to remove the hurtful insects that lurk within their beauteous petals, and threaten them with decay. In this process so light and rapid are the motions of its ethereal pinions, that they seem rather to fan and cool the flower, than injure its fragile loveliness, while the dreamy murmuring of the bird, lulling the insects to repose, hastens the moment of their destruction. Instantly as the delicate bill of the bird enters the flower cup, the enemy is drawn

* Charles Waterton's Wanderings, p. 114

forth and dispatched in a moment, when the bird departs, after sipping a little of the liquid honey gratefully given by the flower to its champion. This beautiful creature seems to possess great activity of flight. " The whole structure of these birds is adapted for flight; their feet are very small, their tail is large, their wings are very long and narrow." *   Sometimes, the humming of its wings telling its approach, it is seen within a few feet, when one is suddenly astonished at the rapidity with which it soars, and is out of sight and hearing in a moment. Its flight is performed in long undulations. It does not alight on the ground, but settles on twigs and branches, where it moves sideways in prettily measured steps, often opening and shutting its wings in "silent ecstasy." After pluming and shaking, as if arranging its splendid apparel, it is fond of spreading one wing at a time, and passing each of the feathers through its bill, the wing being thus rendered extremely transparent, and glittering in the light. Not unfrequently it is chased by a large kind of humble bee, of which it haughtily disdains to take notice, as in a minute its rapid journeying leaves the drone far behind. Its nest is of a peculiarly delicate nature, the outer parts being of a light gray

* White's Popular History of Birds, p. 66.

lichen, so neatly arranged on the branches of the trees, as to seem a portion of the stem to which it is fixed. The next coating is of a cotton substance, and the innermost of the silky pods of various plants, extremely soft and comfortable. No sooner are the young able to provide for themselves, than they associate with other broods, and perform their migrations apart from the old birds. Enterprising as travellers, they are possessed of singular hardihood, as well as marvellous beauty, visiting dreary and inclement regions, such as Patagonia and Canada. Twenty or thirty young ones may be seen sporting amidst a group of flowers, and not a single old one to be found. They receive a portion of sustenance from most plants, but are especially fond of the sweet trumpet flower and honeysuckle. They sip the nectar, in order to allay their thirst, making their meals of more substantial nourishment. As the humming bird does not shun mankind like the more timid of the feathered tribes, it is often imprisoned and supplied with artificial flowers, in the corollas of which honey, with water, or dissolved sugar is placed. On this diet, however, it seldom lives many months, owing probably to the absence of its general food—the minute insects found in or among living flowers.

Rivalling these in splendour are the cinnyris or

sun birds, of which the rich and dazzling hues
seen gleaming in the light, have earned for them
the graceful and appropriate appellation of
" atoms of the rainbow."

"Ethereal, gay, and sprightly in their motions,
flitting briskly from flower to flower, they assume
a thousand lovely and agreeable attitudes. As
the sunbeams glitter on their bodies, they sparkle
like so many precious stones, and exhibit as
they turn a variety of bright and iridescent
hues. Some are emerald-green, some vivid violet, and others yellow with crimson wing."*
But it is to the gorgeous vegetation of the east
that these matchlessly attired songsters lend their
brilliance, where, lingering midst the rich blossoms, they gleam, outrivalling the flowers dyed
in crimson, violet, or gold.

* Adams in Belcher, Voyage XI.

CHAPTER VIII.

IN a certain section on the Mississippi River, there is an extensive swamp, interesting to all lovers of natural philosophy, from its rare and curious abundance of birds, animals, and reptiles. This swamp follows the windings of the Yazoo, till that river breaks off to the north-east, forming at that point the stream named Cold Water River. Audubon, during his rambles about its banks, chanced to meet with a squatter's cabin. The owner, like most other settlers in such districts, was a lover of adventure, and so well versed in the chase, as to be intimately acquainted with the habits of birds and quadrupeds. Audubon, immediately on entering the hut, conversed with the settler respecting the situation and productions of the swamp. The answers he received were such as to increase his interest on the spot. He then requested the favour that his host would guide him through the morasses, and welcome guest as he was, instantly found this, like all his other wishes was cordially assented to. An evening of pleasant quietude, during which, many an entertaining recital was alternately made, closed at length into night, when all betook themselves to their pallets of bearskin, on the floor of the only apartment the hut contained. With the return of dawn, Audubon was awakened by the settler's call to his dogs, of which the numbers had been greatly diminished—he was informed on joining his host—by the ravages of the cougar or American panther, which frequented the neighbourhood. Added to these devastations it had committed many feats of singular audacity, all which were related by the settler, in order to impress upon Audubon the formidable character of the animal.

But the Naturalist, nothing daunted, was delighted by the description, and equally to the surprise and satisfaction of his host, assured him how pleased he should be to assist in the attack, and, if possible, the destruction of the enemy. The suggestion was gratefully received, and the settler after scouring the country in search of candidates for the adventure, at length succeeded in appointing a day of meeting. Accordingly, one morning as the sun rose brightly, five hunters on horseback, fully equipped for the chase, presented themselves at the door of the cabin. They were soon joined by Audubon and his companion, mounted on trusty animals—the whole cavalcade followed, not only by the settler's dogs, but the packs which attended the strangers. Intent upon their enterprise, the party proceeded in silence till they arrived at the edge of a swamp, when eall agreed to disperse and separately seek the track of the panther, with the condition that the triumphant discoverer should remain to keep guard on the spot, till joined by the rest of the retinue. They had not long to wait the exciting signal. In less than two hours the horn was distinctly heard. Guided by its repeated call, the place of rendezvous was soon reached. The most reliable dog was then sent forward to scent the track of the formidable cougar, and its course was told as the whole pack, following their leader, bore towards the interior of the swamp. The huntsmen with their rifles in great trim pressed on their rear, determined to have the panther or nothing for their prey.

The dogs continued to quicken their pace and increase their noise, when suddenly their barking altered, from which it was evident that the animal was treed, that is, he had ascended a tree for safety or to rest for a few moments.* Should it not be shot when thus situated, a long chase must ensue. At this critical moment, the hunt-

---

* When "treed," panthers will ascend to the highest limbs of the tallest trees to gain a perfect security.

ers, repressing their eagerness, moved their well-trained horses cautiously forward. A shot was heard. The cougar leapt to the ground, but again bounded off, the dogs now darting in pursuit, with deafening cries, still towards the centre of the swamp. A slight trail of blood upon the ground convinced the pursuers that the monster had not been aimed at in vain.

On sped the hounds, till the horses, spurred forwards and emulating their swift march, began to pant in the chase. The panther being wounded, the wily hunters well knew he would soon ascend another tree for refuge. Dismounting then their weary horses, the combatants, nothing disheartened, pressed forward on foot. Pools, one after another, still larger and more stagnant, fallen trees and tangled brushwood, which covered acres of the ground, were soon crossed. After a march of two hours again, the exciting cry of the hounds was heard. Stimulated still more in the chase, each one, elated with the hope of being the first to terminate the career of the terrible cougar, seemed animated with the indomitable ambition of Hercules, Theseus, or St. George. At last, from the peculiar barking of the dogs, they knew the cougar was again treed, and this time, as they approached, beheld the ferocious animal distinctly, lying across the huge trunk of a cottonwood tree. His eyes alternately glanced at his pursuers, and the dogs around and beneath him. His wounded fore-leg hung loosely, as he crouched, with his ears close to his head, as though designing to remain undiscovered. On a given signal, three balls were discharged; when the monster, smitten with the agony of the blow, sprung a few feet from the tree, and then fell headlong to the earth.

Attacked on all sides, he fought with infuriated desperation; till the bold settler, advancing in front of the cavalcade, struck him a fatal blow. For a moment he writhed in agony, the next lay dead, as shouts from the combatants told the victory was won.

To celebrate it, the cougar was despoiled of his skin for a trophy, and a camp festival was held on the spot by the victors. Beside a blazing fire, with venison and whisky for their cheer, stories and songs went round; till, wearied with the toils of war, they laid themselves down, and were soon asleep. The only booty of, the fray, the cougar's skin, remained in the possession of the settler, in order that, while gazing on it, he might congratulate himself on the extinction of the much dreaded destroyer of his stock.

An incident, not less memorable than this encounter with the cougar, occurred to Audubon while on another occasion penetrating the formidable interior of an American swamp. A sultry noon rendered it dangerous to linger midst the pernicious effluvia with which excessive heat impregnates the dense atmosphere of their morasses.

Audubon, therefore, laden with the double burden of his weighty gun, and a rich booty of wood ibises, directed his course towards home. Unexpectedly he came upon the banks of a miry pool. As he could not ascertain the depth of the water, owing to its muddiness, he thought it best, while wading through it, to dispense with his burden, which he flung to the opposite margin. Then drawing his knife, as a defence against alligators, he plunged into the pool, followed by his faithful Plato.

Soon he had reason to think that alligators were not the only enemies to be feared. Scarcely had he reached the shore, when his dog exhibited unmistakeable signs of terror at some discovery he was the first to make. Audubon supposing his fear to proceed from the scent of some bear or wolf, put his hand on his gun, when he was enlightened as to the cause of alarm by a loud voice, which commanded him to " stand still, or die." Astonished and indignant at so singular and peremptory a mandate, he determined to resist it, no matter from whom it proceeded; and instantly cocked his gun, though unable to perceive the hidden challenger.

Presently a stout negro emerged from his lurking place, where he had crouched in the brushwood, and repeated his command in a still more threatening tone.

Audubon perceiving, however, the worthlessness of the gun which his enemy was about to aim at his breast, forbore to use his own, and only gently tapped his trusty Plato. He had no reason to regret the forbearance, for the negro, instead of endeavouring to take advantage of it, seemed entirely disarmed by such generosity. In answer to Audubon's inquiries, his simple story was soon told, and the energetic demonstrations of the poor runaway were seemingly fully accounted for by other than guilty motives. In constant apprehension of pursuit, his dread of capture caused him at the least signal of alarm, he said, to stand on the defensive. "Master," he continued, my tale is short and sorrowful. My camp is close by. You cannot reach home to-night. If you will follow me, depend upon my honour that you shall be safe until the morning, when, if you please, I will carry your birds for you to the Great Road." As he spoke, the benevolence of his intelligent eyes, with the attraction of his voice and manner, so assured

THE FUGITIVE. Page 100.

Audubon—never unnecessarily suspicious—that he assented, with a slight emphasis, however, on the phrase that he would follow him.

The negro, observing it, in order to put his companion at ease, then threw away the flint and priming of his gun. His knife he presented to Audubon, who, desirous of showing equal generosity, refused it. On they went through the woods together, Audubon not failing to observe that the course they pursued was directly contrary to his homeward road. After travelling some distance, the negro leading the way, with the accuracy of a redskin, over tangled swamps, and stagnant streams, Audubon was startled by a loud shriek from his companion. Involuntarily he again levelled his gun. "No harm, master," said the negro in answer, "I only give notice to my wife and children of my approach." The signal was answered in gentler tones from female lips, when an expression of delight, which disclosed his ivory teeth, lightened across the negro's countenance. "Master," he said, with a winning simplicity, "my wife, though black, is as beautiful to me as the President's wife is to him. She is my queen, and our young ones are our princes. But you shall see them, for here they all are, thank God." They soon reached the very heart of a cane brake, and here the poor fugitives had formed their camp,

9*

the few possessions of which were neatly and carefully disposed. The kindly demeanour of the negro, together with the amiable expression of his affection for his family, had now completely won Audubon's confidence. Convinced of his host's good intentions, and the sincerity of his hospitality, he did not hesitate to remain beneath his roof. While he received every attention which could ensure his comfort, the children caressed his dog, and after partaking heartily of a savoury repast, he eagerly listened to the painful recital of the negro's trials.

The master to whom he and his family had at first belonged, had been obliged, in consequence of some heavy losses he had sustained, to offer them for sale. The negro was purchased by a planter—his wife became the possession of another, a hundred miles distant, and the children were hurried to different places. The loving heart of the slave was overwhelmed with grief at the calamity of this great loss. For a time entirely prostrated by the misfortune, he sorrowed in the deepest dejection, without energy or hope. At length the powers of resistance awakened. He resolved to act boldly and without delay. One stormy night, when the fury of the hurricane favoured him, by causing every one to seek the shelter of his dwelling, he effected his escape, his intimate knowledge of the neighbouring swamps and brakes facilitating his design. A few nights afterwards he had again the joy of embracing his beloved wife—the next day they wandered together.

Through his caution and unwearied assiduity, he succeeded in obtaining one after another the children, till at length all the cherished objects of his affection were gathered, like a tender brood, beneath the sheltering wings of the bird, under his care. But with the joy of this renewed protection was mingled a painful sense of responsibility, wandering in dreary wilds, where scarcely subsistence for one, much less for five human beings could be found. He was tormented, moreover, by dread of seizure, for he well knew that since his disappearance the forest had been daily ransacked by armed pursuers. Yet driven by extreme privation he was compelled to brave discovery in search of a precarious provision of wild fruits and game. On one of these excursions, as was said, he had been surprised by Audubon. After thus relating to him their secret, both, with tears in their eyes, implored his exertions on behalf of them and their children, who sweetly slumbering, appealed by their helplessness and innocence no less powerfully for protection.

Most cordially Audubon promised them all the assistance in his power. On the following day, accompanied by the run away and his family, he departed from the hut, leaving the ibises hung around the walls of the hut, and many a notch in the neighbouring trees as a memento of his presence. They then bent their way towards the dwelling of the negro's first master. On arriving there, they were received with the most generous kindness. At the request of Audubon, according to the desire of the fugitives, they were repurchased from their late master, and admitted once again into the benevolent planter's family, were ever after regarded as a part of it, and gratefully remembered the good fortune which had brought Audubon to them as a guest.

Rich in interest as are the environs of the Mississippi, not less so is the extraordinary river itself, exhibiting on the recurrence of certain seasons, that truly marvellous spectacle, appalling in its splendour, known as a Flood. With the sudden melting of the snow which had enwrapt the mountains during the severity of winter, an enormous volume of water, turbid and swollen, inundates its broad channels. Its magnitude may be imagined, from the gigantic dimensions of this stream, the course of which is several thousand miles in extent. At the periods of inundation, the waters of the Ohio sometimes mingle with those of the Mississippi, and then it is when in combination, when vast rivers are booming on in their united force, that they are seen in all their magnificence. The waters, having reached the upper part of the banks, then rush forth, overspreading the whole of the adjacent swamps, till all appears one vast ocean, above which a few tall forest trees show their tops, all else submerged beneath the waste, till at length undermined, they are seen to give way and disappear; while stupendous eddies engulph whole tracts of the land. Foaming, seething, and boiling, the torrent rushes, one huge and overpowering mass, fraught with terror and destruction, impetuously and irresistibly on, swallowing for ever the horses, bears and deer, which attempt to cross its relentless surface. Eagles and vultures, the grim attendants of mortality alone are seen, unmindful of the flood, and intent upon their prey.

Meanwhile, the inhabitants, terror-stricken at the sudden inundation, their ingenuity quickened by the terrible doom it threatens, exert their utmost to escape the horrors of the raging element. The Indian hastens to the hills of the interior. Dwellers on the banks of the river may be seen removing themselves and their possessions on rafts, which they fasten with ropes or grape vines to the larger trees, hurrying to unknown homes, while witnessing the melancholy sight of the destruction of their houses by the current. Boats are tossed like playthings by the waters, and even the steam-vessels groan, distressed by the number of logs and branches, which float alongside, impeding their course.

Here and there along the shore, the entire population of a district congregate to strengthen and repair the artificial barrier or levée, as it is called, several feet above the general level of the ground, which prudence has raised as a defence against the overflow. Yet sometimes, in spite of all exertions, a *crevace* or channel opens, and the water bursting in, lays waste all the crops lately luxuriating in the bloom of spring. In the vast tracts of the interior country, over-whelmed by the waters, all is silent and melan-choly. The mournful bleating of the deer alone is heard, or the dismal scream of the ravens or eagles, which, brooding over the desolation, allay their ravenous appetites on the wretched remnants of the catastrophe. Bears, cougars, and lynxes crouch among the topmost branches of the trees, glaring down with ferocious, restless glance; for, agonized perhaps with the pangs of hunger, though beholding around them abundance of animals as their prey, they dare not brave the glistening sheet of waters beneath. At such times they would quietly stand the hunter's fire, preferring instant destruction to the misery of a lingering doom midst the desolation of the earth.

With the subsiding of the waters, at length carried to the ocean, a thick deposit of loam is left on those parts which the flood has visited; from which, in warm weather, an exhalation like a dense fog arises. Extraordinary are the transformations effected by the inundation. Large streams appear where none were supposed to exist. Sand banks whirled by the waters have been deposited in fresh places, and trees have disappeared from the margin of streams, while the upper portions of islands appear like a bulwark of floating trunks and branches. Soon, however, all is fresh life and vigour. Lamentation for the devastations is exchanged for activity in repairing them.

The settler shoulders his rifle and searches the morass in the hope of discovering some of his scattered possessions. New defences are raised and new habitations erected. Lands are ploughed and fresh crops are raised. Yet many a disappointment and many a mis-adventure impends from the catastrophe, and many a traveller finds a bank of sand which, seemingly secure, suddenly gives way beneath his horse, which it engulphs to the chest, leaving his master not in the situation he would choose.

During several weeks these floods rise at the

rate of a foot a-day. When at the highest they undergo little fluctuation for some days, after which they gradually subside. Their usual duration, from four to six weeks, is occasionally protracted to two months.

CHAPTER IX.

NOTWITHSTANDING years of toil devoted by Audubon to ensure the achievement of his cherished plan, disappointments and impediments continued long to test the strength of his resolution and the power of his faith. Yet such was the vigour and elevation of his genius that vicissitudes seemed only to increase the elasticity of his naturally buoyant spirits, and impart a more indomitable fervour to his enthusiasm.

Irrepressible by trial from without—the chill of uncongenial contact or contest with the harsh inexorable conditions of expediency, his genius possessed an imperishable spring within itself which no opposing external force could destroy. Intrinsically it was the source of unequalled pleasures and satisfactions—themselves a rich reward, a perpetual consolation and assistance. From the arguments of interested or sordid policy, the coldness of skepticism, the apathy of ignorance or selfishness, he took refuge in the seclusion of his beloved woods. There, in

10

boundless freedom, he found a congenial atmosphere, and enjoyed that simpathy which too frequently failed him among men, in the melodious language of the forest songsters. Contemplating, moreover, the wisdom and unerring compassion of the Creator in the splendour of his works, his constancy was renewed by reliance. At night his rude couch was the verdure-fringed margin of a brook, the interior of some untravelled forest, or the soft sands of the sea-shore. Aroused at early dawn, he was invigourated by healthful sleep, to wander for days and weeks in the pure air, partaking of his simple repasts under the shelter of green boughs. As evening approached, sending the birds to their retreats, and darkness enshrouded the earth, the naturalist, grateful to the Divine protection in his solitude, knelt in prayer. Then as he dreamily sunk into repose pleasant images of dear friends and home filled his fancy, and kindly wishes his heart. The strength of his physical constitution was thus retained and even increased. To this was doubtless owing much of that undiminished energy and moral fortitude which enabled him to combat so successfully the ordeals of his career. The inability to publish his illustrations in America was naturally a source of the deepest regret. As the subject of his patriotic pride, the scene of his efforts and discoveries, associated too with all his most cherished remembrances and best delights, he desired there first to witness the inauguration of his hopes. Yet, in Philadelphia, it was the opinion that his drawings could never be engraved. In New York he met with no better success.

At length he determined to try the fate of his collection in Europe, whither in 1826, he directed his steps. Whether owing to rare modesty as to his endowments, or an exaggerated estimate of intellect on our side of the Atlantic, he seems to have been overwhelmed on approaching English shores, with a sense of diffidence—"imagining," he says, "that every individual he was about to meet might be possessed of talents superior to those of any one in America!" Visiting for the first time a foreign country, often pictured in his imagination, its resources and acquisitions magnified by contemplation, regarding it moreover with peculiar interest as an arena for the decision, as it were, of his destiny, such feelings might naturally arise in the unsophisticated heart of the American woodsman. Without friend or acquaintance he could not anticipate a single welcome on his arrival. Soon, however, his position was such as to cause all his scruples to vanish. The letters of introduction which he carried speedily procured him a large and influential circle of friends.

At Liverpool, his first resting-place, " honours were freely accorded to him, which Philadelphia had refused." Of the hospitality of the Rathbone family he retained an especially grateful remembrance, and mentions with an enthusiasm equal to that of his fellow countryman Irving, the benevolent kindness of Mr. Roscoe, in remembrance of whom he afterwards named the Sylvia Roscoe, a little bird rarely met with, and which was discovered by Audubon midst the cypresses and pines of one of the Mississippi swamps.

The first great difficulty of his career surmounted, a new path full of promise seemed to open before him. His drawings had been exhibited, and, tried by the impartial test of public criticism, had been universally approved. Under the genial influence of this budding success he was disposed to appreciate all the novelty and interest arising from his European tour. He pursued his journey to Scotland along the north-western shores of England, delighted with the celebrated cathedrals of our island, " hung with her glories," as well as with the picturesque beauty of the Scottish capital, where he was cordially welcomed by all the distinguished scientific and literary characters of the day. Here he produced his first number of " The Birds of America," engraved by Lizars. Thence he proceeded to the several towns on the road to London, and following the example of Wilson in America, exhibited there the engravings of his work. This measure, to which he was greatly disinclined, he resolved to take from the conviction of its expediency, as it promised a more immediate recognition than he could otherwise obtain. In his crowded reception-room he listened to the varied remarks of his visitors, and was recompensed for the sacrifice of his feelings by the numerous subscriptions thus received. In Manchester he obtained upwards of twenty in one week, and had the good fortune to form there, moreover, several friendships which continued with him through life.

Through Chester, Birmingham, and classic Oxford he continued his tour, until, with alternating hope and fear, he approached the great metropolis of England. With mingled admiration and horror this citizen of the new world beheld its sharp contrast of wretchedness and magnificence—raising his eyes from squalid poverty and despairing crime to noble monuments and mansions of aristocratic pomp. As the bearer of numerous introductions to European celebrities, from statesmen and others of distinction, in his own country, he had seemingly a good foundation on which to establish an intercourse favourable to his intentions. But the busy unceasing engrossment of London existence subjected him to delay and disappointment. Wandering early and late, not a single one of those he sought could he find at home! Gradually, however, through different mediums, his aim was accomplished. An intimacy with Lord Stanley led to his acquaintance with others of the nobility. Soon he was elected member of the Linnæan and Zoological Societies, and before long artists, men of science, and professors, were among the list of his subscribers.

During 1828 he again visited Paris, where, investigating the many objects of interest in the great museum, enjoying intercourse with the illustrious Cuvier and his enlightened guests, the time, pleasantly and profitably spent, passed quickly away. He returned to England for the winter, and in 1829 sailed once more for his native soil. Notwithstanding the gratifying reception he had met with in Europe, the kindly courtesy with which he had been welcomed, and the honours with which he had been distinguished, the charm of novelty and the excitement of gay scenes, " with indescribable pleasure," he tells us, " he watched the outspread wings of the first American wanderer which hovered over the waters, and joyfully leapt again upon the shores of the New World. Scouring the woods with a hunter's zeal he speedily traversed the middle states, and at length reached his favourite Louisiana.

In 1830, Audubon, accompanied by his wife, visited New Orleans. Sauntering there one morning, he observed a gentlemen, whose singular appearance attracted his attention. Assuming to be another " odd fish" he determined to make his acquaintance.

The exterior of this original might reasonably account for the conclusion.

A huge straw-hat covered his head. The unusually broad frill of a shirt fluttered about his breast, and a very remarkable collar, which left his neck exposed negligently to the weather, fell over the top of his light green coat. The delicate hue of this garment harmonized well with the yellow of his glowing nankeens, and was brightened by a pink waistcoat, from the bosom of which, lurking amidst a bunch of the splendid magnolia flower, part of an alligator protruded, which seemed anxious to escape its gentle imprisonment in folds of the finest cambric.

In one of his hands the gentleman held a cage, plentifully furnished with nonparcils as richly plumed as himself—in the other sportively handled a silk umbrella, on which could be plainly read the words, " stolen from I," painted in large white characters.

With a conscious air, he strutted along, hum-

ming "My love is but a lassie yet," in such
purely native fashion, that Audubon would
gladly have pronounced him a true Scot, but
for his unmistakably American tournure. This
conviction excited his curiosity still more, till
at length he was compelled to gratify it, by
accosting the stranger with, " Pray, sir, will you
allow me to examine the birds you have in that
cage?" At this request the owner of them
stopped, straightened his body, almost closed his
left eye, spread his legs apart, and, with an irresistibly comic look, answered, " Birds, sir, did you
say birds?" On the question being repeated, he
continued, "What do you know about birds, sir?"
" Sir," replied Audubon, I am a student of nature, and admire her works, from the crawling
reptile you have in your bosom to the "human
form divine." "Ah!" replied he, "a—a—a naturalist, I suppose." He then handed the cage,
which Audubon inspected, and was about to
take his departure, when the stranger requested
that he would accompany him to his lodgings.

On arriving there, they entered a long room,
where the most prominent objects were a number of pictures along the walls, a table covered
with painting apparatus, and a large easel with
a full length portait yet unfinished upon it.
Each of the drawings told the touch of a superior
artist. Audubon felt convinced it could be no

other than his new companion, and complimented him accordingly. " Ay," said he, " the world is pleased with my work, I wish I were so too ; but time and industry are necessary, as well as talents to make a good painter. If you have leisure, and will stay awhile, I will show you how I paint, and will relate to you an incident of my life, which will prove to you how sadly situated an artist is sometimes." On receiving an assent, he continued: " Sir, if you should ever paint, and paint portraits, you will often meet with difficulties. For instance, the brave commodore of whom this is the portrait," pointing to the picture occupying the easel before him, " the brave commodore, though an excellent man at everything else, is the worst sitter I ever saw. The first morning that he came to me, he was in full uniform, and with a sword at his side. After a few minutes conversation, and when all was ready on my part, I bade him ascend this throne, place himself in an attitude which I contemplated, and assume an air becoming an officer of the navy.

" Well, he mounted, placed himself as I had desired, but merely looked at me as if I had been a block of stone. I waited a few minutes, when, observing no change in his countenance, I ran the chalk over the canvass to form a rough outline. This done, I looked up to his face again, and opened a conversation which I thought would warm his warlike nature, but in vain. I waited and talked, waited and talked, until my patience, sir—you must know I am not overburdened with it—my patience being exhausted, I rose, threw my pallet and brush on the floor, stamped, walked to and fro about the room, and vociferated such fearful calumnies against our navy, that I startled the good commodore. Yet he still looked at me with a plain countenance, and, as he told me since, thought I had lost my senses. But I observed him all the while, and fully as deter-mined to carry my point as he would be to carry off an enemy's ship, I gave my oaths additional emphasis, addressed him as a representative of the navy, and, steering somewhat clear of per-sonal insult, played off my batteries against the craft. At last, the commodore walked up to me, placed his hand on the hilt of his sword, and told me in a resolute manner, that if I had intended to insult the navy, he would instantly cut off my ears. His features exhibited all the spirit and animation of his noble nature, and as I had now succeeded in rousing the lion, I judged it time to retreat. So, changing my tone, I begged his pardon, and told him he now looked precisely as I wished to represent him. He laughed, and re-turning to his seat, assumed a bold countenance, and so, sir, see the picture!"

From New Orleans, Audubon proceeded again

to London, where he was presented with a diploma from the Royal Society. In addition, he received a general letter of recommendation to the authorities in the British Colonies from the Duke of Sussex, with many of a similar nature from · Lord Stanley and others.

In August he proceeded a second time to the United States, and landed at New York, where he passed a few days before proceeding to Philadelphia.

Everywhere he was received with honours and courtesies. Subscriptions and diplomas were lavished upon him, and at Washington he was presented by the government with numerous letters of assistance and protection along the frontier, which it was his intention to visit. After a visit to Charleston, he sailed for Florida, where he wintered during 1831.

In that fertile and beautiful country, where the naturalist may luxuriate midst the rare abundance of curious and interesting objects, with which it is endowed, Audubon willingly loitered. While sojourning there, many important additions to his collection were made. Wandering on the beach, fenced by its beautiful coral, stretching like a giant wall along the shore, he could at leisure contemplate rising from the clear depths of the water, its curious inhabitants glittering in a thousand richly spangled dyes, emulating the sea itself in the exquisite harmony of their colouring. Raising his gaze, he could look upon the glowing flamingo, the rosy-hued curlew, the snowy ibis, the purple heron, and the dusky cormorant and pelican. Or in the interior, midst tangled groves, dazzling with gorgeous flowers, strange plants, and luxuriant trees, where the pure salubrious air, impregnated with fragrance, steals like balmy breath along, he was greeted by gayer songsters, gambolling among the bushes, or gliding over the fresh green waters.

Continually some strange aerial pilgrim, with which he was unacquainted, would gladden his sight. With the various species of doves to be met with in Florida, he was particularly delighted. The peculiarly gentle and loving disposition of these sweet birds, the constancy of their attachment to each other, and the anxious care exhibited by them for their young, are all characteristics which render them of especial interest. For Audubon, moreover, there existed associations with them, which had for him an irresistible charm, which doubtless led him to ask, as he does with an exquisite sensibility and simplicity, "Who can approach a sitting dove, hear its notes of remonstrance, or feel the feeble stroke of its wings, without being convinced that he is committing a wrong act?" His first attempt at drawing had been from the preserved specimen of a dove. Of this he had often been reminded, too young at the time of his first essay to remember it in after years himself.

The Zenaida dove, a visitor to East Florida from the West India Islands, is remarkable for the indescribably plaintive tenderness of its cooing. So touching is its utterance, that even to the heart, hardened by a life of crime, it is irresistible.

A notorious pirate, linked with a band of desperadoes, who menaced the Florida coast, chancing to hear its soft melancholy notes, lingered till feelings to which he had long been a stranger, subdued his spirit, and melted it to repentance. It was effectual too, for, resolved to lead a different career for the future, at the cost of difficulty and danger, he effected his escape, and returned like the prodigal to a rejoicing home.

The male bird which first appears in Florida, may be heard cooing for his companion for about a week before she arrives. They choose for their resting place spots thickly covered with grasses and low shrubs, in the heart of which they form their nests, glad if protected in addition by a hedge of sturdy mangroves. This meek, unambitious bird seldom soars high, and when crossing the sea flies close over the surface

of the water. Though so timid, they are con-
fiding, and will permit a person's near approach.
Thus Audubon, once hoped to become the possessor of one alive, and imagined himself on the
point of a triumphant capture, when the dove
turned upon him her beautiful eye, and he found
that his intention was discovered. Gently she
glided aside in her nest, then suddenly took to
wing. Hovering around, she would alight within a few yards of her beloved nest—her wings
drooping in sorrow, and her whole form trembling as if from severe cold. "Who could bear
such a scene of despair?" exclaims Audubon.
"I left the mother in security with her off-
spring."

In the morning, while concealed beneath some
low spreading branch, her love-notes are given
forth. Then, when with the freshness of the
morn, the opening flowers spread out all their
fragrance, and the sun with increasing ardour
glances through the evergreen and thickly leaved
oaks, to escape which the owl, swiftly flying
close over the earth, hastens to his retreat, and
the heavy winged bat undulates through the
dewy air, then the melodious accents of her
most enchanting voice may best be heard.

The ground dove, closely resembling the
Zenaida dove in its habits, is another visitor of
the middle portions of the East Florida coast.

But the most beautiful, perhaps, of all its species is the Key West pigeon, first seen by Audubon at the place after which it is named. "How I gazed," he tells us, "on its resplendent plumage! —how I watched the expression of its richly coloured, large, and timid eye, as the poor creature gasped its last breath. Ah! how I looked at the lovely bird, I handled it, turned it, examined its feathers and form, its bill, its legs, its claws, weighed it, and after a while formed a winding sheet for it of a piece of paper. Did ever Egyptian pharmacopolist employ more care in embalming the most illustrious of the Pharaohs, than I did, in trying to preserve from injury this most beautiful of the woodland covers. The brilliant plumage of these birds glitters with the most magnificent ever changing metallic hues, and appears especially splendid when they are seen in flocks of from five to six at a time, performing their low, swift, protracted flight, hovering so closely over the surface of the sea, as to seem on the point of falling into it, or speeding to escape danger, towards the forests.

Early in the morning they emerge from the thickets to cleanse themselves in the shelly sands, surrounding the numerous islands, which protect, like fortifications, the Florida shore.

They usually prefer the darkest solitudes for their habitations.

CHAPTER X.

THROUGHOUT the most part of the so-called forests of East Florida, there exist districts which, thinly clad with woodlands, having an undergrowth of grass and shrubs, interspersed with a few tall pines, are denominated Pine Barrens. The sole objects which here diversify the continuous flatness of the soil, are a few sluggish pools, around which the cattle congregate to allay their thirst, and the various kinds of game abundant in their wilds. After a course of miles over these dreary barrens, the traveller is delighted to behold again the sight of sheltering vegetation in wide-spreading oaks and other trees. In their vicinity the air is purer and more cool, luxuriant flowers diffuse their fragrance, the songs of birds re-echo through their shade, and already he seems refreshed at the sight, even of a clear spring, of which the waters are heard rippling through the undergrowth.

Then beneath the covert of innumerable vines, he may seek a pleasant resting-place, above which the jessamine and bignonia fondly intertwine.

Presently he sees the wood-cutters, who, lightly attired, shouldering their bright axes, proceed to their toils. On the opposite sides of some far-spreading oak they station themselves, while, with continuous blows of their keen-edged implements, they strive to cleave its mossy far-shooting roots. One of their companions ascends another tree stem. Proceeding cautiously, he climbs to the height of perhaps forty feet from the ground, then stops—measures himself on the trunk of which he boldly stands, and wields with strong muscular arm his well-tempered steel, till soon the trunk remains connected only by a thin stripe. Then shaking with all his might, the huge log is seen to swing, suddenly give way, and striking the earth with its weight, the crash of its fall is heard to re-echo throughout the neighbouring space. Then, when the wood-cutter has slidden by the aid of a grape-vine to the ground, the rest of his party congregate to examine the fallen trunk.

This they cut at either end, and if it is proved sound, they proceed to take its measurement, and lay out the timber for use by the aid of models, showing the different forms and sizes required. On the discovery of a good plantation, the cutters, or Live Oakers as they are called, build themselves log dwellings, in which to slumber by night, and take their repast by

11*

day; having generally an excellent provision of beef, biscuits, rice, fish and some genuine whisky. Arriving from the eastern and middle districts, they annually visit the Floridas. During summer they return to their families, but at the approach of winter again set forth for their toils, from the first of December to the beginning of March, being the season for cutting. Sometimes strange misadventures befall them on these journeyings, when fogs so dense are accustomed to overspread the country, as to make it impossible to see further than thirty or forty yards onwards. In the monotony of woods, moreover, where the trees present exact resemblances to each other, and the grass is so tall that a man of ordinary stature cannot see over it, so difficult is it to follow even a well known-track, that the most practised woodsman is not unfrequently bewildered. A Live Oaker of East Florida, employed on St. John's River, left one day his cabin on the banks of that stream, to proceed to the swamps where he was accustomed to labour.

After travelling some hours, he felt convinced he must have passed the spot proposed.

On the dispersion of the fog, he beheld with astonishment the sun at meridian height, and dismayed, found himself unable to recognize a single object around. Resolved then to pursue a different course, he turned his back to the sun.

Gradually as time past, he saw him descend in the west, and still all about him continued a mystery. The huge gray trees spread their quaint boughs, the rank grass extended on all sides, not a living being crossed his path, all was silent and still— like a dull and dreary dream of the land of oblivion. On, on, he wandered like a forgotten ghost, which failing to reach the spirit land, un-heeded by the grim ferryman, lingered still upon the Stygian shore. The hope of extri-cation heightened his imagination. Each fresh object he fancied he could recognize, and search-ing for land-marks, wandered in reality still fur-ther from the right course.

As evening approached, myriads of insects buzzed through the air. The squirrel retired to his hole, the crow to its roost, the harsh croaking of the heron told, that full of anxiety it sought its retreat in the miry interior of some distant swamp, the woods resounded to the shrill cries of the owl, and all nature warned the wan-derer to seek some place of refuge, as the breeze sweeping through the forest came laden with heavy dews. No moon appeared to irradiate the scene and cheer the solitude with silvery light, which, "kissing dead things to life," sheds beauty over all. The lost one, despairing and weary, laid himself on the damp ground, to wait with feverish anxiety the return of day, his sole consolation prayer to that Being ever peculiarly mindful of the disconsolate and distressed. Dawn brought a return of the fog which had so misled the wanderer on the preceding day.

With heavy heart he continued his way, which seemed at every step still more a labyrinth than before. Bewildered with fatigue and misery, well nigh despairing, onward he sped, now without the most faintly marked track to guide him, till night closed again upon his path. Terror then took possession of him, while the debility arising from his toils and sufferings prostrated him beneath his anguish, at the dreadful reality of his situation, increased too by the horrors of an excited fancy.

That he should be left alone there to perish of agony and hunger—such he felt assured would be his fate. Almost frantic at the supposition, beating his breast and tearing his hair, he threw himself down, famished as he was, to feed on the weeds and grass around. Another night was passed in indescribable misery. More than fifty miles he had traversed without meeting a single brook from which to quench his thirst, or allay the burning fever of his parched lips. One day among the Barrens, he caught sight of a tortoise. Although convinced that were he to follow it, he must at length find some water, such was the fearful craving of his thirst and hunger, that he was compelled at once to gratify both, by eating its flesh and drinking its blood.

The following morning, somewhat refreshed, he renewed his endless march. The sun rose brightly, and he followed the direction of its shadows. Day after day, weeks even passed, and the poor Live Oaker still toiled hopelessly on, feeding on weeds, frogs, or snakes.

Gradually he became more and more emaciciated, till at last he could scarcely crawl. After the lapse of forty days he reached the banks of a river. There reposing, he awaited the endurance of his last hour, unmitigated by human sympathy or human help. With the ebbing consciousness of reality around, more busy became the dreams of fancy. Borne upon its wings were reminiscences strange and sweet. His friends, his home, his youth, hours of delight and days long past crowded upon his thought—when amidst the visions of returning joy, the sounds of oars seemed to fall on the silent river. He listened, but the sounds soon died away on his fainting ears. Was it the delusion of a dying hour? Again he listened eagerly, and again came the plash of oars. It was reality—a saving reality, for now when the light of life was about to he quenched for ever in the poor wanderer, the quickening fulness of returning hope, a sudden joy to the sinking spirit renewed its vitality. Human voices in exclamation thrilled the sufferer's heart, as round the headland covered with tangled brushwood the little boat, pushed by its hardy rowers, boldly advanced. A scream of joy and fear falls upon their ears. They pause and look around. Again it comes, but more feebly than before. At length they behold the wanderer, whose strange and terrible appearance they could scarcely recognize as human.

With tattered garments, hanging like rags about him, his face obscured by neglected beard, his hair matted, and his emaciated frame covered only by shrivelled skin, like a skeleton with parchment, there he lay with fluttering heart, gasping breath and reeling brain. Yet the lost one was soon regained, and, soon restored to the loving hearts and kindly solicitude of home, in renewed health and happiness often in after years gratefully told the tale of his adventure, and excited the sympathy of his listeners by the painful recital of his sufferings.

A class of men whose calling, no less than that of the Live Oakers, exposes them to strange incidents and often to peril, are the Turtlers, who frequent the various islets about Florida. The Tortugas, a group of eighty miles from Key West, consisting of a few uninhabitable banks of shelly sands, intersected by deep intricate channels, are especially resorted to by them; and many a luckless mariner called to that dangerous coast has met his end from careless contact of his vessel with the great coral reefs adjacent.   To these islet banks, thickly spread with corals, sea gems, and the fanciful jewelry of the deep, turtles of various sizes resort to deposit their eggs in the sand; with flocks, arriving every spring of the sea-fowl. Multitudes of beautiful fishes fill the neighbouring waters. Perhaps no more interesting scene could be imagined than that presented by these famous islands beneath the influence of their gorgeous sunsets.   The brilliant orb of day seems there to triple its dimensions; partially sunk beneath the waves, glittering through their transparence with crimson flush, it irradiates their iris hues, while in its encircling splendour the whole heavens are transfigured as by a flood of golden light, purpling the distant clouds which hover over the horizon.   A marvellous blaze of splendour is poured over the west, and even the masses of vapour appear like mountains of molten gold, till gradually their brilliance disappears behind the sable veil of night.

The hawk, hovering on noiseless wing, enjoys the gentle sea-breeze; the terns settle on their nests, and the pelicans hasten to their homes among the mangroves. Skimming the surface of the waters, glistening in the moonlight, the broad forms of the turtles are then seen, their anxiety and fear told by their hurried breathing, heard in the silence as they toil along. On nearing the shore the turtle raises her head, looks round and carefully examines the objects on it. Observing anything which seems to measure her proceedings, she utters a loud hissing sound by which to intimidate her enemies, then instantly sets sail and wades to a considerable distance. On the contrary, should she find everything quiet and propitious she crawls on the beach, and having found a convenient spot, again gazes cautiously round. With the utmost ingenuity she alternately raises and scatters the sand till a hole is dug to the depth of eighteen inches or, sometimes, two feet. After depositing her eggs and leaving the hatching of them to the heat of the sun, she launches once more into the deep. Those who search for the eggs are provided with a light stiff cane or ram-rod with which they probe the sands along the shore, endeavouring to keep as near as possible to the tracks of the animal, which, however, it is not always easy to ascertain, often obliterated as they are by winds and heavy rains. The turtlers employ various methods of capture. Sometimes nets are placed across the entrance of streams, formed of intricate meshes, into which the poor turtles once entrapped are only the more entangled the more they attempt to extricate themselves. Frequently they are harpooned in the usual way.

The turtlers, men of humble birth, must necessarily possess energy and enterprise for their vocation. These qualities not unfrequently raise to higher stations, and a naval officer with whom Audubon met had formerly been a turtler. He was accustomed to relate many an exciting adventure which gave proof of the perils to which those who engage in such a career are exposed. Among them was the following :—

The Turtler's Story.

In the calm of a fine moonlight night as I was admiring the beauty of the heavens, and the broad glare of light that flamed from the trembling surface of the water around, I chanced to be paddling along a sandy shore which I thought well fitted for my repose, being covered with tall grass, and as the sun was not many degrees above the horizon, I felt anxious to pitch my musquito bar or net, and spend the night in the wilderness. The bellowing notes of thousands

12

of bull-frogs in a neighbouring swamp might lull me to rest, and I looked upon the flocks of blackbirds that were assembling as sure companions in this secluded retreat. I proceeded up a little stream to insure the safety of my canoe from any sudden storm, when as I gladly advanced a beautiful yawl came unexpectedly in view. Surprised at such a sight in a part of the country then scarcely known, I felt a sudden check in the circulation of my blood. My paddle dropped from my hands, and fearfully indeed, as I picked it up, did I look towards the unknown boat. On reaching it, I saw its sides marked with stains of blood, and looking with anxiety over the gunwale, I perceived to my horror two human bodies covered with gore. Pirates or hostile Indians I was persuaded had perpetrated the foul deed, and my alarm naturally increased; my heart fluttered, stopped, and heaved with unusual tremors, and I looked towards the setting sun in consternation and despair.

How long my reveries lasted I cannot tell: I can only recollect that I was roused from them by the distant groans of one apparently in mortal agony. I felt as if refreshed by the cold perspiration that oozed from every pore, and I reflected that though alone, I was well armed, and might hope for the protection of the Almighty! Humanity whispered to me that, if not surprised and disabled, I might render assistance to some sufferer, or even be the means of saving a useful life. Buoyed up by this thought, I urged my canoe on shore, and seizing it by the bow pulled it at one spring high among the grass. The groans of the unfortunate persons fell heavy on my ear, as I cocked and reprimed my gun, determined to shoot the first who should rise from the grass. As I cautiously proceeded a hand was raised over the reeds, and waved in a most supplicatory manner. I levelled my gun about a foot below it, when the next moment the head and breast of a man were convulsively raised, and a faint hoarse voice asked of me mercy and help! A deathlike silence followed his fall to the ground. I surveyed every object around, with eyes intent and ears impressible by the slightest sound, for my situation at that moment, I thought as critical as any I had ever been in. The croaking of the frogs and the last blackbirds alighting on their roosts, were the only sounds or sights. I now proceeded towards the object of my mingled alarm and consternation. Alas! the poor being who lay prostrate at my feet was so weakened by loss of blood that I had nothing to fear from him.

My first impulse was to run back to the water, and having done so, I returned with my cap filled to the brim. I felt at his heart, washed his face and breast, and rubbed his temples with the contents of a phial which I kept about me as an antidote for the bites of snakes. His features, seamed by the ravages of time, looked frightful and disgusting; but he had been a powerful man, as his broad chest plainly showed. He groaned in the most appalling manner as his breath struggled through the mass of blood that seemed to fill his throat. His dress plainly disclosed his occupation: a large pistol he had thrust in his bosom, a naked cutlass lay near him on the ground, a red silk handkerchief was bound over his projecting brows, and over a pair of loose trousers he wore fisherman's boots. He was, in short, a pirate. My exertions were not in vain, for as I continued to bathe his temples he revived, his pulse regained some strength, and I began to hope he might survive the deep wound he had received. Darkness, deep darkness now enveloped us. I spoke of making a fire. "Ah! for mercy's sake," he exclaimed "don't." Knowing that under existing circumstances it was expedient for me to do so, I left him, went to his boat, and brought the rudder, the benches, and the oars, which, with my hatchet, I soon splintered. I then struck a light and presently stood in the glare of a blazing fire. The pirate seemed struggling between terror and gratitude for my assistance; he desired me several times to put out the flames, but after a draught of strong spirits became more composed. I tried to staunch the blood that flowed from the deep gashes in his shoulders and side. I expressed my regret that I had no food about me, but when I spoke of eating he sullenly moved his head.

My situation was one of the most extraordinary I had ever been placed in. I naturally turned my talk towards religious subjects, but, alas, the dying man hardly believed in the existence of a God. "Friend," said he, "for friend you seem to be; I never studied the ways of Him of whom you talk. I am an outlaw, perhaps you will say a wretch,—I have been for many years a pirate. The instructions of my parents were of no avail to me, for I always believed I was born to be a most cruel man. I now lie here about to die midst these woods, because, long ago, I refused to listen to their many admonitions. Do not shudder when I tell you these now useless hands murdered the mother whom they had embraced. I feel I have deserved the pangs of the wretched death that hovers over me, and I am thankful that only one of my kind will witness my last gaspings."

A feeble hope that I might save his life, and perhaps assist in procuring his pardon, induced me to speak to him on the subject. " It is all in vain, friend—I have no objection to die—I

12*

am glad that the villains who wounded me were not my conquerors. I want no pardon from *any one*—give me some water, and let me die alone."

With the hope that I might learn from his conversation something that might lead to the capture of his guilty associates; I returned from the creek with another capful of water, nearly the whole of which I managed to introduce into his parched mouth, and begged him, for the sake of his future peace, to disclose his history to me. " It is impossible," said he, " there will be no time, the beatings of my heart tell me so. Long before day these sinewy limbs will be motion-less. Nay, there will hardly be a drop of blood in my body. My wounds are mortal, and I must and will die without what you call confession."

The moon rose in the east. The majesty of her placid beauty impressed me with reverence. I pointed towards her, and asked the pirate if he could not recognize the hand of God there.

" Friend, I see what you are driving at," was his answer, " you, like the rest of our enemies, feel the desire of murdering us all. Well—be it so--to die is, after all, nothing more than a jest, and were it not for the pain, no one, in my opinion, need care a jot about it. But as you have really befriended me I will tell you all that is proper."

Hoping his mind might take a useful turn, I again bathed his temples, and washed his lips with spirits. His sunken eyes seemed to dart fire at mine—a heavy and deep sigh swelled his chest and struggled through his blood-choked throat, as he asked me to raise him a little. I did so, when he addressed me as follows :—

" First tell me how many bodies you found in the boat, and what sort of dresses they had on." I mentioned their number and described their apparel. " That's right," said he, they are the bodies of the scoundrels who followed me in that infernal Yankee barge. Bold rascals they were. For when they found the water too shallow for their craft, they took to it and waded after me. All my companions had been shot, and to lighten my own boat I flung them overboard, but as I lost time in this, the two ruffians caught hold of my gunwale, and struck on my head and body in such a way that I was scarcely able to move. The other villain carried off our schooner and one of our boats, and perhaps ere now have hung all my companions whom they did not kill at the time. I always hated the Yankees, and only regret that I did not kill more of them. I sailed from Matanzas—I have often been in concert with others. I have money without counting, but it is buried where it will never be found, and it would be useless to tell you of it." His throat filled with blood, his voice failed, the cold hand of death was on his brow, feebly and hurriedly he muttered, " I am a dying man, farewell!"

Alas! it is painful to me, death in any shape; in this it was horrible, for there was no hope. The rattling of his throat announced the moment of his dissolution, and already did the body fall on my arms with a weight which was insupportable. I laid him on the ground. A mass of dark blood poured from his mouth, then came a frightful groan, the last breathing of that foul spirit, and all that now lay at my feet, in that wild desert, was a mangled mass of clay!

The remainder of that night was passed in no enviable mood, but my feelings cannot be described. At dawn I dug a hole with the paddle of my canoe, rolled the body into it, and covered it. On reaching the boat, I found several buzzards feeding on the bodies, which I in vain attempted to drag to the shore. I therefore covered them with mud and reeds, and launching my canoe, paddled from the cove, with a secret joy at my escape, shadowed with the gloom of a mingled dread and abhorrence

CHAPTER XI.

RETURNING from Florida, enriched by numerous and important discoveries, Audubon proceeded to Philadelphia. There he had the happiness to be reunited to his family. Anxiety for their welfare induced him to shorten his stay in that city, then afflicted by the terrible pestilence of cholera. They continued their journey to Boston. During his sojourning there, 1832, he was engaged in making the drawings requisite to the completion of his "Illustrations"—his son leaving the family gathering to superintend their publication in London. At the noble city of Boston Audubon lingered to indulge his admiration of it, as well as to enjoy the pleasure afforded him by the warm and generous reception he met with from its inhabitants. "The outpouring of kindness at Boston," he tells us, " exceeding all with which he had ever met." This so justly admired capital was naturally a source of honourable pride to him. With the utmost enthusiasm he speaks of the laudable characteristics of this people, the fitting citizens of a free land; of its churches, its universities, its harbours, the beauty of the adjacent country, brightened by glimpses of neat and elegant habitations—and dwells with loving complacency on the numerous places distinguished by association with the glorious chronicle of his far-famed history.

Audubon's next excursion was to explore the British Provinces of New Brunswick. Proceeding to Frederickton along St. John's River, he was delighted with the aspect of its shores, bounded by verdurous hills, here and there picturesquely interspersed with sharp rocky banks. They were adorned, moreover, with the "yellow fruitfulness" of autumn, waving luxuriant fields of corn, glowing fruits which hung clustering in the orchards, and lustrous tints gilding the forest of carmine and gold.

On the broad unruffled waters the canoes of the Indian swiftly glided, scaring the timid water-fowl. The sprightly Canada jay sprung from branch to branch; the kingfisher took to flight, while the fish-hawk and eagle spread their broad wings over the waves.

Returning eastward, Audubon passed the winter at Boston, again occupied in making drawings of the birds that migrate thither from the colder regions of the north, and in May, 1833, set sail for Labrador. Approaching its coast appeared what seemed to be hundreds of snow-white sails sporting over the waters, but which proved to be masses of drifted snow and ice filling every nook and cove of the rugged shores.

The coast of Labrador, like that of the Floridas, is dotted with numerous islands, the resorts of winged creatures. Some hover along the huge rocks which there project like a giant bulwark over the sea, others flap their sable wings over its surface; the raven spreads her pinions, and the golden eagle soars majestically aloft, moving in wide circles through the air.

Before his visit to Labrador, Audubon had met with but a single one of the species of the Esquimaux curlew. Coming from the north, these birds arrive in flocks as dense as the passenger pigeons, directing their course to the sterile mountainous tracts. They feed in Labrador on the curlew berry, a small black fruit, found on a creeping plant, abundantly covering the rocks. While in search of food they fly in close masses, sometimes high, sometimes low, but always with remarkable swiftness, and with the most elegant evolutions. When on wing they perpetually repeat a soft whistling note, but immediately on alighting become silent. They may be seen running all in the same direction, picking up the berries in their way, when, at the slightest intimation of danger, at a single whistle from any one of the flock, they all instantly fly off, rising from the ground by one quick spring, undulating backwards and forwards, and round, in the most curious manner, now and then pausing in the air, like the hawk, for a few minutes against the wind, as though for the pleasantness of meeting the breeze.

Beautiful as are the various species of terns, the roseate probably surpasses them all, with its glossy head of raven blackness and the delicate loveliness of its rosy tinted breast. So light and graceful are the movements of these birds, too, as in gatherings of hundreds they dance through the air, that they may with justice be called the humming-birds of the sea. Now flocking together, they disperse again, and hover round, or, if in anger, plunge with a sudden dash, uttering cries of wrath.

Traversing the solitudes of Labrador, the unbroken silence which reigns around seems like the mournfulness of a deserted land, and, combined with the melancholy grandeur of the scenery, is peculiarly impressive. Stupendous masses of rock, hundreds of feet in height, look down frowningly, their curious carvings appearing like devices wrought by superhuman hands.

The few dwarf pines and the stunted vegetation add to the singular aspect of the landscape, which seems as though stricken into barrenness by some enchantment. The gull and grim raven brood among the cliffs. Yet has the power of enterprise peopled even these wilds.

Audubon, while lying at anchor, directed his attention one day to the pinnacle of a small island, separated only by a narrow channel from the main land, and beheld a man with clasped hands, bended knees and heavenward gaze, before a mount of rough stones, supporting a wooden cross. This attitude was unmistakably that of prayer, and at once arrested Audubon's attention, awakening that reverential regard which cannot fail to impress the soul in the presence of another, seeking communion with its Creator. In the desolation of these northern lands, moreover, it appeared peculiarly affecting, where human creatures far removed from the assistance of their fellow-creatures, in simple confidence sought it in the more immediate agency of an Almighty hand. Audubon felt his curiosity and interest awakened. Landing upon the rock, he scrambled to the spot where he had observed the man upon his knees, who still, on Audubon's approach, continued his devotions. On their conclusion Audubon inquired his reasons for choosing so dreary a sanctuary.

" Because," answered he, " the sea lies before

me, and from it I receive my spring and summer sustenance."

Struck with the reply, Audubon desired a further acquaintance with his new companion, and accordingly accepted the invitation to his abode. Low and small it was, formed of stones, plastered with mud. The roof was composed of a sort of thatching of weeds and moss. A large Dutch stove filled nearly one half of the place—a small port-hole served as a window. The bed was a pile of deer skins. A bowl, a jug, and an iron pot placed on a rude shelf, three old and rusty muskets, their locks fastened by thongs, stood in a corner; and buck-shot, powder, and flints were tied up in skins. Eight Exquimaux dogs leaped about this uninviting abode.

With the courtesy of his nation (for the rustic of these wilds was a Frenchman) he invited his guest to refreshment, and Audubon, during the preparation of his repast, wandered out of doors to enjoy the glorious landscape afforded by the majestic scenery around, ornamented by a marvellous luxuriance in plants and grasses, which clothed the valley where the settler dwelt contentedly in his chosen home. There, throughout ten returning dreary winters, he had resided, subsisting on the annual sale of furs, eiderdowns, and seal-skins, to the traders who sought their merchandise in these inclement regions.

"With the exception of the loss of a barrel of rum," said Pierre, "he had never experienced a single sorrow, and felt as happy as a lord!" To Audubon's inquiry how he managed to feed the dogs, he replied, "Why, sir, during spring and summer they ramble along the shores, where they meet with abundance of dead fish, and in winter they eat the flesh of seals which I kill late in the autumn, when those animals return from the north. As to myself, everything eatable is good, and when hard pushed, I assure you I can relish the fare of my dogs just as they do themselves." To this simple standard of satisfaction, the poor settler was reduced from the lofty expectations which had led him, with a greater credulity than that of Whittington, to leave his native land, in the conviction of becoming a millionaire in the north! Yet he was happy, and the realization of his best wishes could have brought him no more enviable destiny.

Proceeding along the indentations of the bay, Audubon perceived several neat-looking habitations which gladdened the prospect, proving that a similarity of taste or intention had induced many besides the settler to seek the seclusion of these inhospitable shores.

The next adventurer, however, proved an entire contrast to Pierre. His demeanour instantly bespoke the gentleman and polished citizen of the world. He immediately recognized the name of Audubon, and declared that he had been expecting to greet him during the last three weeks, having read in the journals of his intention to visit Labrador. He then cordially welcomed him to his elegant mansion, and its pleasant inmates. A chosen collection of books, with newspapers from all quarters, evinced that no contracting influences of seclusion had chilled their sympathies or deadened their interest in that *society* from which they were removed. "How had they thus hidden themselves from the world, with every incentive to mingle pleasantly and profitably in it?" inquired Audubon.

"Having mixed once in society," replied his companion, "he never wished to return to it. The country around," he continued, "is all my own, much farther than you can see. No fees, no lawyers, no taxes are *here*. I do just as I choose. My means are ample through my own industry. Vessels come here for seal skins, seal oil, and salmon, and give me in return all the necessaries, and, indeed, comforts of the life I love to follow. And what else could the world afford? My wife and I teach the children all that is necessary for them to know, and is not that enough? My girls will marry their countrymen, my sons the daughters of my neighbours, and I hope all of them will live and die in this country."

In such unambitious happiness, ignorant alike of the aspirations and evils of so-called civilization, dwell the settlers of Labrador!

Frequenting the coast of this interesting country are a class of men, who, the scourge of the feathered species, were regarded by Audubon as the scandal of their own. These buccaneers, whose vocation it is to despoil the nest of every wild bird, in order to dispose of its produce, are known as Eggers.

Their cruel occupation is rendered still more vicious, from the propensity they exhibit to destroy the poor creatures whom they have robbed, adding the crime of inhumanity to that of injustice. In their unwashed shallops, plastered and patched often with the remnants of some luckless vessel plundered by these pirates, they skulk behind the frowning rocks, a refuge for myriads of winged creatures, who there seek unmolested repose. Like evil phantoms of the waters, the boats are stealthily pushed along, manned by their reckless crews, intent on evil.

On their approach towards some island for their prey, clouds of birds rising, thicken the air, wheeling and screaming around, as though in defiance of their dreaded enemies. Some in the vain hope of saving their cherished young

13*

remain still. But instantly the reports of muskets loaded with heavy shot are heard, and the dead and wounded fall in numbers to the earth. Collecting their prey, they then return to their vessels, to celebrate with drunken orgies their brutal triumph. Stripping off their beautiful feathered apparel, while the flesh of their victims is yet warm, they throw them on the coals. Then filling repeatedly their rum flasks, with shouting and revelry the night is far spent, till at length tumbling and snoring, the crazy crew fall into uneasy slumbers. With the return of morning they are again on the alert, when the sun shines brightly on the snow-clad mountains, and fresh breezes shake the heavy dew-drops from the boughs.

Startled by the pure eye of day upon them, the Eggers arise, and make for some other spot sheltered as before, where, undisturbed, they may betake themselves again to their ferocious employment. Thus passing their days in cruelty, and their nights in revelry, the marauders spend weeks in these occupations. Touching in succession at every island along the coast, propitious to their guilty purposes, ample gatherings are made by them to satisfy their sordid minds. Sometimes, enraged at competition in their degraded traffic by a band of desperadoes like themselves, a challenge is given, musketry is discharged, and careless of the lives of their fellow-creatures, as they are of those of the helpless inhabitants of the air, they fight like wild beasts for a contested prey. Not till fractured skulls and wounded limbs give evidence of the fray, is it brought to a satisfactory conclusion, when fraternising, they divide the booty.

Not only against their rivals do the ruffians wage war, but against mariners, who in the dauntlessness of innocence boldly traverse the waters. Often they are surprised and robbed by these lawless crews, who infest the coast whenever a covert may be found. Yet not unfrequently they meet with a merited punishment. In a company of a hundred, perhaps, the fishermen gallantly advance their boats. Disdaining to carry other weapons, they use the sufficient ones of their fists and oars. They prepare boldly to ascend the rock, where they are awaited by the enemy—a dozen Eggers armed with guns and bludgeons. Loud cheers re-echo through the air, a fierce contest ensues, but the vanquished Eggers are generally left bruised upon the ground.

So unremitting are these pirates in their depredations, as to threaten the entire extinction of various species of birds, once abundant in resorts which they abandon in search of unmolested retreats. Gulls, guillerots, and puffins are espccally massacred in vast numbers, on account of their feathers. Eventually, however, this unrelenting persecution will be the means of its own extinction, when the multitude of birds, once a prey to these pirates, no longer exist to attract them to their haunts.

Returning from Labrador, Audubon, as he sailed along the northern coast of Newfound-land, while others beguiled themselves with various amusements, enjoyed a satisfaction which was for him unequalled—that of beholding the grandeur of creation displayed in the majestic scenery of those shores, softened by a fertility unknown in Labrador. Here, though along the foot of huge projections of rock, which, like fragments of mountains overhang the sea, the waters dash with terrific force; more distant valleys clad with verdure, intermingling with which are gently swelling hills, prove the luxuriance of vegetable growth.

Numerous habitations add to the cheerfulness of the aspect, while the boats, with their white sails expanded to the breeze, flutter like silvery sea-birds about the inlets which every now and then appear. Clouds of curlews dash through the air as they wing their way to the south. Nearer, the pleasant sight of cattle feeding in cultured meadows, and people busy at their avocations continue to gladden the view.

As Audubon and his companions landed, an unusual excitement seemed to prevail, which, with reason, they attributed to the curiosity raised among the good people by their arrival, as with arrows and hunting accoutrements, in guise half Indian, half civilized, they made their appearance. In return for the interest they excited, they met, however, with kind greetings and abundance of good cheer. Grateful for the welcome, on betaking themselves at nightfall again to their floating habitations, they serenaded with repeated glees and madrigals the amiable inhabitants of the village; who on the following day sent a deputation to request that the whole party would favour with their company a ball, which was to take place in the evening; desiring, also, that in order to give additional zest to the festivities, they would bring their musical instruments. At the fashionable hour of ten o'clock, accordingly, the party—some carrying flutes, others violins, and Audubon a flageolet stuck in his pocket—were lighted to the dancing hall— (the ground floor of a fisherman's house) by paper lanterns.

The hostess, completely at her ease and *en négligé*, like the apartment, curtseyed with the agility if not with the elegance of a Cerito, and full of activity, as well as intent on cordiality, proceeded in the presence of her visitors to arrange matters for their comfort. Perambulating the apartment, she held in one hand a bunch of candles, in the other a lighted torch, distributing the candles along the wall, and by the application of the torch producing a blaze of illumination. She then proceeded to empty the contents of a tin vessel into a number of glasses, placed on the only table in the room.

The chimney, black and capacious, was ornamented around and above with coffee-pots, milk-bowls, cups and saucers, and all the *et cetera* necessary for the festival.

Some primitive wooden benches were placed around the apartment for the accommodation of the belles of the village.

It was not long before the Arctic beauties appeared, flourishing in the rosy exuberance which proved the beneficial influence of a northern climate. Their decorations might have vied with the Queen of Otaheite herself, in possession of brilliant beads, feathers, gaudy flowers, and flowing ribbons, which mingled with their ebony tresses, and ornamented their finely-developed forms. Soon arrived their partners, who, returning from fishing, skipped up, without ceremony, a kind of partially screened loft adjoining the room of assembly, to exchange their drenched garments for apparel more suited to the elegant usages of the dance.

At each pause of the musicians, refreshments were handed round, not the slightest surprise being manifested at the evident alacrity with which glasses of pure rum were swallowed by the robust ladies of that inclement clime.

To the surprise of Audubon, who naturally supposed them to be entirely free from *mauvaise honte*, some of them whom he and his companions afterwards met in their rambles, fled from them like "gazelles before jackalls." One bearing a pitcher of water, dropped it, and ran to the woods.

Another in search of a cow, took to the water, and waded through it more than waist deep, and then made for home with the speed of a frightened hare. So marvellous is the transformation effected by the genial influence of that extraordinary occurrence—a ball in that portion of Newfoundland.

After a few days of delightful wanderings over the mossy hills, and many a pleasant row up the indentures of the beautiful bay of St. George, he bade adieu to the rude, but most hospitable English and French of that isolated port, and a few days of easy sailing saw the Ripley at anchor a few miles from Pictou, and a boat, containing all the party but the captain and crew of the schooner, was pulled cherrily on to the beach, where Audubon, followed by the youths of the expedition, having hired a cart from the nearest farmer, to bring their baggage, walked, with his long strides, some twelve miles into town, there to be taken by the hand, and receive the friendship of Professor McCulloch and his sons.

The whole collection of these gentlemen was placed at his disposal, and one or two exceedingly rare species he accepted, though what he most prized, were notes of the observations of birds, made by Thomas McCulloch. But October was at hand, and he traversed rapidly the road towards Windsor, and on a substantial, but slow British steamer, he proceeded down the Bay of Fundy (on its extraordinary ebb of 80 feet in height at Windsor) to St. Johns, New Brunswick, where he was received with cheerful welcome by Edward Harris, Esq., his old and good friend, who had come from Philadelphia to await his return to Eastport, Maine. Many were the kindly greetings he received, as once again he travelled to New York, there to meet his wife, and, with her, to loiter slowly on through the inland route, to Charleston, to fulfil a promise to his friend, the Rev. Dr. Backman— that he would again visit him before a return to Europe. This winter was to him alternate hard work, and the relaxation of the gun and chase, enjoyed with " Friend Backman," at the homes

of the hospitable, warm-hearted, South Caroli-
nians; so happy were those days, that Dr. Backman was want to sigh, and say: " Ah, old man,
this is *too* much happiness for this world—it
makes us forget ourselves." But he rested not;
and we find him once again in London, where
he, with his eldest son, assorted the drawings,
made during two years absence, into numbers;
and, making his final arrangements as to what
birds were still wanted from the works of previous authors, he returned to Edinburgh, his
favourite resort in Great Britain, where he published the third volume of the Ornithological
Biographies.

14

CHAPTER XII.

WITH untiring zeal Audubon continued to work out his great plan—a source to him of perpetual anxiety in alternating hopes and fears. The unfaltering enterprise and powers of endurance, both mental and physical, required in the ceaseless labours necessary to the accomplishment of his task, alone constituted an ordeal that few could sustain. Often days, and even weeks, were passed without the slightest results to his researches. Hundreds of miles were traversed, woods and shores ransacked in arduous toil, and not a single discovery made! Hunger, weariness, disappointment, would necessarily press upon the wanderer suffering deprivation in solitude, where unprotected he was exposed to the inclemency of the atmosphere, and the ruthlessness of the elements. At such times, when prostrated with fatigue, and wearied with the delayed fulfilment of his hopes, imagination too would scare him with her cruel phantoms. Sometimes, betaking himself to repose in the dreary recesses of the forest, he would be stricken

by the dread of illness, which should quell for
ever his aspirations, and destroy all hope of
further achievement. The fancied yell of the
Indians and their murderous threats would tor-
ture him, or visions of loathsome snakes entwin-
ing him with fatal embrace, while vultures impatiently eyed the scene, or dreams would re-
enact the sorrowful realities of the past. For
actual poverty had more than once compelled
him to entertain the idea of throwing away
his pencils, destroying his drawings, and betaking himself at once to some more immediately
lucrative engagement.

Added to these physical trials, were those of
a moral influence—the objections, the incredulity, the persuasions or the censures of others.
These, though unable to deter him from his designs—ever warmly cherished—had yet the ill
result of increasing the actual difficulties of the
case. The effect of their perpetual representation, moreover, was naturally to depress and an-
noy.

" At one period," says Audubon, " not a single
individual seemed to have the least hope of my
success." On delivering his first drawings to
the engraver, he had not a single subscriber.
Nevertheless, he persevered, and with what success has been seen. Nor did prosperity persuade
him to relax in his endeavours.

Working early and late he continued to improve as far as possible his drawings, as well as diligently to collect from his portfolio all that related to the habits of the birds represented. At length, after years of anxiety, he was presented with the first volume of the Birds of America. This was in 1835. So far, at least, he had the delightful assurance of the triumph of his hopes. Scrupulously comparing the plates, he felt convinced too of their improvement as they proceeded, and looked forward confidently to the completion of the second volume.

Subsequently he visited London and Edinburgh, receiving from his friends in those cities, the most kindly assistance, as well as numerous interesting additions to his collections in some rare and beautiful specimens of birds. He was especially delighted traversing the highlands of Scotland. The rocky shores of their magnificent lakes, the splendour of their mountains, and the roar of the torrents, the romantic glens, and picturesque passes, gorgeous landscapes and heather-purpled hills, with clusters of the lichen and red-berried mountain ash, awakened his liveliest admiration.

In the third volume of his illustrations it was Audubon's object to give a description of the water birds. Owing to the large size of these species, in comparison with those of the land, the representations were fewer in this, than in either of the preceding volumes. The colouring and engravings, however, were considered as superior. It contains an account of not less than sixty new species of water-birds, to be met with along the shores and streams of the United States.

The honour which attaches to these discoveries is considerably enhanced when we consider the peculiar difficulties attending the study of the aquatic species. Through rough and tangled forest tracts, and over dreary pathless plains the land bird must patiently be followed, but the water bird as it sweeps the ocean, or scours the rocks, resorts to retreats which are almost inaccessible. This Audubon proved, when compelled to urge his boat onwards, for miles, perhaps, beneath a burning sun, tormented the while with swarms of insects—to lie on the edge of a precipice some hundred feet above the waters, or to crawl along its brink in order to procure a single specimen!

American ornithology is rich in the aquatic tribes. Of the heron it contains numerous species. It possesses also the cormorant, the pelican, the ibis, the curlew, the tern, the petrel, the gull, and others.

Of the cormorants the double-crested is the

14*   L

most distinguished. It resorts every spring to the islets of Labrador, after sojourning for the winter on the eastern coasts. In long lines, sometimes forming angles, it hovers close over the waters in its flight. Occasionally it may be seen to sail in a beautiful manner at a considerable height above the surface. In order to rise from the water, in which it sinks so as to be covered when swimming, it runs beating the waves as it goes for many yards, as though to receive an impetus before it mounts on wing. It is fond of sunning itself with extended wings, when the glossy blended plumage of this beautiful bird, shining in the light, is seen to great advantage. Though differing in size, as well as in the structure of its plumage, it closely resembles the cormorant of Florida. It has another temporary distinction during the breeding season, in the crest or tuft, which consists of a single line of feathers curved downwards.

The Florida cormorant is a constant resident in the country after which it is named. Occasionally it proceeds as far as Cape Hatteras. Seldom venturing out far to sea, or over land, it is found in bays and inlets, always thus following the windings of the shores, though its course should be extended in this way to three times the necessary length for reaching a given spot. This is the only one of its kind observed to alight on trees. Among the branches of the dark mangrove its nest is formed. Its flight, which is more rapid than that of others of its kind, is performed during its migrations by continued flappings; but at other times, sailing more sportively, it is combined with the most elegant aerial movements. In cloudy weather, these birds soar in wide circles high into the air, frequently uttering a note not unlike that of the raven. Should the atmosphere suddenly change to cold, they may be seen in groups of fifty or a hundred, as though assembled for council, when arranging themselves in angular double lines, in marching order, as if by unanimous consent they fly swiftly southwards. In fair calm weather they betake themselves in flocks to some rocky isle or cluster of trees, where, spreading their wings, they bask in the sunlight for hours. Swimming and diving with great expertness—their food consists principally of fishes, with which they satisfy the cravings of their enormous appetites. Similar in its powers of flight, its habits and diet, is the common cormorant, found along the coast of Labrador, and rarely seen further than the limits of Maryland.

In fertile Louisiana the elegant great blue heron may be seen on the margins of the beautiful streams and inland ponds, his graceful neck extended, as with his golden eye he

glances watchfully around. Cautiously he proceeds till the appearance of his prey—a perch,
perhaps—which, troubling the waters, immediately the heron transfixes with his bill, then
spreads his broad wings for flight. Possessing
an acuteness of vision equal to that of the fal-
con, with a disposition extremely suspicious and
timid, that should he perceive a person approaching, he will instantly take to wing. Only
during the love season are these herons seen in
pairs, at other times exhibiting a morose desire
of seclusion, each one securing to himself a certain portion as a feeding ground, from which he
chases all the rest. The excuse may be the
enormous appetite of these birds, which will not
permit a division of any booty that may be
obtained.

At the commencement of the love season,
when their plumage is in full perfection, they
show the utmost anxiety to render themselves
attractive to their companions. Should any
competition arise, the rivals instantly become
combatants, when, opening their powerful bills
and spreading their wings, they rush furiously
upon each other. For half an hour the contest
continues, blows are returned for blows, and
strokes are parried with the skill of accomplished swordsmen. At length the vanquished
one, felled to the earth, is there left to recover

himself, the victor departing with the prize. In plantations, thickly matted with grasses, roofed with the sombre cypress, their nests are found, sometimes on the tops of the highest trees, sometimes a few feet from the ground, or even on it. The male and female sit alternately, receiving food from each other, which consists of fish, frogs, birds, and even the smaller animals. In the Carolinas, where are a number of reservoirs and streams containing fish, which intersect the rice fields, these birds are in great abundance.

The Louisiana heron, a constant resident in the Carolinas, is found also in the southern parts of the Floridas. So delicate and beautiful is it in attire and form as to be denominated by Audubon the Lady of the Waters. With graceful motion, and light and measured tread, this lovely bird in dignified ease leisurely traverses the Florida beaches, with so fairylike a step as to leave no trace upon the sand. In this way it exhibits to perfection the glowing tints of its pendant crest, the beautifully blended plumage of its back and wings and its gracefully falling train. Always sociable, this bird migrates in company with the blue heron, or night egret, and frequently associates also with the white, the yellow crowned, and the night herons. Light, irregular, and swift in flight, it moves with its fellow birds in an undulating manner, in long lines, rather widely separated.

The night heron as well as the snowy heron closely resemble in their habits the rest of the species, the blue heron emulating that of Louisiana, in the ease and grace of its motions.

Frequenting the Floridas, abounding more towards the south, are the brown pelicans, the most interesting of their species. Hovering over the waters, diving for prey, or slumbering midst the mangrove's branches, these birds there exist in multitudes. Despite their weighty proportions, they possess great powers of flight, being able not only to remain many hours on wing, but to rise high in the air, where they perform the most beautiful evolutions. In genial weather, congegrating in groups, as though for social enjoyment, they rise, flock after flock, in broad circles, till they reach, perhaps, the height of a mile, when with their wings constantly extended, they float gracefully, coursing each other, as if in an aerial labyrinth, for an hour or more at a time. Suddenly with wonderful velocity they dart downwards and settle on the waters, where they ride like a dusky fleet along the billows. Or sometimes alighting among their favourite mangroves, they spread their wings to the breeze. When about to repose, they rest upon the sand, or remain standing, when they draw their head

between their shoulders, raise one of their feet,
place their bills upon their backs, and so betake
themselves to slumber. Immediately on the return of the tide, of which they have a most
unerring intuition, they all start up, and spreading their ample pinions, soar in search of prey.
They are also in a remarkable degree weather-
wise, and should they be seen fishing in retired
places, it is the sure precursor of a storm. On
the contrary, when they venture out to see, it is
a certain indication of fair weather.

The frigate pelicans are closely allied in their
habits, as in many of their characteristics, to the
vulture. Like it rapacious, ferocious, and sloth-
ful, their predominating traits are anything but
attractive. Unscrupulously these birds pillage
each other's nests, in order to construct their
own with less exertions; lord it over others
weaker than themselves, and even devour indis-
criminately the young of every species. They
exhibit extraordinary dexterity in collecting
materials for the construction of their nests,
and when flitting swiftly on wing they break
off the twigs of trees in passing, just as though
for amusement, by a single snap of their powerful bills.

The frigate pelican possesses a power of flight
equalled by few other birds, surpassing as it
does that of the gull, the tern, and the hawk in

its velocity. Darting from on high in pursuit of its prey, which the keenness of its vision enables it to perceive at a great distance, it boldly contests the possession of it with any rival that may approach. In that·case, glancing from side to side, it surrounds the enemy with such strategic skill, as effectually to cut off all hope of retreat, until at length he is found to drop the prey from his open bill. Several of his own species then observing the good fortune of the pelican, smitten with envy, enclose him for a combat. Dashing towards him on widely extended wings, they writhe around in wide circles, each one as it overtakes him lashing him with its pinions, and fighting for the treasure. In this manner, passing from bill to bill, the poor captive is carried through the air. With the early dawn, this bird commences his pilgrimage in search of prey. Before the awakening of any of the more amiable songsters, he emerges from his roosting place steathily. Onwards he sails towards the deep, when the richly-tinted green waters lie still ungladdened by the sun. Then flapping his pinions far into the pure azure he soars and floats around. Again descending with half closed wing he makes towards the sea, and having secured his food shoots away.

Or in the gloom of a gathering hurricane,

when the misty air and lurid sky, muttering thunder, and angrily rolling billows, all give evidence of its approach, he may be seen gallantly awaiting the storm. Should he not be able to force a passage against its fury, he keeps his ground by ballancing himself in the air like the hawk. For three successive springs the plumage of this bird increases in beauty, the green, purple, and bronze tints acquiring greater distinctness.

Another species of these birds is the American white pelican, so named by Audubon in distinction to the white pelican of Europe; it varies but slightly in its habits from the rest of its tribe.

Its snowy plumage, when unsoiled, as on rising from the water, is extremely beautiful, as well as its broadly expanded crest and eyes of diamond brightness.

America possesses a variety of the ibis in the scarlet, the white, the brown, the glossy, and the wood ibis. The latter frequents the banks of forest pools, swamps, and the pine barrens. In desolate recesses, where the abounding cypresses, hung with lichens, form a complete labyrinth of shade, it is seen. In many respects it resembles the pelican and vulture, as in the greediness with which it feeds; after which it remains for hours in a state of reple-

15

tion. Its appearance is beautiful, from the fine contrast of its pure white plumage with its raven tipped wings. When at rest it places the bill against the breast, in the manner of the pelican.

The American flamingo resembling the ibis in some of its traits, frequents the coasts of Florida. It is remarkable for the splendour of its apparel, being entirely scarlet, with the exception of the bill, the half of which, as well as the points of each wing, is of black. Its eyes are blue.

One of the most curious amidst the feathered tribes of which the New World boasts, is the oyster catcher. It may be considered a constant resident in the States, and has an extensive range, being found successively along the coast, from Maryland to the Gulf of Mexico—the shores of the Floridas, the Middles States, North Carolina and Labrador. Remaining among the sands or rocky shores of streams and bays, it is never found inland. This species is seldom seen in greater numbers than from one to three or four pairs, except indeed in winter, when they assemble cosily in parties of twenty-five or thirty. Remarkably dignified in its demeanour, this bird is attractive as well as interesting in its appearance, from the peculiarity of its long, slender, but powerful bill, and its handsome plumage, the beauty of which is especially exhibited when on wing. Similar in the colours of its apparel to the ivory-billed woodpecker, the snowy hue of the lower portions is rendered more effective from the brilliant tints of its coral bill, and the transparent whiteness of its wings, with the blended jets of their tips, altogether present a most striking combination. Its flight, swift and graceful, is also powerful and sustained, sometimes accompanied also by the most extraordinary evolutions. When in groups they pass impetuously, wheeling; then, suddenly checking their course, return, not low over the surface of the water as before, but soaring high. Then forming themselves into ranks, presenting a broad front, in a moment, as though alarmed, again they close, and dive towards the sands or the waves. Should they be aimed at then, the shot generally strikes more than one, but the rest, as soon as aware of danger, meet in a straggling line, and are soon out of sight or reach. Vigilant and timid, this bird is constantly on the alert. Should it perceive any one watching it, immediately it sends forth a loud, shrill cry of alarm, and on being approached, flies entirely out of view. Thus the only means of observing its habits, Audubon found, was in the use of the telescope. When quietly pursuing its occupations, it is observed often to probe the sand to the full length of its bill. This weapon, too, it ingeniously insinuates between the shell like a chisel; in this manner seizing and devouring the oysters which are found in shallow waters. Sometimes it dashes the shell against the sand, until broken, and thus the contents are obtained. Swimming for yards at a time, it catches up shrimps and crabs, and may be seen patting the sand, to force out the insects which it greedily swallows.

It does not form any regular nest, but merely scratches the sand till a hollow is formed, where the eggs are deposited. On these, during the heat of the sun, it does not sit. Sometimes, however, when laid on the bare rock, as found on the coast of Labrador, and the bay of Fundy, the bird broods in the fashion of others of the feathered species. It must not be censured as entirely careless of its young, as it always seeks for places in which to deposit its eggs, spots covered with fragments of shells, or sea weeds, in order that they may be hidden. Should it be molested when sitting, moreover, it screams loudly, at the same time flying over and around the enemy, so as to evince the utmost solicitude.

Equally interesting, from its curious habits, is the anhinga or snake bird. In the most secluded swamps, among the forest branches, or on the margin of streams and lakes it is found. It frequents Louisiana, Georgia, Alabama and the Floridas.

On the bough of the tallest cypress, the female may be seen closely brooding over her eggs. Meanwhile her partner, with outspread wings, his fan-like tail extended, soars afar, glancing alternately at his companion, then keenly around for their enemies. Higher and higher in wide bold circles he floats upward until, a mere speck, he mingles with the azure expanse. Suddenly with closed wings he dashes downward, and alighting on the edge of the nest, gazes fondly on his beloved.

As the young develop in strength, they may be seen to test it by standing upright in the nest, and flapping their wings for several minutes at a time. Soon after they are forced by their parents to leave the home of their infancy, in order that another brood may be reared in their stead. The anhinga seldom frequents the immediate vicinity of the sea, preferring rivers and lakes in the lower and level parts of the country. The Floridas, from their number of stagnant streams and pools, possessing abundance of fish, reptiles, and insects, especially attract it. Never is it met with on clear or rapid waters, and a singular fact in connection with its habits is, that

15*

in never selects sojourning places where it is debarred the means of escape from its enemies.

Thus it never frequents a pool completely enclosed by trees. Preferring the most impenetrable morasses, it lurks amidst the topmost boughs of some trees growing from out a pond in its centre, as in this commanding situation, it is the better enabled to perceive the approach of an enemy. In securing its prey, it never plunges from an eminence, though sometimes it drops silently into the water, but only for the purpose of swimming, and afterwards diving for booty. Invariably it returns to the same roosting places, generally on the shore of a stream, or else directly over the water.

To these retreats it hastens after feeding, where basking in the sun, it stands erect, its long wings and large fan-like tail extended, throwing out its slender head and neck in the most curious manner, with sudden jerks, while with its beautiful bright eyes it glances around. The anhinga is a very expert diver, plunging, and instantly disappearing so lightly as not even to cause a ripple on the surface. Though usually but partially emerged when swimming, on the least alarm it sinks further, so as to hide itself from sight. From the peculiar motions of its head and neck, which cause it to resemble the form of a snake, it takes its name.

CHAPTER XIII.

THE Scottish capital, above all other cities, seems to have been associated by Audubon with pleasant and grateful recollections.

He had wandered among the exquisite scenes of the highlands, delighted with the natural beauties of this northern land, where, as an additional charm, dwelt not a few of his warmest admirers and steadfast friends. The most affectionate testimony appears in his "Biography," to the kindness and assistance received from them, in various ways, and a special tribute of thanks is offered to Dr. Argyle Robertson, as well as to Mr. William Macgillivray, whose talents Audubon acknowledges to have been of the most important service to him in the production of his great work.

Nor was a less earnest remembrance of Audubon retained by his friends, numbering among them Christopher North, whose pages contain the following happy delineation of an evening spent with the great naturalist :—*

* Noctes Ambrosianæ.

"We were sitting one night, lately," he says, "all alone by ourselves, almost unanimously eyeing the embers, fire without flame, in the many-visioned grate, but at times aware of the symbols and emblems there beautifully built up of the ongoings of human life, when a knocking, not loud, but resolute, came to the front door. At first we supposed it might be some late home-going knight-errant, from a feast of shells, in a mood between 'malice and true love,' seeking to disquiet the slumbers of old Christopher, in expectation of seeing his night-cap (which he never wears) popped out of the window, and hearing his voice (of which he is chary, in the open air) simulating a scold upon the audacious sleep-breaker. So we benevolently laid back our head on our easy chair, and pursued our speculations on the state of affairs in general, and more particularly on the floundering fall of that inexplicable people—the Whigs. We had been wondering—and of our wondering found no end—what could have been their chief reasons for committing suicide. It appeared a case of very singular *felo de se*—for they had so timed the 'rash act,' as to excite suspicion in the public mind, that his majesty had committed murder. Circumstances, however, had soon come to light that proved to demonstration, that the ministry had laid violent hands on itself, and effected its purpose by strangulation. There was the fatal black ring visible round the neck—though a mere thread; there were the bloodshot eyes protruding from the sockets; and there, sorriest sight of all, was the ghastly suicidal smile, last relic of the laughter of despair! But the knocking would not leave off; and listening to its character, we felt assured it came from the fist of a friend. So we gathered up our slippered feet from the rug, lamp in hand, stalked along the lobbies, unchained and unlocked the oak which our faithful night-porter, Somnus, had sported—and lo! a figure, muffled up in a cloak, and furred like a Russ, advanced familiarly into the hall, extended both hands, bade God bless us, and pronounced, with somewhat of a foreign accent, the name in which we and the world rejoiced, 'Christopher North!' We were not slow in returning the hug fraternal, for who was it, but the ' American woodsman?' —even Audubon himself—fresh from the Floridas, and breathing of the pure air of far-off Labrador!

" Three years, and upwards, had fled since we had taken farewell of the illustrious ornithologist —on the same spot—at the same hour; and there was something ghost-like in such return of a dear friend from a distant region, almost as from the land of spirits. It seemed as if the same moon looked at us—but then, she was wan, and somewhat sad—now, clear as a diamond, and all the starry heavens wore a smile. 'Our words, they were no mony feck'—but in less time than we have taken to write it we two were sitting cheek by jowl, and hand in hand, by that essential fire—while we showed by our looks that we both felt, now they were over, that three years are but as one day! The cane coal-scuttle, instinct with spirit, beeted the fire of its own accord, without word or beck of ours, as if placed there by the hands of one of our wakeful Lares; in globe of purest crystal the Glenlivet shone; unasked, the bright brass kettle began to whisper its sweet under-song; and a centenary of the fairest oysters, native to our isle, turned towards us their languishing eyes, unseen the Nereid that had on the instant wafted them from the procreant cradle-beds of Prestonpans. Grace said, we drew in to supper, and hobnobbing, from elegant long-shank, down each natural-ist's gullet graciously descended, with a gurgle, the mildest, the meekest, the very Moses of ales.

"Audubon, ere half an hour had elapsed, found an opportunity of telling us that he had never seen us in a higher state of preservation —and in a low voice whispered something about the 'eagle renewing his youth.' We acknowl-

edged the kindness by a remark on bold bright
birds of passage, that find the seasons obedient
to their will, and wing their way through worlds,
still rejoicing in the perfect year. But too true
friends were we, not to be sincere in all we
seriously said; and while Audubon confessed
that he saw rather more plainly than when we
parted the crowfeet in the corners of our eyes,
we did not deny that we saw in him an image
of the Falco Leucocephalus, for that looking on
his ' carum caput,' it answered his own description of that handsome and powerful bird, viz.,
' the general colour of the plumage above is dull
hair brown, the lower parts being deeply brown,
broadly margined with greyish white.' But here
he corrected us, for ' surely, my dear friend,'
quoth he, ' you must admit I am a living specimen of the adult bird, and you remember my
description of him in my first volume.' And
thus blending our gravities and our gayeties,
we sat facing one another, each with his last
oyster on the prong of his trident, which disappeared like all mortal joys, between a smile
and a sigh.

"It was quite a noctes. Audubon told us—
by snatches—all his travels, history, and many
an anecdote interspersed of the dwellers among
the woods, birds, beasts, and man."

This enthusiastic record is equalled by that of

the travellers,* who, during a journey by canal route from Philadelphia, chanced, through good fortune, to have Audubon for their companion.

Through the noise and bustle, round about them, of the crowd on board the boat, his well-known name sounded on their ears.

"Mr. Audubon is last on the list," observed the speaker, "I fear he will not get a bed, we are so crowded."

"What, is it possible, Mr. Audubon can be on board?" they rejoined, "the man of all others in the world we wanted most to see. Where? Which is he?"

"He is actually in this very cabin," said their informant, "there," he added, pointing to a huge pile of blankets and fur, which, stretched upon one of the benches, looked like the substantial bale of some western trader. "What, *that* Mr. Audubon!" exclaimed the travellers—whose names were at the moment called out by the captain as entitled to the first choice of berths. This privilege they openly renounced in favour of Audubon. And now the green ball stirred a little, half turned upon its narrow resting-place, after awhile sat erect, and showed that there was a man inside of it! A patriarchal

* Talk about birds and Audubon.—*North American Review.*

beard fell white and wavy down his breast; a pair of hawklike eyes gleamed sharply out from the frizzy shroud of cap and collar. The lookers on drew near, with a thrill of irrepressible curiosity. The moment their eyes beheld the noble contour of that Roman face, they felt it could be *he*, and no one else. Audubon it was, in this wilderness garb, hale and alert with sixty winters on his shoulders, like one of his old eagles, " feathered to the heel." He looked, as they had dreamed, the antique Plato, with his fine classic head and lofty mean, the valorous and venerable sage.

The travellers, soon on intimate terms with their admired companion, were delighted in listening to the ever fresh relation of his exploits, discoveries, and experiences, instructive from the singular stores of knowledge and profound accuracy of information the naturalist displayed. Somewhat silent in general, his conversation was impulsive and fragmentary. A mellow Gallic idiom marked his speech.

When ashore the travellers found he outstripped in walking, with perfect ease, his considerably younger companions; while the clearness and power of his vision showed how entirely the vigour of his constitution was retained. One clear, fine morning, when passing through a particularly picturesque region, his keen eyes,

16

with an abstracted intense expression peculiar to them, were gazing over the scenery, when suddenly he pointed with his finger to the fence of a field, about two hundred yards off, with the exclamation, " See, yonder is a fox-squirrel, running along the top rail, it is not often I have seen one in Pennsylvania."

As not one other person in the group who looked in the direction with him, could detect the creature at all, his companions felt some skepticism as to whether he could discern the object so distinctly, as to discover its species, and curiously asked him if he were *sure* that it was a *fox squirrel?*

Audubon smiled, as flashing his eagle's glance upon them, he answered, "Ah! I have an eagle's eyes."

CHAPTER XIV.

SPITE the enthusiastic admiration of Audubon for the Scottish highlands, and the numerous attractions, as well as grateful associations that linked him to the English metropolis, which he subsequently visited, his heart yearned for the majestic woods of his beloved land.

Previous to his departure for America, however, the gladness of anticipated return to his native shores, the satisfaction of witnessing the increasing success of his work, and the encouragement afforded him by a still extending circle of subscribers in Europe, were sources of happiness alloyed by one distress—anxiety respecting the precarious health of his wife. The thought of separation too, and his approaching absence heightened his solicitude, denied that dearest consolation of watching over its object. But at this trying juncture, he was solaced by the ready sympathy and benevolence of friendship, in the unfailing kindness of Mr. Philips, at that time the medical adviser of his family, whom he had but recently numbered among the subscribers to his work. The liberality and kindness of this excellent man is recorded with the warmest eulogy by Audubon, who gratefully makes mention of his services, together with those received from his excellent friends, Dr. Argyle Robertson, Dr. Roscoe, and Dr. Carswell.

The courtesies of acquaintance between Mr. Philips and Audubon soon ripened into intimacy, and many an instance occurred which proved to the naturalist, not only the worth of his friend's attachment, but the value of his enlightenment, experience, and superior medical skill. Audubon's situation at the time, moreover, caused him to receive, as well as to remember, with especial gratitude, the generous assistance which it was in the power of his friend, by unremitting professional attention, to afford. Thus assured of an unceasing watchfulness during his absence, over the delicate condition of his wife's health, he was enabled to leave the English shores with a peaceful assurance of heart, to which he would otherwise have been a stranger.

In August, therefore, (1836,) he proceeded on his voyage. Lingering at Philadelphia, he had the gratification of meeting Nuttall, distinguished alike for his acquirements in zoology, botany, and mineralogy, who arrived at the city from his recent excursion over the Rocky Mountains to the Pacific, during Audubon's stay. Endowed

with the most disinterested zeal for science, he
at once generously presented Audubon with
every prize of ornithological discovery in his
possession, inscribing at the same time, in his
journal, all that related to the habits of the several species.

At Philadelphia, he anxiously sought access
to the scientific treasury of Townsend, indefatigable in his endeavours to concentrate in his
own publication the fruits of all previous re-
search. As before, however, Philadelphia afforded him but little encouragement, many of
its inhabitants, though the self-styled lovers of
science, so far from assisting his efforts, objecting
even to his viewing the collection of Townsend,
as well as to his desire of incorporating its discoveries with his own.

Such opposition was the more uncalled for,
since it was entirely at variance with the wishes
of the possessor of the specimens in question,
who, absent at that time, afterwards evinced the
warmest desire to render his acquisitions of service to Audubon, who, spite of all obstacles, at
length succeeded in his hopes regarding them.
From Philadelphia, he bent his course towards
Baltimore, and from thence to Charleston. While
here, he received the intelligence of his having
been elected a member of the Ornithological
Society of London.

16*

From New Orleans, down the Mississippi, through its south-west pass, he proceeded, and arrived in April, (1837,) at the Mexican Gulf, pausing now and then for the purpose of exploring the islands dotting its inlets.

In these excursions often he wandered through muddy swamps for whole days, exposed in addition to the terrible ordeal of a scorching sun, rendered still more unendurable by the swarms of insects which prevailed. At a later date, during several cross journeyings over the country, he was compelled to wade through uncultivated wastes, by tracks more resembling quagmires than roads; plodding thus daily, supported only by whatever chance provision the barbarity of the land might afford.

At night the arduous enterprise was exchanged, not for the refreshment of downy bed and pillows, but the miserable shelter, perhaps, of a cart, in which, lying cramped, he was slowly jolted onwards till dawn, when his researches were again renewed! Though not a single discovery resulted from his toilsome wanderings at this period, they proved, nevertheless, profitable, as well as interesting, since he thus obtained not only a more accurate knowledge of the migratory movements of several species, already known to him, but understood more distinctly their geographical distribution.

Touching in his homeward course at Baltimore, Philadelphia, and New York, where he remained a fortnight, he again paused at Liverpool, for the pleasure of once more greeting his numerous friends there, before proceeding to join his family in London. This meeting we readily conceive to have been productive of unusual gratification and delight. After an interval of anxious separation, doubly joyful for Audubon, was reunion to the beloved companion of his life. The gladness of the family gathering, too, we imagine to have been increased, by the especial interest and hilarity natural to the occasion—the introduction of one in her newly formed several relations, a daughter, a sister, and a bride; for the son of Audubon, who had accompanied him in his recent expedition, had but lately been united to the daughter of his friend, Dr. Bachman.

The "Birds of America" proceeded satisfactorily, though several subscribers manifested impatience for the completion of the work, and some even discontinued their subscription. Out of deference to the wishes of these, Audubon was induced to crowd, occasionally, a number of species into one plate, and fortunate it was that a laudable regard for his cherished plan prevented him from further acquiescence to its detriment.

He was honoured shortly after this date by a diploma from the Literary and Historical Society of Quebec. Aided by the diligence of his friend, Mr. Robert Havel, the engraver of the "Birds of America," to whose assiduity and care Audubon frequently bears grateful testimony, he was enabled to offer his illustrations with unfailing punctuality to the public, till the completion of the fourth volume.

The beautiful meadow lark of America may be found in the Floridas, Louisiana, and Carolina, where it abounds during the winter. Its resorts are grassy spots where flowers in rich luxuriance give forth their fragrance beneath golden floods of sunlight. In retreats like these, ere yet the moon has disappeared in the west, or the crystal dew-drops of the morning are brushed from off the boughs, and the many warblers of the forest still slumber in wood and brake, the buoyant lark arises on light pinions, and gladly launches into the pure air. His powers refreshed by repose, he awaits with joy-glowing breast the answering notes of his beloved, whom he implores with the heart-touching melody of his song. She yet lingers—to his singing accents, loud and clear, comes no reply.

Impatiently he then glances round, and irritated at her continued absence, seeks the refuge of some verdurous shade in which to indulge his

chagrin. Loudly he then calls, as if reproach-
fully, or even in anger, when suddenly all is
changed to tenderness at the timid gentle tones
which tell the coming of his love. His wings
are spread immediately, and with sprightly bliss
he flies to meet her.

Precious moments of mutual rapture are then
passed, and the tale of their affection is melodi-
ously told, when sweet assurance of undying
fidelity are given in answer to gentle chidings
for delay. The flight of the meadow lark is
peculiar. Suddenly springing from the ground,
with the flittering movement of a young bird, it
pauses for a while in its course, glancing at the
same time backwards, as though suspicious of
danger.

If pursued, it moves more swiftly, sailing and
beating its wings alternately, until it floats far
away into the bright azure, like a spirit of gladness. Migrating always by day, it is sometimes
seen in groups of fifty or a hundred, flying above
the tallest forest trees. Cases of single combat
not unfrequently occur by the way, when the
fugitive foes who have wandered from the track
to indulge their wrath, are all at once reconciled
—hasten their flight to overtake their companions in their course, and the march is peaceably continued. On the approach of Spring,
these flocks are broken up, and the male birds

continue the migration alone. At this season, the beauty of their plumage, as well as the elegance of their motions, is much increased, their notes flow forth in rapturous intricate harmony of soul-moving joy, and the grace of every external indication proves the refining, elevating influence of the passion which thrills their breasts.

A cavity scooped in the ground serves to form their nest. It is lined with the softest verdurous substances, and matted leaves are placed around to conceal it. The meadow lark displays the utmost solicitude for its young, and an intuitive benevolence seems to prevail with regard to this tender, loving bird, the farmer, while cutting his hay, always, it is said, respecting the tuft in which its nest is placed, which is seldom destroyed by children even.

Frequenting the vicinity of the sea, the shore lark is found on the high wild tracts of Labrador. Amidst the curious vegetation of this inclement land, where from out gorgeous cliffs clad with dangling snow-drifts furious cataracts pour towards the plain, it seeks a home. Amongst the mosses and lichens which, in snowy tufts or tinted embroidery of green, cover the dark granitic-looking expanse of the country, the shore lark places her nest so carefully, as to make it appear a part of the natural vegetation, the similarity of colour between the mosses and the attire of the bird forming an additional defence for it. The nest, which is composed of the finest grasses, forms, as it were, a bed about two inches thick, and is rendered additionally comfortable, from its soft inner lining of feathers.

The male of this species has a very sweet song, though not protracted. Springing from the rock, it soars for about forty yards, then, after performing a few evolutions, returns to the ground, during which time, its chaunt is begun and ended. Another, and one of the most interesting among the specimens of American Ornithology, is the mango humming bird, emulating, in the splendour of its apparel, the gem-like lustre of that celestial pilgrim, the most beautiful among the feathered inhabitants of the Indian Isles, known as the bird of paradise.

The mango humming bird is thus described. "In those warm climates, where the bignonians and other tubular flowers that bloom throughout the year, and innumerable insects that sport in the sunshine, afford an abundance of food, these lively birds are the greatest ornaments of the gardens and forests. Such in most cases is the brilliancy of their plumage, that I am unable to find apt objects of comparison, unless I resort to the most brilliant gems and the richest metals. So rapid is their flight, that they seem to outstrip the wind.   Almost always on the wing, we scarcely see them in any other position.   Living on the honeyed sweets of the most beautiful flowers, and the minute insects concealed in their corollas, they come to us as ethereal beings, and it is not surprising that they should have excited the wonder and admiration of mankind."

This genus consists of upwards of a hundred species, all of which, it is said, are peculiar to the Continent of America and the adjoining Islands.

Contrasted with these, are those birds which, delighting in rapacity and cruelty, are the terror of the winged tribes.   The evil character of these, superstition has not failed to magnify and invest with a thousand imaginary horrors.   Thus that so-called ominous bird, the raven, is maligned and persecuted.   His usefulness entirely forgotten, a war of extirmination is mercilessly waged against him, and his retreats attacked, even though at the cost of the greatest peril to the invaders, his nest being invariably placed in the most inaccessible cavities of the rock.

In America, the raven which frequents the middle, western, and northern portions of the States, usually resorts to mountains, banks of rivers, rocky shores, and the cliffs of deserted islands.   Species of the crow are also met with. The roosting places of these birds are singularly interesting. "They choose," Audubon tells us, "the margin of ponds, lakes, and rivers, upon the rank weeds."

The observations of other travellers have, however, met with them in very different situations. Among the hills of the Green River country, Kentucky, they may be seen streaming overhead in great numbers. An unusual noise is then produced in the air. On advancing in the direction with them, the sound grows in volume, till it bursts forth in a commingled roar of notes and beating wings, which is absolutely deafening. All around, for the space of half an acre, the cracking trees bend beneath multiplied thousands of crows, shifting and flapping with unceasing movement, every one screaming his vociferous "caw" in boisterous emulation. Resembling a pigeon roost very closely, it differs in this respect, that by the time dark sets in, the crows are all quiet, sitting black and still, in heaped masses, as they are defined against the dim sky. In the pigeon roost, on the contrary, the heavy thundering of myriad wings rolls on without ceasing, till just before day.*

The vulture, with several species of the hawk,

* North American Review.

are also inhabitants of the Western World, the owl, of which there exists a great variety, and the eagle. Among the latter the white-headed eagle is especially distinguished. The noble bird is renowned for his strength, his courage, and his remarkable powers of flight. As winter advances along the shore of the Mississippi, he may be seen. Erect on the summit of the tallest tree, adorning the banks of that proud stream, his keen eye eagerly viewing the expanse around, sits this ruthless monarch among birds, the terror of all aerial and aquatic wanderers. Should everything remain tranquil, he is warned by a cry from his companion to continue patient for a while, to which the eagle replies in tones described as resembling the laugh of a maniac. Silently he watches, regardless of the insignificant teal or widgeon, which crosses the current, until at length he is roused by the sight of a swan, her snowy form moving gracefully, as she sails with majestic ease along the waters. Then it is that the exulting shriek of the eagle is borne over the stream, striking the ear of the swan with terror, as, flapping her large wings, with out-stretched neck and animated eye, she watches the enemy's approach. Darting through the air like a lightning flash, he bears down with resistless destruction on his despairing prey. For a time it struggles, seeks to dash into the stream, but is prevented, and speedily forced by the eagle to the earth. Then crushing the dying bird beneath his feet, he drives his sharp claws deep into its breast, and assured of its dying agonies, the ferocious victor again shrieks with joy. When in pursuit of water fowl, which, the eagles are aware, have it in their power to elude their grasp by diving, exerting the utmost ingenuity, they combine their forces for the capture. On marking their prey, both soar to a certain height, when suddenly one sails swiftly towards the water bird, which dives at his approach.

The pursuer then rises in the air to meet his companion, which, in his turn, flies to intimidate the victim, which emerges for a moment to breathe, but is forced to plunge afresh. . The first eagle then takes the place of his successor, and the poor bird, thus alternately menaced and fatigued, makes for the shore, when instantly both eagles settling upon it, divide it as their booty. So unscrupulous is the rapacity of this bird, that it resorts to the most revolting expedient to gratify it. Its daring is astonishing, and it succeeds in scaring even the vulture and crow. Often it pursues them, and becomes possessor of their loathsome spoil. Tradition tells its frequent attempts to capture children.

Audubon, though unable to verify this from

personal experience, does not doubt its capacity
and inclinction to do so. The white-headed
eagle, which seldom frequents the mountainous
districts, preferring the lowlands or sea-shore, is
a constant resident in the United States, and to
be met with in every part. It is capable of
existing for a long period, even twenty days, it
is said, without food. Its nest, usually placed
on the tallest trees, is also found on rocks. It
manifests a strong attachment to certain localities.

Audubon expresses his regret that this bird
should have been chosen as the emblem of his
country, in accordance with the sentiment of
Franklin, who, in one of his letters, thus gives
his opinion, "I wish," he says, "the white-headed
eagle had not been selected as the representative
of our country. He is a bird of bad moral character, he does not get his living honestly ; you
may have seen him perched on some dead tree,
where, too lazy to fish for himself, he watches
the labour of the fishing hawk, and when that
diligent bird has at length taken a fish, and is
bearing it to his nest for the support of his mate
and young ones, the eagle pursues him and takes
it from him."

With all this injustice he is never in good case,
but, like those among men who live by sharping
and robbing, is generally poor.

In 1831, during Audubon's visit to the Floridas, the caracara eagle was first seen by him. Two years later, he became the possessor of a specimen of the golden eagle, which was purchased by him from Mr. Greenwood, proprietor of the Museum at Boston. With an irresistibly amusing naïveté, he relates the circumstance. "The eagle," he tells us, "was immediately conveyed to my place of residence, covered by a blanket, to save him in his adversity from the gaze of the people. I placed the cage so as to afford me a good view of the captive, and I must acknowledge that as I watched his looks of proud disdain, I did not feel towards him so generously as I ought to have done. At times, I was half inclined to restore to him his freedom, that he might return to his native mountains; nay, I several times thought how pleasant it would be to see him spread out his broad wings, and sail away towards the rocks of his wild haunts; but then, some one seemed to whisper that I ought to take the portrait of this magnificent bird, and I abandoned the more generous design of setting him at liberty, for the express purpose of showing you his semblance.

"I occupied myself a whole day in watching his movements; on the next I came to a determination as to the position in which I might best represent him; and on the third, thought
17*

of how I could take away his life with the least
pain to him. I consulted several persons on the
subject, and among others, my most worthy
and generous friend, Dr. George Parkman, who
kindly visited my family every day. He spoke
of suffocating him by means of burning charcoal,
of killing him by electricity, etc., and we both
concluded that the first method would be probably the easiest for ourselves, and the least painful to him. Accordingly the bird was removed
in his prison to a very small room, and closely
covered with blankets—a pan of lighted charcoal
was introduced, the windows and doors fastened,
and the blankets tucked in beneath the cage. I
waited, expecting every moment to hear him fall
down from his perch; but after listening for
hours, I opened the door, raised the blankets,
and peeped under them amidst a mass of suffocating fumes. There stood the eagle on his
perch, with his bright, unflinching eye turned
towards me, and as lively and vigorous as ever!
Instantly reclosing every aperture, I resumed
my station at the door, and towards midnight,
not having heard the least noise, I again took a
peep at my victim. He was still uninjured, although the air of the closet was insupportable
to my son and myself, and that of the adjoining
apartment began to feel unpleasant. I persevered, however, for ten hours in all, when,

finding that the charcoal fumes would not produce the desired effect, I retired to rest, wearied and disappointed. Early next morning, I tried the charcoal anew, adding to it a quantity of sulphur, but we were nearly driven from our house in a few hours, by the stifling vapours, while the noble bird continued to stand erect, and look defiance at us whenever we approached his post of martyrdom. His fierce demeanour precluded all internal application, and at last I was compelled to resort to a method, always used as a last expedient, and a most effectual one. I thrust a long pointed piece of steel through his heart, when my proud prisoner instantly fell dead, without even ruffling a feather.

"I sat up nearly the whole of another night to outline him, and worked so constantly at the drawing, that it nearly cost me my life. I was suddenly seized with a spasmodic affection, that much alarmed my family, and completely prostrated me for some days."

The golden eagle, which frequents the shores of the Hudson and the upper parts of the Mississippi, was also seen by Audubon over the dreary heights of Labrador.

Though it cannot, like the white-headed eagle, seize its prey when on wing, the keenness of its vision enables it to mark the desired object at a great distance, and driving through the air with the swiftness of a meteor, it is thus unerring in its aim. When it has soared high into the air, its evolutions slowly performed in wide circuits, are most majestic; " becoming," says Audubon, this monarch among birds. Its gyrations are sometimes continued for hours. The nest of this eagle, placed invariably high on some rugged cliffs, must be pillaged at the risk of dire peril to the invader, an instance of which occurred during the revolutionary war. A company of soldiers were stationed near the highlands of the Hudson River. A golden eagle had placed her nest in a cleft of the rocks, midway between the summit and the river. One of the soldiers was let down by his companions, suspended by a rope fastened round his body. On reaching the nest, he found himself suddenly attacked by the eagle. In self defence, he drew the only weapon he had, his knife, and made repeated passes at the bird, when accidently he cut the rope almost off. It began to unravel; when the men above him, hastily drawing him up, relieved him from his perilous position, at the moment he expected to be precipitated to the bottom of the gulf. But so powerful was the effect of the terror experienced by the soldier whilst in danger, that before the lapse of three days, his hair became quite grey.

CHAPTER XV.

WITH the publication of the fifth and last volume of Ornithological Biographies, during the year 1839, Audubon had the happiness to witness the completion of his long pursued and dearly cherished plan. It was the achievement of no ordinary ambition—the gratification of impatience at the consummation of some light essay. In it, he beheld as it were, the fulfilment of his destiny—the realization of constant effort and aspiration—the result of the trials of a life-time, the fruits of an entire dedication of all the faculties of existence to one great and honoured end. The advancement of science was his vocation, and in that vocation he nobly served as the worshipper of his Creator and the benefactor of his kind, which he was, intellectually and morally. For to comparatively few, even to those rarely gifted, is it given to follow from the days of infancy, with single-hearted desire, one great object—that object demanding, moreover, the entire surrender of every other for its attainment. Yet to Audubon was this granted. Unconsious of the weakness of vacillation in purpose or practice for one day, he pursued unflinchingly an absorbing principle of action, not only at the sacrifice of leisure, ease, and indulgence, but at the cost of danger, deprivation, and the most arduous endurance.

The naturalist, compelled to undergo the pain of separation, to wander in solitude, to suffer daily toil and peril, is called upon pre-eminently to "live by faith"—to anticipate with dauntless hope, compensation in the future for temporary ills, and thus living in the exercise of fortitude, patience, and industry, he cannot fail to be strengthened and ennobled.

By this faith it was the happiness of Audubon to live. "My heart was nerved," he tells us, relating the obstacles which attended his career, "and reliance on that power on whom all must depend, brought me bright anticipations of success."

Sixteen years had been the period calculated upon by him for the accomplishment of his task. During that time, with unremitting zeal, he had applied himself to its worthy fulfilment. Visions of this most eagerly desired satisfaction would present themselves to cheer him on his laborious way, while sensibility to the beauties of nature, proportioned to the intensity of his love, was the source of refreshment and delight. As the glorious sun arose, gladdening the earth with its rays, starting to his feet, invigorated by health-ful repose, the naturalist was urged to the pursuits of the day, by the delighting prospect of the successful termination of his toils. Fancy would then load the breeze with the praises of admirers. Or with the sweet serenity of evening, the flower-perfumed air, and the declining melodies of forest warblers, thoughts of home and friends would arise, awakening the dear anticipation of joyful meeting.

Incited ever onwards by pleasing images and hopes such as these, Audubon found himself, he tells us, "furnished as it were with large and powerful wings, when, cleaving the air like an eagle, he would fly off, and by a few joyous bounds overtake the object of his desire."

With no partial achievement could his ambition be content, for the ideal of true genius through the slightest detraction is destroyed. "How often," he exclaims, "I long to see the day on which my labours should be brought to an end"—when hope should be converted into assurance, that devotion to nature so enthusiastic, so untiring, had not been in vain. Thus incited and sustained, the wanderer toiled on, till at length in the completion of his great work, he beheld his rich and abundant reward. This was in the sixty-third year of his age. Once more

he was in the charmed circle of his home, ever
so lovingly remembered, though so little enjoyed. Exulting in the satisfaction of his dearest
earthly wishes, he looked up " with gratitude to
the Supreme Being, and felt that he was happy."
The devoted student of nature, he remained to
the close of his career enjoying the pleasures of
those pursuits from which he had derived his
best delights. Audubon lived to the age of
seventy-six.

On the 27th of January, 1851, the " darkness
of death spread for him a sable curtain" over the
scene of this life, from which the great Naturalist
of America for ever departed.

The traveller was at rest.

CHAPTER XVI.

NOTE AND ADDENDA BY THE AMERICAN PUBLISHERS.

WE have taken the liberty of transposing some portions of the foregoing pages from the London edition, having ascertained that chronological mistakes had been made by the fair authoress in preparing her interesting sketch of Audubon, and we would further say, that as she appears not to have been aware of the publication of his second great work, the " Quadrupeds of North America," (which has not been advertised, we believe, in Europe,) it has been deemed by us essential to mention it, and to subjoin the following particulars:—

When Audubon had finished his great edition of the "Birds of America," and had also published a synopsis of the species inhabiting our country, (which was issued in Edinburgh, in 1839,) leaving the hospitable shores of Britain, and parting with many highly valued friends, he embarked for his native land, and after a tedious, although not otherwise unpleasant voy-

18

age, arrived at New York in the month of September of that year.

Desiring to reproduce his work on the Birds in a small form, so as to place it within the reach of nearly all who might wish to possess it, an octavo edition was soon begun, and this undertaking proved entirely successful, being aided by the subscriptions of men of science and professional reputation, and by the patronage of the wealthy and liberal merchants and gentlemen of our principal cities and towns, in which Audubon was most cordially welcomed.

Soon after this edition of the "Birds" had been commenced, the publication of the "Quadrupeds of North America" was projected, with the advice and aid of the Reverend Dr. Bachman, of Charleston, South Carolina, well known for his zoological researches and discoveries, and who had for some time been connected by the marriage of two of his daughters to Audubon's two sons, with ties even stronger than those which always bind congenial and noble spirits together.

Audubon had, during his journeyings, and whilst in the wilderness, made many notes of the habits of our quadrupeds, as well as some drawings of them, and was very soon interested in this new labour in the cause of natural history, notwithstanding his advanced age and the

difficulties that stood in the way: with his experience, and with his usual energy to help him,
bending his mind to the task he had thus taken
up, he at once began to arrange his plans, and
having decided to bring out the work in a size
sufficient to give figures of all the animals
not larger than the raccoon, of their natural
dimensions; he soon was deeply engaged in
preparing it.

He was aided in this arduous task, not only
by Dr. Bachman, but by his sons, V. G. and
J. W. Audubon, the former painting the back-
grounds, drawings of trees, plants, etc., and
editing the manuscript for the press, and the
latter procuring and drawing some of the animals in Texas, California and elsewhere.

Audubon was also assisted by hosts of friends,
many of whom are named in the introduction
to the work, including Sir George Simpson, of
the Hudson's Bay Company, the Chouteaus, of
the American Fur Company, etc., etc.   This
work involved the necessity of further journeyings, and among the rest, a trip to the Yellow
Stone river and the spurs of the Rocky Mountains, which expedition was made in 1843, and
was productive, besides its results in respect to
the history of the quadrupeds, of further discoveries in ornithology, some twenty new
species of birds having been added by it to the

octavo edition of the "Birds of America," the publication of which was not then completed. The work on the quadrupeds has since been republished by V. G. Audubon, in an octavo form, to correspond in size with the small edition of the Birds, and we have been permitted to make some extracts from it, which we gladly add to the foregoing pages.

THE MINK.

Next to the ermine, the mink is the most active and destructive little depredator that prowls around the farm-yard, or the farmer's duck-pond; where the presence of one or two of these animals will soon be made known by the sudden disappearance of sundry young ducks and chickens. The vigilant farmer may perhaps see a fine fowl moving in a singular and most involuntary manner, in the clutches of a mink, towards a fissure in a rock or a hole in some pile of stones, in the gray of the morning, and should he rush to the spot to ascertain the fate of the unfortunate bird, he will see it suddenly twitched into a hole too deep for him to fathom, and wish he had carried with him his double-barreled gun, to have ended at once the life of the voracious destroyer of his carefully tended poultry. Our friend, the farmer, is not, however, disposed to allow the mink to carry on the sport long, and therefore straightway repairs to the house for his gun, and if it be loaded and ready for use, (as it always should be in every well-regulated farm-house,) he speedily returns with it to watch for the reappearance of the mink, and shoot him ere he has the opportunity to depopulate his poultry-yard. The farmer now takes a stand facing the retreat into which the mink has carried his property, and waits patiently until it may please him to show his head again. This, however, the cunning rogue will not always accommodate him by doing, and he may lose much time to no purpose. Let us introduce you to a scene on our own little place near New York.

There is a small brook, fed by several springs of pure water, which we have caused to be stopped by a stone dam to make a pond for ducks in the summer and ice in the winter; above the pond is a rough bank of stones through which the water filters into the pond. There is a little space near this where the sand and gravel have formed a diminutive beach. The ducks descending to the water are compelled to pass near this stony bank. Here a mink had fixed his quarters with certainly a degree of judgment and audacity worthy of high praise, for no settlement could promise to be more to his mind. At early dawn

18*   o

the crowing of several fine cocks, the cackling of many hens and chickens, and the paddling, splashing, and quacking of a hundred old and young ducks would please his ears; and by stealing to the edge of the bank of stones, with his body nearly concealed between two large pieces of broken granite, he could look around and see the unsuspecting ducks within a yard or two of his lurking place. When thus on the look out, dodging his head backward and forward, he waits until one of them has approached close to him, and then with a rush seizes the bird by the neck, and in a moment disappears with it between the rocks. He has not, however, escaped unobserved, and like other rogues deserves to be punished for having taken what did not belong to him. We draw near the spot, gun in hand, and after waiting some time in vain for the appearance of the mink, we cause some young ducks to be gently driven down to the pond—diving for worms or food of various kinds while danger so imminent is near them—intent only on the objects they are pursuing, they turn not a glance toward the dark crevice where we can now see the bright eyes of the mink as he lies concealed. The unsuspecting birds remind us of some of the young folks in that large pond we call the world, where, alas! they may be in greater danger than our poor ducks or chickens. Now we see a fine hen descend to the water; cautiously she steps on the sandy margin and dipping her bill in the clear stream, sips a few drops and raises her head as if in gratitude to the Giver of all good; she continues sipping and advancing gradually; she has now approached the fatal rocks, when with a sudden rush the mink has seized her; ere he can regain his hole, however, our gun's sharp crack is heard and the marauder lies dead before us.

We acknowledge that we have little inclination to say anything in defence of the mink. We must admit, however, that although he is a cunning and destructive rogue, his next door neighbour, the ermine or common weasel, goes infinitely beyond him in his mischievous propensities. Whilst the mink is satisfied with destroying one or two fowls at a time, on which he makes a hearty meal; the weasel, in the very spirit of wanton destructiveness, sometimes in a single night puts to death every tenant of the poultry-house!

Whilst residing at Henderson, on the banks of the Ohio river, we observed that minks were quite abundant, and often saw them carrying off rats which they caught like the weasel or ferret, and conveyed away in their mouths, holding them by the neck in the manner of a cat.

Along the trout streams of our Eastern and Northern States, the mink has been known to steal fish, that, having been caught by some angler, had been left tied together with a string while the fisherman proceeded farther in quest of more. An angler informed us that he had lost in this way thirty or forty fine trout, which a mink dragged off the bank into the stream and devoured, and we have been told that by looking carefully after them, the minks could be seen watching the fisherman, and in readiness to take his fish, should he leave it at any distance behind him. Mr. Hutson of Halifax informed us that he had a salmon weighing four pounds carried off by one of them.

We have observed that the mink is a tolerably expert fisher. On one occasion, whilst seated near a trout-brook in the northern part of the state of New York, we heard a sudden splashing in the stream, and saw a large trout gliding through the shallow water and making for some overhanging roots on the side of the bank. A mink was in close pursuit, and dived after it; in a moment afterwards it reappeared with the fish in its mouth. By a sudden rush we induced it to drop the trout, which was upwards of a foot in length.

We are disposed to believe, however, that fishes are not the principal food on which the mink subsists. We have sometimes seen it feeding on frogs and cray-fish. In the Northern States we have often observed it with a Wilson's meadow-mouse in its mouth, and in Carolina the very common cotton-rat furnishes no small proportion of its food. We have frequently remarked it coursing along the edges of the marshes, and found that it was in search of this rat, which frequents such localities, and we discovered that it was not an unsuccessful mouser. We once saw a mink issuing from a hole in the earth, dragging by the neck a large Florida rat.

In the vicinity of Charleston, South Carolina, a hen-house was one season robbed several nights in succession, the owner counting a chicken less every morning. No idea could be formed, however, of the manner in which it was carried off. The building was erected on posts, and was securely locked, in addition to which precaution a very vigilant watch-dog was now put on guard, being chained underneath the chicken-house. Still, the number of fowls in it diminished nightly, and one was as before missed every morning.

We were at last requested to endeavour to ascertain the cause of the vexatious and singular abstraction of our friend's chickens, and on a careful examination we discovered a small hole in a corner of the building, leading to a cavity

between the weather-boarding and the sill. On
gently forcing outward a plank, we perceived
the bright eyes of a mink peering at us and
shining like a pair of diamonds. He had long
been thus snugly ensconced, and was enabled to
supply himself with a regular feast without leaving the house, as the hole opened toward the
inside on the floor. Summary justice was in-
flicted, of course, on the concealed robber, and
peace and security once more were restored in
the precincts of the chicken-yard.

This species is very numerous in the salt-
marshes of the Southern states, where it subsists principally on the marsh-hen, the sea-side
finch, and the sharp-tailed finch, which, during
a considerable portion of the year, feed on the
minute shell-fish and aquatic insects left on the
mud and oysterbanks, on the subsiding of the
waters. We have seen a mink winding stealthily
through the tall marsh-grass, pausing occasionally to take an observation, and sometimes lying
for the space of a minute flat upon the mud: at
length it draws its hind-feet far forwards under
its body in the manner of a cat, its back is
arched, its tail curled, and it makes a sudden
spring. The screams of a captured marsh-hen
succeed, and its upraised fluttering wing gives
sufficient evidence that it is about to be trans-

ferred from its pleasant haunts in the marshes to the capacious maw of the hungry mink.

It is at low tide that this animal usually captures the marsh-hen. We have often at high spring tide observed a dozen of those birds standing on a small field of floating sticks and matted grasses, gazing stupidly at a mink seated not five feet from them. No attempt was made by the latter to capture the birds that were now within his reach. At first we supposed that he might have already been satiated with food and was disposed to leave the tempting marsh-hens till his appetite called for more; but we were after more mature reflection inclined to think that the high spring tides which occur, exposing the whole marsh to view and leaving no place of concealment, frighten the mink as well as the marsh-hen; and as misery sometimes makes us familiar with strange associates, so the mink and the marsh-hen like neighbour and brother hold on to their little floating islands till the waters subside, when each again follows the instincts of nature. An instance of a similar effect of fear on other animals was related to us by an old resident of Carolina: some forty years ago, during a tremendous flood in the Santee river, he saw two or three deer on a small mound not twenty feet in diameter, surrounded by a wide sea of waters, with a cougar seated in the midst of them; both parties, having seemingly entered into a truce at a time when their lives seemed equally in jeopardy, were apparently disposed peaceably to await the falling of the waters that surrounded them.

This species prefers taking up its residence on the borders of ponds and along the banks of small streams, rather than along large and broad rivers. It delights in frequenting the foot of rapids and waterfalls. When pursued, it flies for shelter to the water, an element suited to its amphibious habits, or to some retreat beneath the banks of the stream. It runs tolerably well on high ground, and we have found it on several occasions no easy matter to overtake it, and when overtaken, we have learned to our cost, that it was rather a troublesome customer about our feet and legs, where its sharp canine teeth made some uncomfortable indentations; neither was its odour as pleasant as we could have desired. It is generally supposed that the mink never resorts to a tree to avoid pursuit; we have, however, witnessed one instance to the contrary. In hunting for the ruffed-grouse, we observed a little dog that accompanied us, barking at the stem of a young tree, and on looking up, perceived a mink seated in the first fork, about twelve feet from the ground. Our friend, the late Dr. Wright, of Troy, informed us that whilst he was walking on the border of a wood, near a stream, a small animal which he supposed to be a black squirrel, rushed from a tuft of grass, and ascended a tree. After gaining a seat on a projecting branch, it peeped down at the intruder on its haunts, when he shot it, and picking it up, ascertained that it was a mink.

We think, however, that this animal is not often seen to ascend a tree, and these are the only instances of its doing so, which are known to us.

This species is a good swimmer, and like the musk-rat, dives at the flash of a gun; we have observed, that the percussion-cap now in general use is too quick for its motions, and that this invention bids fair greatly to lesson its numbers. When shot in the water, the body of the mink, as well as that of the otter, has so little buoyancy, and its bones are so heavy, that it almost invariably sinks.

The mink, like the musk-rat and ermine, does not possess much cunning, and is easily captured in any kind of trap; it is taken in steel-traps and box-traps, but more generally in what are called dead-falls. It is attracted by any kind of flesh, but we have usually seen the traps baited with the head of a ruffed grouse, wild duck, chicken, jay, or other bird. The mink is exceedingly tenacious of life, and we have found

19

it still alive under a dead-fall, with a pole lying across its body pressed down by a weight of one hundred and fifty pounds, beneath which it had been struggling for nearly twenty-four hours.

This species, as well as the skunk and the ermine, emits an offensive odour, when provoked by men or dogs, and this habit is exercised likewise in a moderate degree whenever it is engaged in any severe struggle with an animal or bird on which it has seized. We were once attracted by the peculiar and well known plaintive cry of a hare, in a marsh on the side of one of our Southern rice-fields, and our olfactories were at the same time regaled with the strong fetid odour of the mink; we found it in possession of a large marsh-hare, with which, from the appearance of the trampled grass and mud, it had been engaged in a fierce struggle for some time.

The mink, when taken young, becomes very gentle, and forms a strong attachment to those who fondle it in a state of domestication. Richardson saw one in the " possession of a Canadian woman, that passed the day in her pocket, looking out occasionally when its attention was roused by an unusual noise." We had in our possession a pet of this kind for eighteen months; it regularly made a visit to an adjoining fish-pond both morning and evening, and returned

to the house of its own accord, where it continued during the remainder of the day. It
waged war against the Norway rats which had
their domicile in the dam that formed the fish-
pond, and it caught the frogs which had taken
possession of its banks. We did not perceive
that it captured many fish, and it never attacked
the poultry. It was on good terms with the
dogs and cats, and molested no one unless its
tail or foot was accidentally trod upon, when it
invariably revenged itself, by snapping at the
foot of the offender.

It was rather dull at mid-day, but very active
and playful in the morning and evening, and at
night. It never emitted its disagreeable odour
except when it had received a sudden and severe
hurt. It was fond of squatting in the chimney-
corner, and formed a particular attachment to an
arm-chair in our study.

The skins of the mink were formerly an
article of commerce, and were used for making
muffs, tippets,, etc.; they sold for about fifty
cents each. Richardson states that they at present are only taken by the traders of the fur company to accommodate the Indians, and that they
are afterwards burnt, as they will not repay the
expense of carriage. The fur, however, although
short, is even finer than that of the marten.

A short time since, we were kindly presented

by Charles P. Chouteau, Esq., with a mink skin of a beautiful silver-gray colour, the fur of which is quite different from the ordinary coat of the animal. These beautiful skins are exceedingly rare, and six of them, when they are united, will make a muff, worth at least a hundred dollars. A skin, slightly approaching the fine quality and colour of the one just mentioned, exists in the Academy of Natural Sciences at Philadelphia, but it is brownish, and the fur is not very good.

CHAPTER XVII.

THE BUFFALO.

WHETHER we consider this noble animal as an object of the chase, or as an article of food for man, it is decidedly the most important of all our contemporary American quadrupeds; and as we can no longer see the gigantic mastodon passing over the broad savannas, or laving his enormous sides in the deep rivers of our wide-spread land, we will consider the buffalo as a link (perhaps sooner to be forever lost than is generally supposed) which to a slight degree yet connects us with larger American animals, belonging to extinct creations.

But ere we endeavour to place before you the living and the breathing herds of buffaloes, you must journey with us in imagination to the vast western prairies, the secluded and most inaccessible valleys of the Rocky Mountain chain, and the arid and nearly impassable deserts of the western table lands of our country; and here we may be allowed to express our deep, though

19*

unavailing regret, that the world now contains only few and imperfect remains of the lost races, of which we have our sole knowledge through the researches and profound deductions of geologists; and even though our knowledge of the osteology of the more recently exterminated species be sufficient to place them before our "mind's eye," we have no description and no figures of the once living and moving, but now departed possessors of these woods, plains, mountains and waters in which, ages ago, they are supposed to have dwelt. Let us however hope, that our humble efforts may at least enable us to perpetuate a knowledge of such species as the Giver of all good has allowed to remain with us to the present day. And now we will endeavour to give a good account of the majestic bison.

In the days of our boyhood and youth, buffaloes roamed over the small and beautiful prairies of Indiana and Illinois, and herds of them stalked through the open woods of Kentucky and Tennessee; but they had dwindled down to a few stragglers, which resorted chiefly to the "Barrens," towards the years 1808 and 1809, and soon after entirely disappeared. Their range has since that period gradually tended westward, and now you must direct your steps " to the Indian country," and travel many hundred miles beyond the fair valleys of the Ohio, towards the great rocky chain of mountains which forms the backbone of North America, before you can reach the buffalo, and see him roving in his sturdy independence upon the vast elevated plains, which extend to the base of the Rocky Mountains.

Hie with us then to the West! let us quit the busy streets of St. Louis, once considered the outpost of civilization, but now a flourishing city, in the midst of a fertile and rapidly growing country, with towns and villages scattered for hundreds of miles beyond it; let us leave the busy haunts of men, and on good horses take the course that will lead us into the buffalo region, and when we have arrived at the sterile and extended plains which we desire to reach, we shall be recompensed for our toilsome and tedious journey; for there we may find thousands of these noble animals, and be enabled to study their habits, as they graze and ramble over the prairies, or migrate from one range of country to another, crossing on their route water-courses, or swimming rivers at places where they often plunge from the muddy bank into the stream, to gain a sand-bar or shoal, midway in the river, that affords them a resting place, from which, after a little time, they can direct their course to the opposite shore, when, having reached it, they must scramble up the bank, ere they can gain the open prairie beyond.

There we may also witness severe combats between the valiant bulls, hear their angry bellowing, and observe their sagacity, as well as courage, when disturbed by the approach of man.

The American bison is much addicted to wandering, and the various herds annually remove from the North at the approach of winter, although many may be found, during that season, remaining in high latitudes, their thick woolly coats enabling them to resist a low temperature, without suffering greatly. During a severe winter, however, numbers of them perish, especially the old, and the very young ones.

When the buffalo bull is working himself up to a belligerent state, he paws the ground, bellows loudly, and goes through nearly all the actions we may see performed by the domesticated bull under similar circumstances, and finally rushes at his foe head foremost, with all his speed and strength. Notwithstanding the violent shock with which two bulls thus meet in mad career, these encounters have never been known to result fatally, probably owing to the strength of the spinous process commonly called the hump, the shortness of their horns, and the quantity of hair about all their fore parts.

When congregated together in fair weather, calm or nearly so, the bellowing of a large herd (which sometimes contains a thousand) may be heard at the extraordinary distance of ten miles at least.

In winter, when the ice has become strong enough to bear the weight of many tons, buffaloes are often drowned in great numbers, for they are in the habit of crossing rivers on the ice, and should any alarm occur, rush in a dense crowd to one place; the ice gives way beneath the pressure of hundreds of these huge animals, they are precipitated into the water, and if it is deep enough to reach over their backs, soon perish. Should the water, however, be shallow, they scuffle through the broken and breaking ice, in the greatest disorder, to the shore.

From time to time small herds, crossing rivers on the ice in the spring, are set adrift in consequence of the sudden breaking of the ice after a rise in the river. They have been seen floating on such occasions in groups of three, four, and sometimes eight or ten together, although on separate cakes of ice. A few stragglers have been known to reach the shore in an almost exhausted state, but the majority perish from cold and want of food rather than trust themselves boldly to the turbulent waters.

Buffalo calves are often drowned, from being unable to ascend the steep banks of the rivers across which they have just swam, as the cows cannot help them, although they stand near the bank, and will not leave them to their fate unless something alarms them.

When a large herd of these wild animals are crossing a river, the calves or yearlings manage to get on the backs of the cows, and are thus conveyed safely over; but when the heavy animals, old and young, reach the shore, they sometimes find it muddy or even deeply miry; the strength of the old ones struggling in such cases to gain a solid footing, enables them to work their way out of danger in a wonderfully short time. Old bulls, indeed, have been known to extricate themselves when they had got into the mire so deep that but little more than their heads and backs could be seen. On one occasion we saw an unfortunate cow that had fallen into, or rather sank into a quicksand only seven or eight feet wide; she was quite dead, and we walked on her still fresh carcase safely across the ravine which had buried her in its treacherous and shifting sands.

The gaits of the bison are walking, cantering, and galloping, and when at full speed, he can get over the ground nearly as fast as the best horses found in the Indian country. In lying down, this species bends the forelegs first, and its movements are almost exactly the same as those of the common cow. It also rises with the same kind of action as cattle.

When surprised in a recumbent posture by the sudden approach of a hunter, who has suc-ceeded in nearing it under the cover of a hill, clump of trees or other interposing object, the bison springs from the ground and is in full race almost as quick as thought, and is so very alert, that one can scarcely perceive his manner of rising on such occasions.

The captain of the steamboat on which we as-cended the Missouri, informed us, that on his last annual voyage up that river, he had caught several buffaloes, that were swimming the river. The boat was run close upon them, they were lassoed by a Spaniard, who happened to be on board, and then hoisted on the deck, where they were butchered *secundum artem*. One day we saw several that had taken to the water, and were coming towards our boat. We passed so near them, that we fired at them, but did not procure a single one. On another occasion, one was killed from the shore, and brought on board, when it was immediately divided among the men. We were greatly surprised to see some of the Indians, that were going up with us, ask for certain portions of the entrails, which they devoured with the greatest voracity. This gluttony excited our curiosity, and being always willing to ascertain the quality of any sort of meat, we tasted some of this sort of tripe, and found it very good, although at first its appearance was rather revolting.

The Indians sometimes eat the carcasses of buffaloes that have been drowned, and some of those on board the Omega one day asked the captain most earnestly to allow them to land and get at the bodies of three buffaloes which we passed, that had lodged among the drift-logs and were probably half putrid. In this extraordinary request some of the squaws joined. That, when stimulated by the gnawings of hunger, Indians, or even whites, should feed upon carrion, is not to be wondered at, since we have many instances of cannibalism and other horrors, when men are in a state of starvation, but these Indians were in the midst of plenty of wholesome food, and we are inclined to think their hankering after this disgusting flesh must be attributed to a natural taste for it, probably acquired when young, as they are no doubt sometimes obliged, in their wanderings over the prairies in winter, to devour carrion, and even bones and hides, to preserve their lives.

During the winter of 1842 and 43, as we were told, buffaloes were abundant around Fort Union, and during the night picked up straggling handfuls of hay that happened to be scattered about the place. An attempt was made to secure some of them alive, by strewing hay as a bait, from the interior of the old fort, which is about two hundred yards off, to some distance from the gateway, hoping the animals would feed along into the enclosure. They ate the hay to the very gate; but as the hogs and common cattle were regularly placed there, for security, during the night, the buffaloes would not enter, probably on account of the various odours issuing from the interior. As the buffaloes generally found some hay scattered around, they soon became accustomed to sleep in the vicinity of the fort, but went off every morning, and disappeared behind the hills, about a mile off.

One night they were fired at, from a four-pounder loaded with musket-balls. Three were killed, and several were wounded, but this disaster did not prevent them from returning frequently to the fort at night, and they were occasionally shot, during the whole winter, quite near the fort.

As various accounts of buffalo hunts have been already written, we will pass over our
20

earliest adventures in that way, which occurred many years ago, and give you merely a sketch of the mode in which we killed them during our journey to the West, in 1843.

One morning in July, our party and several persons attached to Fort Union, (for we were then located there,) crossed the river, landed opposite the fort, and passing through the rich alluvial belt of woodland which margins the river, were early on our way to the adjacent prairie, beyond the hills. Our equipment consisted of an old Jersey wagon, to which we had two horses attached, tandem, driven by Mr. Culbertson, principal at the fort. This wagon carried Mr. Harris, Bell, and ourselves, and we were followed by two carts, which contained the rest of the party, while behind came the running horses or hunters, led carefully along. After crossing the lower prairie, we ascended between the steep banks of the rugged ravines, until we reached the high undulating plains above. On turning to take a retrospective view, we beheld the fort and a considerable expanse of broken and prairie land behind us, and the course of the river was seen as it wound along, for some distance. Resuming our advance we soon saw a number of antelopes, some of which had young ones with them. After travelling about ten miles farther we approached the Fox river, and at this point one of the party espied a small herd of bisons at a considerable distance off. Mr. Culbertson, after searching for them with the telescope, handed it to us and showed us where they were. They were all lying down and appeared perfectly unconscious of the existence of our party. Our vehicles and horses were now turned towards them and we travelled cautiously to within about a quarter of a mile of the herd, covered by a high ridge of land which concealed us from their view. The wind was favourable, (blowing towards us,) and now the hunters threw aside their coats, tied handkerchiefs around their heads, looked to their guns, mounted their steeds, and moved slowly and cautiously towards the game. The rest of the party crawled carefully to the top of the ridge to see the chase. At the word of command, given by Mr. Culbertson, the hunters dashed forward after the bulls, which already began to run off in a line nearly parallel with the ridge we were upon. The swift horses, urged on by their eager riders and their own impetuosity, soon began to overtake the affrighted animals; two of them separated from the others and were pursued by Mr. Culbertson and Mr. Bell; presently the former fired, and we could see that he had wounded one of the bulls. It stopped after going a little way, and stood with its head hanging down and its nose near the ground. The blood appeared to be pouring from its mouth and nostrils, and its drooping tail showed the agony of the poor beast. Yet it stood firm, and its sturdy legs upheld its ponderous body as if naught had happened. We hastened toward it, but ere we approached the spot, the wounded animal fell, rolled on its side, and expired. It was quite dead when we reached it. In the mean time Mr. Bell had continued in hot haste after the other, and Mr. Harris and Mr. Squire had each selected, and were following one of the main party. Mr. Bell shot, and his ball took effect in the buttocks of the animal. At this moment Mr. Squire's horse threw him over his head fully ten feet: he fell on his powder-horn and was severely bruised; he called to some one to stop his horse and was soon on his legs, but felt sick for a few moments. Friend Harris, who was perfectly cool, neared his bull, shot it through the lungs, and it fell dead on the spot. Mr. Bell was still in pursuit of his wounded animal, and Mr. Harris and Mr. Squire joined and followed the fourth, which, however, was soon out of sight. We saw Mr. Bell shoot two or three times, and heard guns fired, either by Mr. Harris or Mr. Squire, but the weather was so hot that, fearful of injuring their horses, they were obliged to allow the bull they pursued to escape. The one shot by Mr. Bell, tumbled upon his knees, got up again, and rushed on one of the hunters, who shot it once more, when it paused, and almost immediately fell dead.

The flesh of the buffaloes thus killed was sent to the fort in the cart, and we continued our route and passed the night on the prairie, at a spot about half way between the Yellow Stone and the Missouri rivers. Here, just before sundown, seven more bulls were discovered by the hunters, and Mr. Harris, Mr. Bell and Mr. Culbertson each killed one. In this part of the prairie we observed several burrows made by the swift fox, but could not see any of those animals, although we watched for some time in hopes of doing so. They probably scented our party and would not approach. The hunters on the prairies, either from hunger or because they have not a very delicate appetite, sometimes break in the skull of a buffalo and eat the brains raw. At sunrise we were all up, and soon had our coffee, after which a mulatto man called Lafleur, an excellent hunter attached to the American Fur Company, accompanied Mr. Harris and Mr. Bell on a hunt for antelopes, as we wanted no more buffaloes. After waiting the return of the party, who came back unsuccessful, we broke up our camp and turned our steps homeward.

20*

The prairies are in some places whitened with the skulls of the buffalo, dried and bleached by the summer's sun and the frosts and snows of those severe latitudes in winter. Thousands are killed merely for their tongues, and their large carcasses remain, to feed the wolves and other rapacious prowlers on the grassy wastes.

When these animals are shot at a distance of fifty or sixty yards, they rarely, if ever, charge on the hunters. Mr. Culbertson told us he had killed as many as nine bulls from the same spot, unseen by these terrible animals. There are times, however, when they have been known to gore both horse and rider, after being severely wounded, and have dropped down dead but a few minutes afterwards. There are indeed instances of bulls receiving many balls without being immediately killed, and we saw one which during one of our hunts was shot no less than twenty-four times before it dropped.

A bull that our party had wounded in the shoulder, and which was thought too badly hurt to do much harm to any one, was found rather dangerous when we approached him, as he would dart forward at the nearest of his foes, and but that his wound prevented him from wheeling and turning rapidly, he would certainly have done some mischief. We fired at him from our six-barrelled revolving pistol, which, however, seemed to have little other effect than to render him more savage and furious. His appearance was well calculated to appal the bravest, had we not felt assured that his strength was fast diminishing. We ourselves were a little too confident, and narrowly escaped being overtaken by him through our imprudence. We placed ourselves directly in his front, and as he advanced, fired at his head and ran back, not supposing that he could overtake us ; but he soon got within a few feet of our rear, with head lowered, and every preparation made for giving us a hoist; the next instant, however, we had jumped aside, and the animal was unable to alter his headlong course quick enough to avenge himself on us. Mr. Bell now put a ball directly through his lungs, and with a gush of blood from the mouth and nostrils, he fell upon his knees and gave up the ghost, falling (as usual) on the side, quite dead.

On another occasion, when the same party were hunting, near the end of the month of July, Mr. Squire wounded a bull twice, but no blood flowing from the mouth, it was concluded the wounds were only in the flesh, and the animal was shot by Mr. Culbertson, Owen McKenzie, and Mr. Squire, again. This renewed fire only seemed to enrage him the more, and he made a dash at the hunters so sudden and unexpected, that Mr. Squire, attempting to escape, rode between the beast and a ravine which was near, when the bull turned upon him, his horse became frightened and leaped down the bank, the buffalo following him so closely that he was nearly unhorsed; he lost his presence of mind and dropped his gun; he, however, fortunately hung on by the mane and recovered his seat. The horse was the fleetest, and saved his life. He told us subsequently that he had never been so terrified before. This bull was fired at several times after Squire's adventure, and was found to have twelve balls lodged in him when he was killed. He was in very bad condition, and being in the rutting season, we found the flesh too rank for our dainty palates and only took the tongue with us.

Soon afterwards we killed a cow, in company with many bulls, and were at first afraid that they would charge upon us, which in similar cases they frequently do, but our party was too large and they did not venture near, although their angry bellowings and their unwillingness to leave the spot showed their rage at parting with her. As the sun was now sinking fast towards the horizon on the extended prairie, we soon began to make our way toward the camping ground and passed within a moderate distance of a large herd of buffaloes, which we did not stop to molest, but increasing our speed reached our quarters for the night, just as the shadows of the western plain indicated that we should not behold the orb of day until the morrow.

Our camp was near three conical hills called the Mamelles, only about thirty miles from Fort Union, although we had travelled nearly fifty by the time we reached the spot. After unloading and unsaddling our tired beasts, all hands assisted in getting wood and bringing water, and we were soon quietly enjoying a cup of coffee. The time of refreshment to the weary hunter is always one of interest: the group of stalwart frames stretched in various attitudes around or near the blazing watch-fires, recalls to our minds the masterpieces of the great delineators of night scenes; and we have often at such times beheld living pictures, far surpassing any of those contained in the galleries of Europe.

There were signs of grizzly bears around us, and during the night we heard a number of wolves howling among the bushes in the vicinity. The service berry was abundant, and we ate a good many of them, and after a hasty preparation in the morning, started again after the buffaloes we had seen the previous evening. Having rode for some time, one of our party who was in advance as a scout, made the customary signal from the top of a high hill, that buffaloes were in sight; this is done by walking the hunter's horse backward and forward several times. We hurried on and found our scout lying close to his horse's neck, as if asleep on the back of the animal. He pointed out where he had discovered the game, but they had gone out of sight, and (as he said) were travelling fast, the herd being composed of both bulls and cows. The hunters mounted at once, and galloped on in rapid pursuit, while we followed more leisurely over hills and plains and across ravines and broken ground, at the risk of our necks. Now and then we could see the hunters, and occasionally the buffaloes, which had taken a direction toward the fort. At last we reached an eminence from which we saw the hunters approaching the buffaloes in order to begin the chase in earnest. It seems that there is no etiquette among buffalo hunters, and this not being understood beforehand by our friend Harris, he was disappointed in his wish to kill a cow. The country was not as favourable to the hunters as it was to the flying herd. The females separated from the males, and the latter turned in our direction and passed within a few hundred yards of us without our being able to fire at them. Indeed we willingly suffered them to pass unmolested, as they are always very dangerous when they have been parted from the cows. Only one female was killed on this occasion. On our way homeward we made towards the coupee, an opening in the hills, where we expected to find water for our horses and mules, as our supply of Missouri water was only enough for ourselves.

The water found on these prairies is generally unfit to drink, (unless as a matter of necessity,) and we most frequently carried eight or ten gallons from the river, on our journey through the plains. We did not find water where we expected, and were obliged to proceed about two miles to the eastward, where we luckily found a puddle sufficient for the wants of our horses and mules. There was not a bush in sight at this place, and we collected buffalo dung to make a fire to cook with. In the winter this prairie fuel is often too wet to burn, and the hunters and Indians have to eat their meat raw. It can however hardly be new to our readers to hear that they are often glad to get any thing, either raw or cooked, when in this desolate region.

Some idea of the immense number of bisons to be still seen on the wild prairies, may be formed from the following account, given to us by Mr. Kipp, one of the principals of the American Fur Company. "While he was travelling from Travers' Bay to the Mandan nation in the month of August, in a cart heavily laden, he passed through herds of buffalo for six days in succession. At another time he saw the great prairie near Fort Clark on the Missouri river, almost blackened by these animals, which covered the plain to the hills that bounded the view in all directions, and probably extended farther.

When the bisons first see a person, whether white or red, they trot or canter off forty or fifty yards, and then stop suddenly, turn their heads and gaze on their foe for a few moments, then take a course and go off at full speed until out of sight, and beyond the scent of man.

Although large, heavy, and comparatively clumsy, the bison is at times brisk and frolicksome, and these huge animals often play and gambol about, kicking their heels in the air with surprising agility, and throwing their hinder parts to the right and left alternately, or from one side to the other, their heels the while flying about and their tails whisking in the air. They are very impatient in the fly and mosquito season, and are often seen kicking and running against the wind to rid themselves of these tormentors.

The different Indian tribes hunt the buffalo in various ways: some pursue them on horseback and shoot them with arrows, which they point with old bits of iron, or old knife blades. They are rarely expert in loading or reloading guns, (even if they have them,) but in the closely contested race between their horse and the animal, they prefer the rifle to the bow and arrow. Other tribes follow them with patient perseverance on foot, until they come within shooting distance, or kill them by stratagem.

The Mandan Indians chase the buffalo in parties of from twenty to fifty, and each man is provided with two horses, one of which he rides, and the other being trained expressly for the chase, is led to the place where the buffaloes are started. The hunters are armed with bows and arrows, their quivers containing from thirty to fifty arrows according to the wealth of the owner. When they come in sight of their game, they quit the horses on which they have ridden, mount those led for them, ply the whip, soon gain the flank or even the centre of the herd, and shoot their arrows into the fattest, according to their fancy. When a buffalo has been shot, if the blood flows from the nose or mouth, he is considered mortally wounded; if not, they shoot a second or a third arrow into the wounded animal.

The buffalo, when first started by the hunters, carries his tail close down between the legs; but when wounded, he switches his tail about, especially if intending to fight his pursuer, and it behooves the hunter to watch these movements closely, as the horse will often shy, and without due care the rider may be thrown, which when in a herd of buffalo is almost certain death. An arrow will kill a buffalo instantly if it takes effect in the heart, but if it does not reach the right spot, a dozen arrows will not even arrest one in his course, and of the wounded, many run out of sight and are lost to the hunter.

At times the wounded bison turns so quickly and makes such a sudden rush upon the hunter, that if the steed is not a good one and the rider perfectly cool, they are overtaken, the horse gored and knocked down, and the hunter thrown off and either gored or trampled to death. But if the horse is a fleet one, and the hunter expert, the bison is easily outrun and they escape. At best it may be said that this mode of buffalo hunting is dangerous sport, and one requires both skill and nerve to come off successfully.

The Gros Ventres, Blackfeet and Assinaboines often take the buffalo in large pens, usually called parks, constructed in the following manner.

Two converging fences built of sticks, logs and brushwood are made, leading to the mouth of a pen somewhat in the shape of a funnel. The pen itself is either square or round, according to the nature of the ground where it is to be placed,

at the narrow end of the funnel, which is always
on the verge of a sudden break or precipice in
the prairie ten or fifteen feet deep, and is made
as strong as possible. When this trap is completed, a young man very swift of foot starts at
daylight, provided with a bison's hide and head,
to cover his body and head when he approaches
the herd that is to be taken, on nearing which
he bleats like a young buffalo calf, and makes
his way slowly towards the mouth of the converging fences leading to the pen. He repeats
this cry at intervals, the buffaloes follow the
decoy, and a dozen or more of mounted Indians
at some distance behind the herd gallop from one
side to the other on both their flanks, urging
them by this means to enter the funnel, which
having done, a crowd of men, women and children
come and assist in frightening them, and as soon
as they have fairly entered the road to the pen
beneath the precipice, the disguised Indian, still
bleating occasionally, runs to the edge of the
precipice, quickly descends, and makes his escape,
climbing over the barricade or fence of the pen
beneath, while the herd follow on till the leader
(probably an old bull) is forced to leap down into the pen, and is followed by the whole herd,
which is thus ensnared, and easily destroyed
even by the women and children, as there is no
means of escape for them.

This method of capturing the bison is especially resorted to in October and November, as the hide is at that season in good condition and saleable, and the meat can be preserved for the winter supply. When the Indians have thus driven a herd of buffalo into a pen, the warriors all assemble by the side of the enclosure, the pipe is lighted, and the chiefs smoke to the honour of the Great Spirit, to the four points of the compass, and to the herd of bisons. As soon as this ceremony has ended, the destruction commences, guns are fired and arrows shot from every direction at the devoted animals, and the whole herd is slaughtered before the Indians enter the space where the buffaloes have become their victims. Even the children shoot tiny arrows at them when thus captured, and try the strength of their young arms upon them.

It sometimes happens, however, that the leader of the herd becomes alarmed and restless while driving to the precipice, and should the fence be weak, breaks through, and the whole drove follow and escape. It also sometimes occurs, that after the bisons are in the pen, which is often so filled that they touch each other, the terrified crowd swaying to and fro, their weight against the fence breaks it down, and if the smallest gap is made, it is immediately widened, when they dash through and scamper off, leaving the Indians in dismay and disappointment. The side fences for the purpose of leading the buffaloes to the pens extend at times nearly half a mile, and some of the pens cover two or three hundred yards of ground. It takes much time and labour to construct one of these great traps or snares, as the Indians sometimes have to bring timber from a considerable distance to make the fences and render them strong and efficient.

The bison has several enemies: the worst is, of course, man; then comes the grizzly bear; and next, the wolf. The bear follows them and succeeds in destroying a good many; the wolf hunts them in packs, and commits great havoc among them, especially among the calves and the cows when calving. Many buffaloes are killed when they are struggling in the mire on the shores of rivers where they sometimes stick fast, so that the wolves or bears can attack them to advantage; eating out their eyes and devouring the unresisting animals by piecemeal.

Every part of the bison is useful to the Indians, and their method of making boats, by stretching the raw hide over a sort of bowl-shaped frame work, is well known. These boats are generally made by the women, and we saw one of them at the Mandan village. The horns are made into drinking vessels, ladles, and spoons. The skins form a good bed, or admirable covering from the

21*

cold, and the flesh is excellent food, whether fresh or dried or made into pemmican; the fat is reduced and put up in bladders, and in some cases used for frying fish, etc.

The hide of the buffalo is tanned or dressed altogether by the women, or squaws, and the children.

The scrapings of the skins, we were informed, are sometimes boiled with berries, and make a kind of jelly, which is considered good food in some cases by the Indians. The strips cut off from the skins are sewed together and make robes for the children, or caps, mittens, shoes, etc. The bones are pounded fine with a large stone and boiled, the grease which rises to the top is skimmed off and put into bladders. This is the favourite and famous marrow grease, which is equal to butter. The sinews are used for stringing their bows, and are a substitute for thread; the intestines are eaten, the shoulder-blades made into hoes, and in fact (as we have already stated) nothing is lost or wasted, but every portion of the animal, by the skill and in dustry of the Indians, is rendered useful

CHAPTER XVIII.

THE OPOSSUM.

TRAVELLERS in unexplored regions are likely to find many unheard-of objects in nature that awaken in their minds feelings of wonder and admiration. We can imagine to ourselves the surprise with which the opossum was regarded by Europeans when they first saw it. Scarcely anything was known of the marsupial animals, as New Holland had not as yet opened its unrivalled stores of singularities to astonish the world. Here was a strange animal, with the head and ears of the pig, sometimes hanging on the limb of a tree, and occasionally swinging like the monkey by the tail! Around that prehensile appendage a dozen sharp-nosed, sleek-headed young, had entwined their own tails, and were sitting on the mother's back! The astonished traveller approaches this extraordinary compound of an animal and touches it cautiously with a stick. Instantly it seems to be struck with some mortal disease: its eyes close, it falls to the ground, ceases to move, and appears to be dead! He turns it on its back, and perceives on its stomach a strange apparently artificial opening. He puts his fingers into the extraordinary pocket, and lo! another brood of a dozen or more young, scarcely larger than a pea, are hanging in clusters on the teats. In pulling the creature about, in great amazement, he suddenly receives a gripe on the hand—the twinkling of the half-closed eye and the breathing of the creature, evince that it is not dead, and he adds a new term to the vocabulary of his language, that of "playing 'possum."

Like the great majority of predacious animals, the opossum is nocturnal in its habits. It suits its nightly wanderings to the particular state of the weather. On a bright starlight or moonlight night, in autumn or winter, when the weather is warm and the air calm, the opossum may everywhere be found in the Southern States, prowling around the outskirts of the plantation, in old deserted rice fields, along water courses, and on the edges of low grounds and swamps; but if the night should prove windy or very cold, the best-nosed dog can scarcely strike a trail, and in such cases the hunt for that night is soon abandoned.

The gait of the opossum is slow, rather heavy, and awkward; it is not a trot like that of the fox, but an amble or pace, moving the two legs on one side at a time. Its walk on the ground is plantigrade, resting the whole heel on the earth. When pursued, it by no means stops at once and feigns death, as has often been supposed, but goes forward at a rather slow speed, it is true, but as fast as it is able, never, that we are aware of, increasing it to a leap or canter, but striving to avoid its pursuers by sneaking off to some thicket or briar patch; when, however, it discovers that the dog is in close pursuit, it flies for safety to the nearest tree, usually a sapling, and unless molested does not ascend to the top, but seeks an easy resting place in some crotch not twenty feet from the ground, where it waits silently and immoveably, till the dog, finding that his master will not come to his aid, and becoming weary of barking at the foot of the tree, leaves the opossum to follow the bent of his inclinations, and conclude his nightly round in search of food. Although a slow traveller, the opossum, by keeping perseveringly on foot during the greater part of the night, hunts over much ground, and has been known to make a circle of a mile or two in one night. Its ranges, however, appear to be restricted or extended according to its necessities, as when it has taken up its residence near a corn field, or a clump of ripe persimmon trees, the wants of nature are soon satisfied, and it early and slowly carries its fat and heavy body to its quiet home, to spend the remainder of the night and the succeeding day in the enjoyment of a quiet rest and sleep.

The whole structure of the opossum is ad-mirably adapted to the wants of a sluggish animal. It possesses strong powers of smell, which aid it in its search after food; its mouth is capacious, and its jaws possessing a greater number and variety of teeth than any other of our animals, evidencing its omnivorous habits; its fore-paws, although not armed with retractile claws, aid in seizing its prey and conveying it to the mouth. The construction of the hind-foot with its soft yielding tubercles on the palms and its long nailless opposing thumb, enable it to use these feet as hands, and the prehensile tail aids it in holding on to the limbs of trees whilst its body is swinging in the air; in this manner we have observed it gathering persimmons with its mouth and fore-paws, and devouring them whilst its head was downwards and its body suspended in the air, holding on sometimes with its hind-feet and tail, but often by the tail alone.

We have observed in this species a habit which is not uncommon among a few other species of quadrupeds, as we have seen it in the raccoon and occasionally in the common house dog—that of lying on its back for hours in the sun, being apparently dozing, and seeming to enjoy this position as a change.   Its usual posture, however, when asleep, is either lying at full length on the side, or sitting doubled up with its head under its fore-legs, and its nose touching the stomach, in the manner of the raccoon.

The opossum cannot be called a gregarious animal.   During summer, a brood composing a large family may be found together, but when the young are well grown, they usually separate, and each individual shifts for himself; we have seldom found two together in the same retreat in autumn or winter.

Although not often seen abroad in very cold weather in winter, this animal is far from falling into that state of torpidity to which the marmots, jumping mice, and several other species of quad-rupeds are subject.   In the southern States, there are not many clear nights of starlight or moonshine in which they may not be found roaming about; and although in their farthest northern range they are seldom seen when the ground is covered with snow, yet we recollect having come upon the track of one in snow a foot deep, in the month of March, in Pennsyl-vania; we pursued it, and captured the opossum in its retreat—a hollow tree.   It may be re-marked, that animals like the opossum, raccoon, skunk, etc., that become very fat in autumn require but little food to support them through the winter, particularly when the weather is cold.

Hunting the opossum is a very favourite amusement among domestics and field labourers on our southern plantations, of lads broke loose from school in the holidays, and even of gentlemen, who are sometimes more fond of this sport than of the less profitable and more dangerous and fatiguing one of hunting the gray fox by moonlight. Although we have never participated in an opossum hunt, yet we have observed that it afforded much amusement to the sable group that in the majority of instances make up the hunting party, and we have on two or three occasions been the silent and gratified observers of the preparations that were going on, the anticipations indulged in, and the excitement apparent around us.

On a bright autumnal day, when the abundant rice crop has yielded to the sickle, and the maize has just been gathered in, when one or two slight white frosts have tinged the fields and woods with a yellowish hue, ripened the persimmon, and caused the acorns, chesnuts and chinquepins to rattle down from the trees and strewed them over the ground, we hear arrangements entered into for the hunt. The opossums have been living on the delicacies of the season, and are now in fine order, and some are found excessively fat; a double enjoyment is anticipated, the fun of catching and the pleasure of eating this excellent substitute for roast pig.

"Come, men," says one, "be lively, let us finish our tasks by four o'clock, and after sundown we will have a 'possum hunt." "Done," says another, "and if an old coon comes in the way of my smart dog, Pincher, I be bound for it, he will shake de life out of him." The labourers work with increased alacrity, their faces are brightened with anticipated enjoyment, and ever and anon the old familiar song of "'possum up the gum tree" is hummed, whilst the black driver can scarcely restrain the whole gang from breaking out into a loud chorus.

The paraphernalia belonging to this hunt are neither showy nor expensive. There are no horses caparisoned with elegant trappings—no costly guns imported to order—no pack of hounds answering to the echoing horn; two or three curs, half hound or terriers, each having his appropriate name, and each regarded by his owner as the best dog on the plantation, are whistled up. They obey the call with alacrity, and their looks and intelligent actions give evidence that they too are well aware of the pleasure that awaits them. One of these humble rustic sportsmen shoulders an axe and another a torch, and the whole arrangement for the hunt

22

is completed. The glaring torch-light is soon
seen dispersing the shadows of the forest, and
like a jack-o'-lantern, gleaming along the skirts
of the distant meadows and copses. Here are
no old trails on which the cold-nosed hound tries
his nose for half an hour to catch the scent.
The tongues of the curs are by no means silent
—ever and anon there is a sudden start and an
uproarious outbreak: "A rabbit in a hollow,
wait, boys, till I twist him out with a hickory."
The rabbit is secured and tied with a string
around the neck: another start, and the pack
runs off for a quarter of a mile, at a rapid rate,
then double around the cotton fields and among
the ponds in the pine lands—"Call off your
worthless dog, Jim, my Pincher has too much
sense to bother after a fox." A loud scream and
a whistle brings the pack to a halt, and presently
they come panting to the call of the black hunts-
man. After some scolding and threatening, and
resting a quarter of an hour to recover their
breath and scent, they are once more hied forward. Soon a trusty old dog, by an occasional
shrill yelp, gives evidence that he has struck
some trail in the swamp. The pack gradually
make out the scent on the edges of the pond, and
marshes of the rice fields, grown up with willows
and myrtle bushes. At length the mingled
notes of shrill and discordant tongues give evi-

dence that the game is up. The race, though rapid, is a long one, through the deep swamp, crossing the muddy branch into the pine lands, where the dogs come to a halt, unite in conclave, and set up an incessant barking at the foot of a pine. "A coon, a coon! din't I tell you," says Monday, "that if Pincher come across a coon, he would do he work?" An additional piece of split light wood is added to the torch, and the coon is seen doubled up in the form of a hornet's nest in the very top of the long-leaved pine, (*P. palustris*). The tree is without a branch for forty feet or upwards, and it is at once decided that it must be cut down: the axe is soon at work, and the tree felled. The glorious battle that ensues, the prowess of the dogs, and the capture of the coon, follow as a matter of course.

Another trail is soon struck, and the dogs all open upon it at once: in an instant they rush, pell-mell, with a loud burst of mingled tongues, upon some animal along the edge of an old field destitute of trees. It proves to be an opossum, detected in its nightly prowling expedition. At first, it feigns death, and rolling itself into a ball, lies still on the ground; but the dogs are up to this " 'possum playing," and seize upon it at once. It now feels that they are in earnest, and are not to be deceived. It utters a low growl or two, shows no fight, opens wide its large mouth, and, with few struggles, surrenders itself to its fate. But our hunters are not yet satisfied, either with the sport or the meat: they have large families and a host of friends on the plantation, the game is abundant, and the labour in procuring it not fatiguing, so they once more hie on the dogs. The opossum, by its slow gait and heavy tread, leaves its footprints and scent behind it on the soft mud and damp grass. Another is soon started, and hastens up the first small gum, oak, or persimmon tree within its reach; it has clambered up to the highest limb, and sits crouching up with eyes closed to avoid the light. "Off jacket, Jim, and shake him down; show that you know more about 'possum than your good-for-nutten fox-dog." As the fellow ascends, the animal continues mounting higher to get beyond his reach; still he continues in pursuit, until the affrighted opossum has reached the farthest twig on the extreme branches of the tree. The negro now commences shaking the tall pliant tree top; while, with its hind hands rendered convenient and flexible by its opposing thumb, and with its prehensive tail, the opossum holds on with great tenacity. But it cannot long resist the rapidly accumulating jerks and shocks: suddenly the feet slip from the smooth, tiny limb, and it hangs suspended for a few moments only by its tail, in the meantime trying to regain its hold with its hind hands: but another sudden jerk breaks the twig, and down comes the poor animal, doubled up like a ball, into the opened jaws of eager and relentless canine foes; the poor creature drops, and yields to fate without a struggle.

In this manner half-a-dozen or more opossums are sometimes captured before midnight. The subsequent boasts about the superior noses, speed, and courage of the several dogs that composed this small motley pack—the fat feast that succeeded on the following evening, prolonged beyond the hour of midnight, the boisterous laugh and the merry song, we leave to be detailed by others, although we confess we have not been uninterested spectators of such scenes.

> "Let not ambition mock their useful toil,
>   Their homely joys and destiny obscure,
> Nor grandeur hear with a disdainful smile,
>   The simple pleasures of the humble poor."

The habit of feigning death to deceive an enemy is common to several species of quadrupeds, and we on several occasions witnessed it in our common red fox. But it is more strikingly exhibited in the opossum than in

22*
R

any other animal with which we are acquainted. When it is shaken from a tree and falls
among grass and shrubbery, or when detected
in such situations, it doubles itself into a heap
and feigns death so artfully, that we have
known some schoolboys carrying home for
a quarter of a mile an individual of this
species, stating that when they first saw it, it
was running on the ground, and they could not
tell what had killed it. We would not, however, advise that the hand should on such
occasions be suffered to come too familiarly
in contact with the mouth, lest the too curious meddler should on a sudden be startled
with an unexpected and unwelcome gripe.

The opossum is easily domesticated when
captured young. We have, in endeavouring to
investigate one of the very extraordinary characteristics of this species, preserved a considerable number in confinement, and our experi-
ments were continued through a succession of
years. Their nocturnal habits were in a considerable degree relinquished, and they followed
the servants about the premises, becoming
troublesome by their familiarity and their
mischievous habits. They associated familiarly
with a dog on the premises, which seemed to
regard them as necessary appendages of the
motley group that constituted the family of

brutes in the yard. They devoured all kinds of food: vegetables, boiled rice, hominy, meat both raw and boiled, and the scraps thrown from the kitchen; giving the preference to those that contained any fatty substance.

On one occasion a brood of young with their mother made their escape, concealed themselves under a stable, and became partially wild; they were in the habit of coming out at night, and eating scraps of food, but we never discovered that they committed any depredations on the poultry or pigeons. They appeared, however, to have effectually driven off the rats, as during the whole time they were occupants of the stable we did not observe a single rat on the premises. It was ascertained that they were in the habit of clambering over fences and visiting the neighbouring lots and gardens, and we occasionally found that we had repurchased one of our own vagrant animals. They usually, however, returned towards daylight to their snug retreat, and we believe would have continued in the neighbourhood and multiplied the species, had they not in their nightly prowlings been detected and destroyed by the neighbouring dogs.

CHAPTER XIX.

THE BEAVER.

THE sagacity and instinct of the beaver have from time immemorial been the subject of admiration and wonder. The early writers on both continents have represented it as a rational, intelligent, and moral being, requiring but the faculty of speech to raise it almost to an equality, in some respects, with our own species. There is in the composition of every man, whatever may be his pride in his philosophy, a proneness in a greater or less degree to superstition, or at least credulity. The world is at best but slow to be enlightened, and the trammels thrown around us by the tales of the nursery are not easily shaken off. Travellers into the northern parts of Europe who wrote marvellous accounts of the habits of the beavers in northern Europe, seem to have worked on the imaginations and confused the intellects of the early explorers of our northern regions. They excited the enthusiasm of Buffon, whose romantic stories have so fastened themselves on the mind of childhood, and have been so generally made a part of our education, that we now are almost led to regret that three-fourths of the old accounts of this extraordinary animal are fabulous; and that, with the exception of its very peculiar mode of constructing its domicile, the beaver is in point of intelligence and cunning greatly exceeded by the fox, and is but a few grades higher in the scale of sagacity than the common musk-rat.

The following account was noted down by us as related by a trapper named Prevost, who had been in the service of the American Fur Company for upwards of twenty years, in the region adjoining the spurs of the Rocky Mountains, and who was the "Patroon" that conveyed us down the Missouri river in the summer and autumn of 1843. As it confirms the statements of Hearne, Richardson, and other close observers of the habits of the beaver, we trust that, although it may present little that is novel, it will, from its truth, be acceptable and interesting to our readers. Mr. Prevost states in substance as follows:

Beavers prefer small, clear water rivers, and creeks, and likewise resort to large springs. They, however, at times, frequent great rivers and lakes. The trappers believe that they can have notice of the approach of winter weather, and of its probable severity, by observing the preparations made by the beavers to meet its rigours; as these animals always cut their wood in good season, and if this be done early, winter is at hand.

The beaver dams, where the animal is at all abundant, are built across the streams to their very head waters. Usually these dams are formed of mud, mosses, small stones, and branches of trees cut about three feet in length and from seven to twelve inches round. The bark of the trees in all cases being taken off for winter provender, before the sticks are carried away to make up the dam. The largest tree cut by the beaver, seen by Prevost, measured eighteen inches in diameter; but so large a trunk is very rarely cut down by this animal. In the instance just mentioned, the branches only were used, the trunk not having been appropriated to the repairs of the dam or aught else by the beavers.

In constructing the dams, the sticks, mud, and moss are matted and interlaced together in the firmest and most compact manner; so much so, that even men cannot destroy them without a great deal of labour. The mud and moss at the bottom are rooted up with the animal's snout, somewhat in the manner hogs

BEAVERS MAKING A DAM. Page 262.

work in the earth, and clay and grasses are
stuffed and plastered in between the sticks,
roots, and branches, in so workmanlike a way
as to render the structure quite water-tight.
The dams are sometimes seven or eight feet
high, and are from ten to twelve feet wide at
the bottom, but are built up with the sides
inclining towards each other, so as to form a
narrow surface on the top. They are occasionally as much as three hundred yards in
length, and often extend beyond the bed of
the stream, in a circular form, so as to overflow all the timber near the margin, which the
beavers cut down for food during winter, heap
together in large quantities, and so fasten to the
shore under the surface of the water, that even
a strong current cannot tear it away; although
they generally place it in such a position that
the current does not pass over it. These piles
or heaps of wood are placed in front of the
lodges, and when the animal wishes to feed, he
proceeds to them, takes a piece of wood, and
drags it to one of the small holes near the
principal entrance running above the water,
although beneath the surface of the ground.
Here the bark is devoured at leisure, and the
wood is afterwards thrust out, or used in repairing the dam. These small galleries are
more or less abundant according to the num-

ber of animals in the lodges. The larger lodges are, in the interior, about seven feet in diameter, and between two and three feet high, resembling a great oven. They are placed near the edge of the water, although actually built on or in the ground. In front, the beavers scratch away the mud to secure a depth of water that will enable them to sink their wood deep enough to prevent its being impacted in the ice when the dam is frozen over, and also to allow them always free egress from their lodges, so that they may go to the dam and repair it if necessary. The top of the lodge is formed by placing branches of trees matted with mud, grasses, moss, etc., together, until the whole fabric measures on the outside from twelve to twenty feet in diameter, and is six or eight feet high, the size depending on the number of inhabitants. The outward coating is entirely of mud or earth, and smoothed off as if plastered with a trowel. As beavers, however, never work in the day-time, no person, we believe, has yet seen how they perform their task, or give this hard-finish to their houses. This species does not use its fore-feet in swimming, but for carrying burdens: this can be observed by watching the young ones, which suffer their fore-feet to drag by the side of the body, using only the hind-feet to propel themselves through the water. Before diving, the beaver gives a smart slap with its tail on the water, making a noise that may be heard a considerable distance, but in swimming, the tail is not seen to work, the animal being entirely submerged except the nose and part of the head; it swims fast and well, but with nothing like the speed of the otter.

The beavers cut a broad ditch all around their lodge, so deep that it cannot freeze to the bottom, and into this ditch they make the holes already spoken of, through which they go in and out and bring their food. The beds of these singular animals are separated slightly from each other, and are placed around the wall or circumference of the interior of the lodge; they are formed merely of a few grasses, or the tender bark of trees: the space in the centre of the lodge being left unoccupied. The beavers usually go to the dam every evening to see if repairs are needed.

They rarely travel by land, unless their dams have been carried away by the ice, and even then they take the beds of the rivers or streams for their roadway. In cutting down trees they are not always so fortunate as to have them fall into the water, or even towards it, as the trunks

23

of trees cut down by these animals are observed lying in various positions; although as most trees on the margin of a stream or river lean somewhat towards the water, or have their largest branches extended over it, many of those cut down by the beavers naturally fall in that direction.

It is a curious fact, says our trapper, that among the beavers there are some that are lazy and will not work at all, either to assist in building lodges or dams, or to cut down wood for their winter stock. The industrious ones beat these idle fellows, and drive them away; sometimes cutting off a part of their tail, and otherwise injuring them. These "Paresseux" are more easily caught in traps than the others, and the trapper rarely misses one of them. They only dig a hole from the water, running obliquely towards the surface of the ground twenty-five or thirty feet, from which they emerge when hungry to obtain food, returning to the same hole with the wood they procure, to eat the bark.

They never form dams, and are sometimes to the number of five or seven together; all are males. It is not at all improbable that these unfortunate fellows have, as is the case with the males of many species of animals, been engaged in fighting with others of their sex, and after having been conquered and driven away from the lodge, have become idlers from a kind of necessity. The working beavers, on the contrary, associate, males, females, and young together.

Beavers are caught, and found in good order at all seasons of the year in the Rocky Mountains; for, in those regions the atmosphere is never warm enough to injure the fur; in the lowlands, however, the trappers rarely begin to capture them before the first of September, and they relinquish the pursuit about the last of May. This is understood to be along the Missouri, and the (so called) Spanish country.

Cartwright found a beaver that weighed forty-five pounds; and we were assured that they have been caught weighing sixty-one pounds before being cleaned. The only portions of their flesh that are considered fine eating, are the sides of the belly, the rump, the tail, and the liver. The tail, so much spoken of by travellers and by various authors, as being very delicious eating, we did not think equalled their descriptions. It has nearly the taste of beef marrow, but is rather oily, and cannot be partaken of unless in a very moderate quantity, except by one whose stomach is strong enough to digest the most greasy substances.

Beavers become very fat at the approach of

autumn ; but during winter they fall off in flesh, so that they are generally quite poor by spring, when they feed upon the bark of roots, and the roots of various aquatic plants, some of which are at that season white, tender, and juicy. During winter, when the ice is thick and strong, the trappers hunt the beaver in the following manner: a hole is cut in the ice as near as possible to the aperture leading to the dwelling of the animal, the situation of which is first ascertained; a green stick is placed firmly in front of it, and a smaller stick on each side, about a foot from the stick of green wood; the bottom is then patted or beaten smooth and even, and a strong stake is set into the ground to hold the chain of the trap, which is placed within a few inches of the stick of green wood, well baited, and the beaver, attracted either by the fresh bark or the bait, is almost always caught. Although when captured in this manner, the animal struggles, diving and swimming about in its efforts to escape, it never cuts off a foot in order to obtain its liberty; probably because it is drowned before it has had time to think of this method of saving itself from the hunter. When trapping under other circumstances, the trap is placed within five or six inches of the shore, and about the same distance below the surface of the water, secured and baited as usual. If caught, the beavers now and then cut off the foot by which they are held, in order to make their escape.

The beaver which we brought from Boston to New York was fed principally on potatoes and apples, which he contrived to peel as if assisted with a knife, although his lower incisors were his only substitute for that useful implement. While at this occupation the animal was seated on his rump, in the manner of a ground-hog, marmot, or squirrel, and looked like a very large wood-chuck, using his fore-feet, as squirrels and marmots are wont to do.

This beaver generally slept on a good bed of straw in his cage, but one night having been taken out and placed at the back of the yard in a place where we thought he would be secure, we found next morning to our surprise that he had gnawed a large hole through a stout pine door which separated him from that part of the yard nearest the house, and had wandered about until he fell into the space excavated and walled up outside the kitchen window. Here he was quite entrapped, and having no other chance of escape from this pit, into which he had unluckily fallen, he gnawed away at the window-sill and the sash, on which his teeth took such effect that on an examination of the premises we found that a carpenter and several dollars' worth of work were

23*

needed, to repair damages. When turned loose in the yard in the day-time he would at times slap his tail twice or thrice on the brick pavement, after which he elevated this member from the ground, and walked about in an extremely awkward manner. He fell ill soon after we had received him, and when killed, was examined by Dr. James Trudeau, who found that he would shortly have died of an organic disease.

It is stated by some authors that the beaver feeds on fish. We doubt whether he possesses this habit, as we on several occasions placed fish before those we saw in captivity, and although they were not very choice in their food, and devoured any kind of vegetable, and even bread, they in every case suffered fish to remain untouched in their cages.

THE JAGUAR.

ALIKE beautiful and ferocious, the jaguar is of all American animals unquestionably the most to be dreaded, on account of its combined strength, activity, and courage, which not only give it a vast physical power over other wild creatures, but enable it frequently to destroy man.

Compared with this formidable beast, the

cougar need hardly be dreaded more than the wild cat; and the grizzly bear, although often quite as ready to attack man, is inferior in swiftness and stealthy coming. To the so much feared tiger of the East he is equal in fierceness; and it is owing, perhaps, to his being nocturnal in his habits to a great extent, that he seldom issues from the deep swamps or the almost impenetrable thickets or jungles of thorny shrubs, vines, and tangled vegetation which compose the chaparals of Texas and Mexico, or the dense and untracked forests of Central and Southern America, to attack man. From his haunts in such nearly unapproachable localities, the jaguar roams forth towards the close of the day, and during the hours of darkness seizes on his prey. During the whole night he is abroad, but is most frequently met with in moonlight and fine nights, disliking dark and rainy weather, although at the promptings of hunger he will draw near the camp of the traveller, or seek the almost wild horses or cattle of the ranchero even during daylight, with the coolest audacity.

The jaguar has the cunning to resort to salt-licks, or the watering-places of the mustangs and other wild animals, where, concealing himself behind a bush, or mounting on to a low or sloping tree, he lies in wait until a favorable opportunity presents itself for springing on his prey.

Like the cougar and the wild cat, he seeks for the peccary, the skunk, opossum, and the smaller rodentia; but is fond of attacking the larger quadrupeds, giving the preference to mustangs or horses, mules, or cattle. The colts and calves especially afford him an easy prey, and form a most important item in the grand result of his predatory expeditions.

Like the lion and tiger, he accomplishes by stealth or stratagem what could not be effected by his swiftness of foot, and does not, like the untiring wolf, pursue his prey with indomitable perseverance at top speed for hours together, although he will sneak after a man or any other prey for half a day at a time, or hang on the skirts of a party for a considerable period, watching for an opportunity of springing upon some person or animal in the train.

Col. Hays and several other officers of the rangers, at the time J. W. Audubon was at San Antonio de Bexar, in 1845, informed him that the jaguar was most frequently found about the watering-places of the mustangs, or wild horses, and deer. It has been seen to spring upon the former, and from time to time kills one; but it is much more in the habit of attacking colts about six months old, which it masters with great ease. Col. Hays had killed four jaguars during his stay in Texas. These animals are

known in that country by the Americans as the
"leopard," and by the Mexicans as the "Mexican tiger." When lying in wait at or near the
watering-places of deer or horses, this savage
beast exhibits great patience and perseverance,
remaining for hours crouched down, with head
depressed, and still as death. But when some
luckless animal approaches, its eyes seem to
dilate, its hair bristles up, its tail is gently waved
backwards and forwards, and all its powerful
limbs appear to quiver with excitement. The
unsuspecting creature draws near the dangerous
spot; suddenly, with a tremendous leap, the
jaguar pounces on him, and with the fury of an
incarnate fiend fastens upon his neck with his
terrible teeth, whilst his formidable claws are
struck deep into his back and flanks. The poor
victim writhes and plunges with fright and pain,
and makes violent efforts to shake off the foe,
but in a few moments is unable longer to
struggle, and yields with a last despairing cry to
his fate. The jaguar begins to devour him while
yet alive, and growls and roars over his prey
until his hunger is appeased. When he has
finished his meal, he sometimes covers the remains of the carcass with sticks, grass, weeds, or
earth, if not disturbed, so as to conceal it from
other predacious animals and vultures, until he
is ready for another banquet.. The jaguar often

lies down to guard his prey, after devouring as much as he can. On one occasion a small party of rangers came across one while feeding upon a mustang. The animal was surrounded by eight or ten hungry wolves, which dared not interfere or approach too near "the presence." The rangers gave chase to the jaguar, on which the wolves set up a howl or cry like a pack of hounds, and joined in the hunt, which ended before they had gone many yards, the jaguar being shot down as he ran, upon which the wolves went back to the carcass of the horse and finished him.

The jaguar has been known to follow a man for a long time. Colonel Hays, whilst alone on a scouting expedition, was followed by one of these animals for a considerable distance. The colonel, who was aware that his footsteps were scented by the animal, having observed him on his trail a little in his rear, had proceeded a good way, and thought that the jaguar had left, when, having entered a thicker part of the wood, he heard a stick crack, and being in an Indian country, "whirled round," expecting to face a wakoe; but instead of a red-skin, he saw the jaguar, about half-crouched, looking "right in his eye," and gently waving his tail. The colonel, although he wished not to discharge his gun, being in the neighborhood of Indians who might hear the report, now thought it high time to shoot, so he fired, and killed him in his tracks. "The skin," as he informed us, "was so beautiful, it was a pleasure to look at it."

These skins are very highly prized by the Mexicans, and also by the Rangers; they are used for holster coverings and as saddle cloths, and form a superb addition to the caparison of a beautiful horse, the most important animal to the occupants of the prairies of Texas, and upon which they always show to the best advantage.

In a conversation with General Houston at Washington city, he informed us that he had found the jaguar east of the San Jacinto river, and abundantly on the head waters of some of the eastern tributaries of the Rio Grande, the Guadaloupe, etc.

These animals, said the general, are sometimes found associated to the number of two or more, together, when they easily destroy horses and other large quadrupeds. On the head waters of the San Marco, one night, the general's people were aroused by the snorting of their horses, but on advancing into the space around could see nothing, owing to the great darkness. The horses having become quiet, the men returned to camp and lay down to rest as usual, but in the morning one of the horses was found to have been killed and eaten up entirely, except the skeleton. The horses on this occasion were hobbled and picketed; but the general thinks the jaguar frequently catches and destroys wild ones, as well as cattle. The celebrated Bowie caught a splendid mustang horse, on the rump of which were two extensive scars made by the claws of a jaguar or cougar. Such instances, indeed, are not very rare.

Capt. J. P. McCown, U. S. A., related the following anecdote to us:—At a camp near the Rio Grande, one night, in the thick, low, level musquit country, when on an expedition after Indians, the captain had killed a beef which was brought into camp from some distance. A fire was made, part of the beef hanging on a tree near it. The horses were picketed around, the men outside forming a circular guard. After some hours of the night had passed, the captain was aroused by the soldier next him saying, "Captain, may I shoot?" and raising himself on his arm, saw a jaguar close to the fire, between him and the beef, and near it, with one fore-foot raised, as if disturbed; it turned its head towards the captain as he ordered the soldier not to fire, lest he should hurt some one on the other side of the camp, and then, seeming to know it was discovered, but without exhibiting any sign of fear, slowly, and with the stealthy, noiseless pace and attitude of a common cat, sneaked off.

The jaguars we examined in a menagerie at Charleston had periodical fits of bad temper: one of them severely bit his keeper, and was ready to give battle either to the Asiatic tiger or the lion, which were kept in separate cages.

The jaguar, according to D'Azara, can easily drag away a horse or an ox; and should another be fastened or yoked to the one he kills, the powerful beast drags both off together, notwithstanding the resistance of the terrified living one. He does not conceal the residue of his prey after feeding: this may be because of the abundance of animals in his South American haunts. He hunts in the stealthy manner of a cat after a rat, and his leap upon his prey is a very sudden, quick spring: he does not move rapidly when retreating or running. It is said that if he finds a party of sleeping travellers at night, he advances into their midst, and first kills the dog, if there is one, next the negro, and then the Indian, only attacking the Spaniard after he has made this selection; but generally he seizes the dog and the meat, even when the latter is broiling on the fire, without injuring the men, unless he is attacked or is remarkably hungry, or unless he has been accustomed to eat human flesh, in which case he prefers it to every other kind. D'Azara says very coolly, "Since I have been here the ya-

24

gouarétés (jaguars) have eaten six men, two of whom were seized by them whilst warming themselves by a fire." If a small party of men or a herd of animals pass within gunshot of a jaguar, the beast attacks the last one of them with a loud roar.

CHAPTER XX.

ROCKY MOUNTAIN GOAT

IN the vast ranges of wild and desolate heights, alternating with deep valleys and tremendous gorges, well named the Rocky Mountains, over and through which the adventurous trapper makes his way in pursuit of the rich fur of the beaver or the hide of the bison, there are scenes which the soul must be dull indeed not to admire. In these majestic solitudes all is on a scale to awaken the sublimest emotions and fill the heart with a consciousness of the infinite Being " whose temple is all space, whose altar earth, sea, skies."

Nothing, indeed, can compare with the sensations induced by a view from some lofty peak of these great mountains, for there the imagination may wander unfettered, may go back without a check through ages of time to the period when an Almighty power upheaved the gigantic masses which lie on all sides far beneath and around the beholder, and find no spot upon which to arrest the eye as a place where once dwelt man! No; we only know the Indian as a wanderer, and we cannot say here stood the strong fortress, the busy city, or even the humble cot. Nature has here been undisturbed and unsubdued, and our eyes may wander all over the scene to the most distant faint blue line on the horizon which encircles us, and forget alike the noisy clamour of toiling cities and the sweet and smiling quiet of the well cultivated fields, where man has made a "home" and dwelleth in peace. But in these regions we may find the savage grizzly bear, the huge bison, the elegant and fleet antelope, the large-horned sheep of the mountains, and the agile fearless climber of the steeps—the Rocky Mountain goat.

This snow-white and beautiful animal appears to have been first described, from skins shown to Lewis and Clark, as "the sheep," in their general description of the beasts, birds, and plants found by the party in their expedition. They say, "The sheep is found in many places, but mostly in the timbered parts of the Rocky Mountains. They live in greater numbers on the chain of mountains forming the commencement of the woody country on the coast, and passing the Columbia between the falls and the rapids. We have only seen the skins of these animals, which the natives dress with the wool, and the blankets which they manufacture from the wool. The animal, from this evidence, appears to be of the size of our common sheep, of a white colour. The wool is fine on many parts of the body, but in length not equal to that of our domestic sheep. On the back, and particularly on the top of the head, this is intermixed with a considerable portion of long, straight hairs. From the Indian account, these animals have erect, pointed horns."

The Rocky Mountain goat wanders over the most precipitous rocks, and springs with great activity from crag to crag, feeding on the plants, grasses, and mosses of the mountain sides, and seldom or never descends to the luxuriant valleys, as the big horn does. This goat, indeed, resembles the wild goat of Europe, or the chamois, in its habits, and is very difficult to procure. Now and then the hunter may observe one browsing on the extreme verge of some perpendicular rock almost directly above him, far beyond gunshot, and entirely out of harm's way. At another time, after fatiguing and hazardous efforts, the hungry marksman may reach a spot from whence his rifle will send a ball into the unsuspecting goat; then slowly he rises from his hands and knees, on which he has been creeping, and the muzzle of his heavy gun is "rested" on a loose stone, be-

24*

hind which he has kept his movements from being observed, and now he pulls the fatal trigger with deadly aim. The loud, sharp crack of the rifle has hardly rung back in his ear from the surrounding cliffs when he sees the goat, in its expiring struggles, reach the verge of the dizzy height: a moment of suspense and it rolls over, and swiftly falls, striking, perchance, here and there a projecting point, and with the clatter of thousands of small stones set in motion by its rapid passage down the steep slopes which incline outward near the base of the cliff, disappears, enveloped in a cloud of dust in the deep ravine beneath, where a day's journey would hardly bring an active man to it, for far around must he go to accomplish a safe descent, and toilsome and dangerous must be his progress up the gorge within whose dark recesses his game is likely to become the food of the ever prowling wolf or the solitary raven. Indeed, cases have been mentioned to us in which these goats, when shot, fell on to a jutting ledge, and there lay, fifty or a hundred feet below the hunter, in full view, but inaccessible from any point whatever.

Notwithstanding these difficulties, as portions of the mountains are not so precipitous, the Rocky Mountain goat is shot and procured tolerably easily, it is said, by some of the Indian tribes, who make various articles of clothing out of its skin, and use its soft, woolly hair for their rude fabrics.

THE BLACK BEAR.

THE black bear, however clumsy in appearance, is active, vigilant, and persevering, possesses great strength, courage, and address, and undergoes with little injury the greatest fatigues and hardships in avoiding the pursuit of the hunter. Like the deer it changes its haunts with the seasons, and for the same reason, viz., the desire of obtaining suitable food, or of retiring to the more inaccessible parts, where it can pass the time in security, unobserved by man, the most dangerous of its enemies.

During the spring months it searches for food in the low rich alluvial lands that border the rivers, or by the margins of such inland lakes as, on account of their small size, are called by us ponds. There it procures abundance of succulent roots and tender juicy plants, upon which it chiefly feeds at that season. During the summer heat, it enters the gloomy swamps, passes much of its time in wallowing in the mud like a hog, and contents itself with crayfish, roots, and nettles, now and then seizing on a pig. or perhaps a sow, a calf, or even a full-grown cow. As soon as the different kinds of berries which grow on the mountains begin to ripen, the bears betake themselves to the high grounds, followed by their cubs.

In retired parts of the country, where the plantations are large and the population sparse, it pays visits to the corn-fields, which it ravages for a while. After this, the various species of nuts, acorns, grapes, and other forest fruits, that form what in the western States is called *mast*, attract its attention. The bear is then seen rambling singly through the woods to gather this harvest, not forgetting, meanwhile, to rob every *bee-tree* it meets with, bears being expert at this operation.

The black bear is a capital climber, and now and then *houses* itself in the hollow trunk of some large tree for weeks together during the winter, when it is said to live by sucking its paws.

At one season, the bear may be seen examining the lower part of the trunk of a tree for several minutes with much attention, at the same time looking around, and snuffing the air. It then rises on its hind-legs, approaches the trunk. embraces it with the fore-legs, and scratches the bark with its teeth and claws for several minutes in continuance. Its jaws clash against each other until a mass of foam runs down on both sides of the mouth. After this it continues its rambles.

Most writers on the habits of this animal have stated that the black bear does not eat animal food from choice, and never unless pressed by hunger. This we consider a great mistake, for in our experience we have found the reverse to be the case, and it is well known to our frontier farmers that this animal is a great destroyer of pigs, hogs, calves, and sheep, for the sake of which we have even known it to desert the pecan groves in Texas. At the same time, as will have been seen by our previous remarks, its principal food generally consists of berries, roots, and other vegetable substances. It is very fond also of fish, and during one of our expeditions to Maine and New Brunswick, we found the inhabitants residing near the coast unwilling to eat the flesh of the animal on account of its fishy taste. In our western forests, however, the bear feeds on so many nuts and well tasted roots and berries, that its meat is considered a great delicacy, and in the city of New York we have generally found its market price three or four times more than the best beef per pound. The fore-paw of the bear when cooked presents a striking re- semblance to the hand of a child or young person, and we have known some individuals to be hoaxed by its being represented as such.

Perhaps the most acrid vegetable eaten by the bear is the Indian turnip, which is so pungent that we have seen people almost distracted by it, when they had inadvertently put a piece in their mouth.

The black bear is a remarkably swift runner when first alarmed, although it is generally "treed," that is, forced to ascend a tree, when pursued by dogs and hunters on horseback. We were, not very long since, when on an expedition in the mountains of Virginia, leisurely making our way along a road through the forest after a long hunt for deer and turkeys, with our gun thrown behind our shoulders and our arms resting on each end of it, when, although we had been assured there were no bears in that neighbourhood, we suddenly perceived one above us on a little acclivity at one side of the road, where it was feeding, and nearly concealed by the bushes. The bank was only about fifteen feet high, and the bear not more than twenty paces from us, so we instantly disengaged our gun, and cocking both barrels, expected to "fill our bag" at one shot, but at the instant and before we could fire, the bear, with a celerity that astonished us, disappeared. We rushed up the bank and found the land on the top nearly level for a long distance before us, and neither very thickly wooded nor very bushy; but no bear was to be seen, although our eye could penetrate the woods for at least two hundred yards. After the first disappointing glance around, we thought bruin might have mounted a tree, but such was not the case, as on looking everywhere nothing could be seen of his black body, and we were obliged to conclude that he had run out of sight in the brief space of time we occupied in ascending the little bank.

As we were once standing at the foot of a large sycamore tree on the borders of a long and deep pond, on the edge of which, in our rear, there was a thick and extensive "cane-brake," we heard a rushing, roaring noise, as if some heavy animal was bearing down and passing rapidly through the canes, directly towards us. We were not kept long in suspense, for in an instant or two, a large bear dashed out of the dense cane, and plunging into the pond without having even seen us, made off with considerable speed through the water towards the other shore. Having only bird-shot in our gun we did not think it worth while to call his attention to us by firing at him, but turned to the cane-brake, expecting to hear either dogs or men approaching shortly. No further noise could be heard, however, and the surrounding woods were as still as before this adventure. We supposed the bear had been started at some distance, and that his pursuers, not being able to follow him through the almost impenetrable canes, had given up the hunt.

Being one night sleeping in the house of a friend, who was a planter in the state of Louisiana, we were awakened by a servant bearing a light, who gave us a note, which he said his master had just received. We found it to be a communication from a neighbour, requesting our host and ourself to join him as soon as possible, and assist in killing some bears at that moment engaged in destroying his corn. We were not long in dressing, and on entering the parlour, found our friend equipped. The overseer's horn was heard calling up the negroes. some were already saddling our horses, whilst others were gathering all the cur-dogs of the plantation. All was bustle. Before half an hour had elapsed, four stout negro men, armed with axes and knives, and mounted on strong nags, were following us at a round gallop through the woods, as we made directly for the neighbour's plantation.

The night was none of the most favourable, a drizzling rain rendering the atmosphere thick and rather sultry; but as we were well acquainted with the course, we soon reached the

house, where the owner was waiting our arrival.
There were now three of us armed with guns,
half a dozen servants, and a good pack of dogs
of all kinds. We jogged on towards the de-
tached field in which the bears were at work.
The owner told us that for some days several
of these animals had visited his corn, and that
a negro who was sent every afternoon to see at
what part of the enclosure they entered, had
assured him there were at least five in the field
that night. A plan of attack was formed: the
bars at the usual entrance of the field were to
be put down without noise; the men and dogs
were to divide, and afterwards proceed so as to
surround the bears, when, at the sounding of
our horns, every one was to charge towards the
centre of the field, and shout as loudly as possible, which it was judged would so intimidate
the animals as to induce them to seek refuge
upon the dead trees with which the field was
still partially covered.

The plan succeeded: the horns sounded, the
horses galloped forward, the men shouted, the
dogs barked and howled. The shrieks of the
negroes were enough to frighten a legion of
bears, and by the time we reached the middle
of the field we found that several had mounted
the trees, and having lighted fires, we now saw
them crouched at the junction of the larger

branches with the trunks. Two were immediately shot down. They were cubs of no great size, and being already half dead, were quickly dispatched by the dogs.

We were anxious to procure as much sport as possible, and having observed one of the bears, which from its size we conjectured to be the mother of the two cubs just killed, we ordered the negroes to cut down the tree on which it was perched, when it was intended the dogs should have a tug with it, while we should support them, and assist in preventing the bear from escaping, by wounding it in one of the hind-legs. The surrounding woods now echoed to the blows of the axemen. The tree was large and tough, having been girded more than two years, and the operation of felling it seemed extremely tedious. However, at length it began to vibrate at each stroke; a few inches alone now supported it, and in a short time it came crashing to the ground.

The dogs rushed to the charge, and harassed the bear on all sides, whilst we surrounded the poor animal. As its life depended upon its courage and strength, it exercised both in the most energetic manner. Now and then it seized a dog and killed him by a single stroke. At another time, a well administered blow of one of its fore-legs sent an assailant off, yelping

so piteously that he might be looked upon as
hors du combat. A cur had daringly ventured
to seize the bear by the snout, and was seen
hanging to it, covered with blood, whilst several
others scrambled over its back. Now and then
the infuriated animal was seen to cast a revenge-
ful glance at some of the party, and we had already determined to dispatch it, when, to our
astonishment, it suddenly shook off all the dogs,
and before we could fire, charged upon one of
the negroes, who was mounted on a pied horse.
The bear seized the steed with teeth and claws,
and clung to its breast. The terrified horse
snorted and plunged. The rider, an athletic
young man, and a capital horseman, kept his
seat, although only saddled on a sheep-skin
tightly girthed, and requested his master not to
fire at the bear. Notwithstanding his coolness
and courage, our anxiety for his safety was
raised to the highest pitch, especially when in
a moment we saw rider and horse come to the
ground together; but we were instantly relieved on witnessing the masterly manner in which
Scipio dispatched his adversary, by laying open
his skull with a single, well directed blow of his
axe, when a deep growl announced the death of
the bear.

In the state of Maine the lumbermen (wood-
cutters) and the farmers set guns to kill this

animal, which are arranged in this way : A funnel-shaped space about five feet long is formed by driving strong sticks into the ground in two converging lines, leaving both the ends open, the narrow end being wide enough to admit the muzzle of an old musket, and the other extremity so broad as to allow the head and shoulders of the bear to enter. The gun is then loaded and fastened securely, so as to deliver its charge facing the wide end of the enclosure. A round and smooth stick is now placed behind the stock of the gun, and a cord leading from the trigger passed around it, the other end of which, with a piece of meat or a bird tied to it (an owl is a favourite bait), is stretched in front of the gun, so far that the bear can reach the bait with his paw. Upon his pulling the meat towards him, the string draws the trigger and the animal is instantly killed.

On the coast of Labrador we observed the black bear catching fish with great dexterity, and the food of these animals in that region consisted altogether of the fishes they seized on the edge of the water inside the surf. Like the Polar bear, the present species swims with ease and rapidity, and it is a difficult matter to catch a full-grown bear with a skiff, and a dangerous adventure to attempt its capture in a canoe, which it could easily upset.

We were once enjoying a fine autumnal afternoon on the shores of the beautiful Ohio, with two acquaintances who had accompanied us in quest of some swallows that had built in a high sandy bank, when we observed three hunters about the middle of the river in a skiff, vigorously rowing, the steersman paddling, too, with all his strength, in pursuit of a bear which, about one hundred and fifty yards ahead of them, was cleaving the water, and leaving a widening wake behind him on its unrippled surface as he made for the shore, directly opposite to us. We all rushed down to the water at this sight, and launching a skiff we then kept for fishing, hastily put off to intercept the animal, which we hoped to assist in capturing. Both boats were soon nearing the bear, and we, standing in the bow of our skiff, commenced the attack by discharging a pistol at his head. At this he raised one paw, brushed it across his forehead, and then seemed to redouble his efforts. Repeated shots from both boats were now fired at him, and we ran alongside, thinking to haul his carcase triumphantly on board; but suddenly, to our dismay, he laid both paws on the gunwale of the skiff, and his great weight brought the side for an instant under water, so that we expected the boat would fill and sink. There was no time to be lost: we all

25*

threw our weight on to the other side, to coun-
terpoise that of the animal, and commenced a
pell-mell battery on him with the oars and a
boat-hook; the men in the other boat also attacked him, and driving the bow of their skiff
close to his head, one of them laid his skull
open with an axe, which killed him instanter.
We jointly hurraed, and tying a rope round his
neck, towed him ashore behind our boats.

CHAPTER XXI.

THE GRIZZLY BEAR.

WE passed many hours of excitement, and some, perchance, of danger, in the wilder portions of our country; and at times memory recals adventures we can now hardly attempt to describe; nor can we ever again feel the enthusiasm such scenes produced in us. Our readers must therefore imagine the startling sensations experienced on a sudden and quite unexpected face-to-face meeting with the savage grizzly bear —the huge shaggy monster disputing possession of the wilderness against all comers, and threatening immediate attack!

Whilst in a neighbourhood where the grizzly bear may possibly be hidden, the excited nerves will cause the heart's pulsations to quicken if but a startled ground-squirrel run past; the sharp click of the lock is heard, and the rifle hastily thrown to the shoulder, before a second of time has assured the hunter of the trifling cause of his emotion.

But although dreaded alike by white hunter

and by red man, this animal is fortunately not very abundant to the eastward of the Rocky Mountains, and the chance of encountering him does not often occur. We saw only a few of these formidable beasts during our expedition up the Missouri river, and in the country over which we hunted during our last journey to the west.

The Indians, as is well known, consider the slaughter of a grizzly bear a feat second only to scalping an enemy, and necklaces made of the claws of this beast are worn as trophies by even the bravest among them.

On the 22d of August, 1843, we killed one of these bears, and as our journals are before us, and thinking it may be of interest, we will extract the account of the day's proceedings, although part of it has no connection with our present subject. We were descending the Upper Missouri river.

"The weather being fine, we left our camp of the previous night early, but had made only about twelve miles when the wind arose and prevented our men from making any headway with the oars; we therefore landed under a high bank amongst a number of fallen trees and some drifted timber. All hands went in search of elks. Mr. Culbertson killed a deer, and with the help of Mr. Squires brought the meat to the boat. We saw nothing during a long walk we took, but hearing three or four gun-shots which we thought were fired by some of our party, we hastened in the direction from whence the reports came, running and hallooing, but could find no one. We then made the best of our way back to the boat and dispatched three men, who discovered that the firing had been at an elk, which was, however, not obtained. Mr. Bell killed a female elk and brought a portion of its flesh to the boat. After resting ourselves a while and eating dinner, Mr. Culbertson, Mr. Squires, and ourselves walked to the banks of the Little Missouri, distant about one mile, where we saw a buffalo bull drinking at the edge of a sand-bar. We shot him, and fording the stream, which was quite shallow, took away the 'nerf;' the animal was quite dead. We saw many ducks in this river. In the course of the afternoon we started in our boat and rowed about half a mile below the Little Missouri. Mr. Culbertson and ourselves walked to the bull again and knocked off his horns, after which Mr. Culbertson endeavoured to penetrate a large thicket in hopes of starting a grizzly bear, but found it so entangled with briars and vines that he was obliged to desist, and returned very soon. Mr. Harris, who had gone in the same direction and for the same purpose, did not return with him. As we were approaching the boat we met Mr. Sprague, who informed us that he thought he had seen a grizzly bear walking along the upper bank of the river, and we went towards the spot as fast as possible. Meantime the bear had gone down to the water, and was clumsily and slowly proceeding on its way. It was only a few paces from and below us, and was seen by our whole party at the same instant. We all fired, and the animal dropped dead without even the power of uttering a groan. Mr. Culbertson put a rifle ball through its neck, Bell placed two large balls in its side, and our bullet entered its belly. After shooting the bear we proceeded to a village of 'prairie dogs,' and set traps in hopes of catching some of them. We were inclined to think they had all left, but Mr. Bell seeing two, shot them. There were thousands of their burrows in sight. Our 'patroon,' assisted by one of the men, skinned the bear, which weighed, as we thought, about four hundred pounds. It appeared to be between four and five years old, and was a male. Its lard was rendered, and filled sundry bottles with 'real bear's grease,' whilst we had the skin preserved by our accomplished taxidermist, Mr. Bell."

The following afternoon, as we were descending the stream, we saw another grizzly bear, somewhat smaller than the one mentioned above.

It was swimming towards the carcass of a dead
buffalo lodged in the prongs of a "sawyer" or
"snag," but on seeing us it raised on its hind
feet until quite erect, uttered a loud grunt or
snort, made a leap from the water, gained the
upper bank of the river, and disappeared in an
instant amid the tangled briars and bushes there-
abouts. Many wolves of different colours—
black, white, red, or brindle—were also intent
on going to the buffalo to gorge themselves on
the carrion, but took fright at our approach, and
we saw them sneaking away with their tails
pretty close to their hind-legs.

The grizzly bear generally inhabits the
swampy, well covered portions of the districts
where it is found, keeping a good deal among
the trees and bushes, and in these retreats it has
its "beds" or lairs. Some of these we passed by,
and our sensations were the reverse of pleasant whilst in such thick, tangled, and dangerous
neighbourhoods; the bear in his concealment
having decidedly the advantage in case one
should come upon him unawares. These animals ramble abroad both by day and night. In
many places we found their great tracks along
the banks of the rivers where they had been
prowling in search of food. There are seasons
during the latter part of summer, when the wild
fruits, that are eagerly sought after by the bears,

are very abundant. These beasts then feed upon them, tearing down the branches as far as they can reach whilst standing in an upright posture. They in this manner get at wild plums, service berries, buffalo berries, and the seeds of a species of *cornus* or dog-wood which grows in the alluvial bottoms of the northwest. The grizzly bear is also in the habit of scratching the gravelly earth on the sides of hills where the vegetable called " pomme blanche" is known to grow, but the favourite food of these animals is the more savoury flesh of such beasts as are less powerful, fleet, or cunning than themselves. They have been known to seize a wounded buffalo, kill it, and partially bury it in the earth for future use, after having gorged themselves on the best parts of its flesh and lapped up the warm blood.

We have heard many adventures related, which occurred to hunters either when surprised by these bears, or when approaching them with the intention of shooting them. A few of these accounts, which we believe are true, we will introduce: during a voyage (on board one of the steamers belonging to the American Fur Company) up the Missouri river, a large she-bear with two young was observed from the deck, and several gentlemen proposed to go ashore, kill the dam, and secure her cubs. A small

boat was lowered for their accommodation, and
with guns and ammunition they pushed off to
the bank and landed in the mud.   The old bear
had observed them and removed her position to
some distance, where she stood near the bank,
which was there several feet above the bed of
the river.   One of the hunters having neared
the animal, fired at her, inflicting a severe
wound.   Enraged with pain the bear rushed
with open jaws towards the sportsmen at a rapid
rate, and with looks that assured them she was
in a desperate fury.   There was but a moment's
time; the party, too much frightened to stand
the charge, " ingloriously turned and fled," without even pulling another trigger, and darting to
the margin of the river jumped into the stream,
losing their guns, and floundering and bobbing
under, while their hats floated away with the
muddy current.   After swimming a while they
were picked up by the steamer, as terrified as if
the bear was even then among them, though the
animal on seeing them all afloat had made off,
followed by her young.

The following was related to us by one of the
" engagés" at Fort Union: a fellow having
killed an Indian woman, was forced to run away,
and feared he would be captured, started so
suddenly that he took neither gun nor other
weapon with him; he made his way to the Crow
26

Indians, some three hundred miles up the Yellow Stone river, where he arrived in a miserable plight, having suffered from hunger and exposure. He escaped the men who were first sent after him, by keeping in ravines and hiding closely; but others were despatched, who finally caught him. He said that one day he saw a dead buffalo lying near the river bank, and going towards it to get some of the meat, to his utter astonishment and horror a young grizzly bear which was feeding on the carcass, raised up from behind it and so suddenly attacked him that his face and hands were lacerated by its claws before he had time to think of defending himself. Not daunted, however, he gave the cub a tremendous jerk, which threw it down, and took to his heels, leaving the young savage in possession of the prize.

The audacity of these bears in approaching the neighbourhood of Fort Union at times was remarkable. The waiter, "Jean Battiste," who had been in the employ of the company for upwards of twenty years, told us that while one day picking peas in the garden, as he advanced towards the end of one of the rows, he saw a large grizzly bear gathering that excellent vegetable also. At this unexpected and startling discovery, he dropped his bucket, peas and all, and fled at his fastest pace to the Fort. Immediately

the hunters turned out on their best horses, and
by riding in a circle, formed a line which enabled
•them to approach the bear on all sides. They
found the animal greedily feasting on the peas,
and shot him without his apparently caring for
their approach. We need hardly say the bucket
was empty.

The following is taken from Sir John Richardson's Fauna Boreali Americana: "A party of
voyagers, who had been employed all day in
tracking a canoe up the Saskatchewan, had
seated themselves in the bright light by a fire,
and were busy in preparing their supper, when
a large grizzly bear sprung over their canoe,
that was placed behind them, and seizing one
of the party by the shoulder, carried him off.
The rest fled in terror, with the exception of a
Metis, named Bourapo, who, grasping his gun,
followed the bear as it was retreating leisurely
with its prey. He called to his unfortunate
comrade that he was afraid of hitting him if he
fired at the bear, but the latter entreated him to
fire immediately, without hesitation, as the bear
was squeezing him to death. On this he took a
deliberate aim and discharged the contents of
his piece into the body of the bear, which instantly dropped its prey to pursue Bourapo.
He escaped with difficulty, and the bear ultima-
tely retired to a thicket, where it was supposed

to have died ; but the curiosity of the party not being a match for their fears, the fact of its decease was not ascertained. The man who was rescued had his arm fractured, and was otherwise severely bitten by the bear, but finally recovered. I have seen Bourapo, and can add that the account which he gives is fully credited by the traders resident in that part of the country, who are best qualified to judge of its truth from the knowledge of the parties. I have been told that there is a man now living in the neighbourhood of Edmonton House who was attacked by a grizzly bear, which sprang out of a thicket, and with one stroke of its paw completely scalped him, laying bare the skull and bringing the skin of the forehead down over the eyes. Assistance coming up, the bear made off without doing him further injury, but the scalp not being replaced, the poor man has lost his sight, although he thinks that his eyes are uninjured."

Mr. Drummond, in his excursions over the Rocky Mountains, had frequent opportunities of observing the manners of the grizzly bear, and it often happened that in turning the point of a rock or sharp angle of a valley, he came suddenly upon one or more of them. On such occasions they reared on their hind legs and made a loud noise like a person breathing quick,

but much harsher. He kept his ground without attempting to molest them, and they, on
their part, after attentively regarding him for
some time, generally wheeled round and galloped
off, though, from their disposition, there is little
doubt but he would have been torn in pieces
had he lost his presence of mind and attempted
to fly. When he discovered them from a distance, he generally frightened them away by
beating on a large tin box, in which he carried
his specimens of plants. He never saw more
than four together, and two of these he supposes
to have been cubs; he more often met them
singly or in pairs. He was only once attacked,
and then by a female, for the purpose of allow-
ing her cubs time to escape. His gun on this
occasion missed fire, but he kept her at bay with
the stock of it, until some gentlemen of the
Hudson's Bay Company, with whom he was
travelling at the time, came up and drove her
off. In the latter end of June, 1826, he observed a male caressing a female, and soon afterwards they both came towards him, but whether
accidentally, or for the purpose of attacking him,
he was uncertain. He ascended a tree, and as
the female drew near, fired at and mortally
wounded her. She uttered a few loud screams,
which threw the male into a furious rage, and
he reared up against the trunk of the tree in

26*

which Mr. Drummond was seated, but never attempted to ascend it. The female, in the meantime, retired to a short distance, lay down, and as the male was proceeding to join her, Mr. Drummond shot him also.

The following is from notes of J. W. Audubon, made in California in 1849 and 1850: "High up on the waters of the San Joaquin, in California, many of these animals have been killed by the miners, now overrunning all the country west of the Sierra Nevada. Greatly as the grizzly bear is dreaded, it is hunted with all the more enthusiasm by these fearless pioneers in the romantic hills, valleys, and wild mountains of the land of gold, as its flesh is highly prized by men who have been living for months on salt pork, or dry and tasteless deer-meat. I have seen two dollars a pound paid for the leaf-fat around the kidneys. If there is time, and the animal is not in a starving condition, the grizzly bear always runs at the sight of man; but should the hunter come too suddenly on him, the fierce beast always commences the engagement. And the first shot of the hunter is a matter of much importance, as, if unsuccessful, his next move must be to look for a sapling to climb for safety. It is rare to find a man who would willingly come into immediate contact with one of these powerful and vindictive brutes.

Some were killed near 'Green Springs,' on the Stanislaus, in the winter of 1849-50, that were nearly eight hundred pounds weight. I saw many cubs at San Francisco, Sacramento city, and Stockton, and even those not larger than an ordinary sized dog showed evidence of their future fierceness, as it required great patience to render them gentle enough to be handled with impunity as pets. In camping at night, my friend Robert Layton, and I, too, often thought what sort of defence we could make should an old fellow come smelling round our solitary tent for supper; but as 'Old Riley,' our pack-mule, was always tied near, we used to quiet ourselves with the idea that while Riley was snorting and kicking, we might place a couple of well-aimed balls from our old friend Miss Betsey, (as the boys had christened my large gun,) so that our revolvers, Colt's dragoon pistols, would give us the victory; but really a startling effect would be produced by the snout of a grizzly bear being thrust into your tent, and your awaking at the noise of the sniff he might take to induce his appetite.

"I was anxious to purchase a few of the beautiful skins of this species, but those who had killed 'an old grizzly' said they would take his skin *home*. It makes a first-rate bed under the thin and worn blanket of the digger.

"The different colours of the pelage of this animal, but for the uniformity of its extraordinary claws, would puzzle any one not acquainted with its form, for it varies from jet black in the young of the first and second winter to the hoary gray of age, or of summer."

In Townsend's " Narrative of a Journey across the Rocky Mountains to the Columbia River, etc.," we find two adventures with the grizzly bear. The first is as follows: The party were on Black Foot river, a small, stagnant stream which runs in a northwesterly direction down a valley covered with quagmires, through which they had great difficulty in making their way. " As we approached our encampment, near a small grove of willows on the margin of the river, a tremendous grizzly bear rushed out upon us. Our horses ran wildly in every direction, snorting with terror, and became nearly unmanageable. Several balls were instantly fired into him, but they only seemed to increase his fury. After spending a moment in rending each wound, (their invariable practice,) he selected the person who happened to be nearest, and darted after him, but before he proceeded far he was sure to be stopped again by a ball from another quarter. In this way he was driven about amongst us for perhaps fifteen minutes, at times so near some of the horses that he

received several severe kicks from them. One
of the pack-horses was fastened upon by the
brute, and in the terrified animal's efforts to
escape the dreaded gripe, the pack and saddle
were broken to pieces and disengaged. One of
our mules also lent him a kick in the head,
while pursuing it up an adjacent hill, which
sent him rolling to the bottom. Here he was
finally brought to a stand. The poor animal
was so completely surrounded by enemies that
he became bewildered. He raised himself upon
his hind feet, standing almost erect, his mouth
partly open, and from his protruding tongue the
blood fell fast in drops. While in this position
he received about six more balls, each of which
made him reel. At last, as in complete desperation, he dashed into the water, and swam several yards with astonishing strength and agility,
the guns cracking at him constantly. But he
was not to proceed far. Just then, Richardson,
who had been absent, rode up, and fixing his
deadly aim upon him, fired a ball into the back
of his head, which killed him instantly. The
strength of four men was required to drag the
ferocious brute from the water, and upon examining his body he was found completely rid-
dled; there did not appear to be four inches of
his shaggy person, from the hips upward, that
had not received a ball. There must have been

at least thirty shots made at him, and probably few missed him, yet such was his tenacity of life, that I have no doubt he would have succeeded in crossing the river but for the last shot in the brain. He would probably weigh, at the least, six hundred pounds, and was about the height of an ordinary steer. The spread of the foot, laterally, was ten inches, and the claws measured seven inches in length. This animal was remarkably lean; when in good condition he would, doubtless, much exceed in weight the estimate I have given.

"In the afternoon one of our men had a some what perilous adventure with a grizzly bear. He saw the animal crouching his huge frame in some willows which skirted the river, and approaching him on horseback to within twenty yards, fired upon him. The bear was only slightly wounded by the shot, and with a fierce growl of angry malignity, rushed from his cover, and gave chase. The horse happened to be a slow one, and for the distance of half a mile the race was hard contested, the bear frequently approaching so near the terrified animal as to snap at his heels, whilst the equally terrified rider, who had lost his hat at the start, used whip and spur with the most frantic diligence, frequently looking behind, from an influence which he could not resist, at his rugged and

determined foe, and shrieking in an agony of
fear, 'shoot him! shoot him!' The man, who
was one of the greenhorns, happened to be
about a mile behind the main body, either from
the indolence of his horse or his own careless-
ness; but as he approached the party in his
desperate flight, and his lugubrious cries reached the cars of the men in front, about a dozen
of them rode to his assistance, and soon succeeded in diverting the attention of his pertina-
cious foe. After he had received the contents
of all the guns, he fell, and was soon despatched.
The man rode in among his fellows, pale and
haggard from overwrought feelings, and was,
probably, effectually cured of a propensity for
meddling with grizzly bears."

THE END.

www.ingramcontent.com/pod-product-compliance
Lightning Source LLC
Chambersburg PA
CBHW021805110726
47902CB00006B/1651